Praise for *A Message to Deliver*

"I was impressed with the depth of the character development, each one having a clear voice and specific goal. The pace of Jeremiah's writing, coupled with the suspense, made it near impossible to put this book down." –Clarice

"*A Message to Deliver* delivers suspense, the realities of spiritual warfare, and above all, a message of hope and forgiveness. The journey of the main character from the innocence of heaven to the reality of the world is captivating."
– Jamie

"Peters paints vivid pictures with his writing that allows the reader to step right into the story and imagine Melissa as she is exploring her new home for the first time or being chased through her work!" – Jonathan

"His use of the supernatural was reminiscent of the writings of Christian fiction author Frank Peretti. There is an element of mystery throughout, causing me to want to keep reading!"
– Christa

"I had a hard time putting this book down once I started reading it! The story is beautifully laid out and written, the characters are so real to life, I found myself getting attached to them!" – Kimberly

A Message to Deliver

A Message to Deliver

By Jeremiah Peters

STONEGATE BOOKS

*To my wonderful wife Jodie,
whose unwavering value of human life shines
through the love and commitment she has always shown to our six children.*

This is not a book of theology. It's a book about forgiveness: Forgiveness from God, forgiveness of others, and forgiveness of self.

• *One* •

Melissa sat on her favorite lakeside hill, amidst a field of daisies of such beautiful colors that it looked like a rainbow stretched across the ground. The celestial city rose up beyond the sparkling water, its spires reaching into the deep blue sky.

A warm breeze caressed her face.

"Hello, child." Jesus, wearing His usual wise and loving smile, strolled up the hill. He always called her child. This wasn't because of her age—whatever that was—but simply as a sign of His great love.

A trio of angels circled high above, shouting, "Glory to the One. The Alpha and Omega."

Melissa raced over and embraced Him, just like always. Some of the others fell on their faces before Him. But not her. It wasn't out of disrespect. No. It was simply that her love for Him was so great, she had to throw her arms around Him.

A strand of hair dangled across her face. Jesus brushed it to the side. "I have a task for you."

Her heart leapt. "The choir. You're going to let me sing with the angelic choir? I love listening to them."

"No. I'm sending you on a mission."

"A mission?" Her eyes widened.

"I have a message I'd like you to deliver."

She clapped her hands against her chest. "I'll be your messenger?"

"Yes."

"I'll be like an angel?" She looked up at the trio and a smile spread across her face.

"No." He spoke with the love and patience a parent would have, explaining something to a small child. "Angels are a different creation. You're human."

"What's the message? Where am I going? This is so exciting!" A dozen questions rolled off her tongue.

The Lord allowed her to ramble on for a moment. Finally, He spoke. "This is the message. Remember, it's important that you get this right."

Melissa bounced and fidgeted.

"Listen." He rested a hand on her shoulder.

She gazed up into His eyes. *He's sending me, a human. It must be terribly important. Otherwise, He'd just send an angel!*

"My message is this: 'The Lord loves you, and I forgive you.'"

It grew quiet, as even the hillside itself seemed to be waiting for more. But nothing else was said.

Is that it?

Jesus gave her a look that seemed to say, *I know what you're thinking.* "Is everything all right?"

"... I was hoping for more." She looked at the ground and nudged a daisy with her foot.

"But that's the greatest message you could ever deliver."

"I guess."

"Are you ready to go?"

She tipped her head and gazed up at Him. "Go where?"

"To Earth. That's where you'll be delivering the message."

Her mouth dropped open. "But I've never been to Earth. At least, not since I came here."

"You'll do fine." Jesus smiled. "Plans have been set in motion. You'll be taken care of."

"You-you usually send angels to Earth."

Was it her imagination, or did Jesus hesitate before answering? "This time, I'm sending you."

Melissa leapt forward and threw her arms around His neck. "This is wonderful. Exciting!"

"Child." The Lord spoke with a loving firmness. "Remember." He gently pulled her away and stared into her eyes. "This is going to be all new —"

"And exciting."

"Yes. And exciting. But remember your mission. And when you need help, I'll be there. Can you remember that?"

The Lord gave her further instructions. For several minutes, He shared things she would have to know. But His voice was soon drowned out by one single thought. *Earth! I've always wanted to go there. Always wanted to see where I came from. Others have memories of Earth, but not me. Now I'll see it for myself.*

"I said, can you remember that?" The Lord patted her shoulder.

She shook herself back from her daydreaming. Jesus was staring at her, waiting for an answer. She nodded, then once again, hugged him. "Thank you for choosing me. I won't let you down."

"I know you won't. Are you ready to go?"

"Now? Right now?"

"Yes. It's time."

Her heart raced. "I'm ready."

Jesus took her by the shoulders, and backed her a step away from Him. "Remember. 'The Lord loves you. I forgive you.' It's important for you to remember that exact message."

"I remember. I promise."

As He spoke, the world began to dissolve. "The Lord loves you."

Colors twisted together.

"I forgive you."

Sound and sight merged.

"Don't forget."

The Lord faded.

· *Two* ·

Everything around her faded. The trees, the bright sky, the celestial city dimmed. Until it was all gone. Vanished. But in an instant was replaced by a different scene.

Trees? Yes. But, somehow, not trees. Melissa tipped her head to the side.

Pretty? Yes ... but not like the ones in Heaven.

A blue sky ... yet different. Not as brilliant. The objects around her were shrouded — pale shadows, mere images of the heavenly.

This is the Earth?

She looked down at her arms, long and slender, extending from her body. Real and yet somehow unreal. She reached up and felt her head, pulling long strands of blonde hair in front of her eyes. She must have always had arms and hair ... but she never bothered to look at them before. They hadn't seemed to matter.

Over the next couple of minutes, the sights and sounds of this new reality came into focus and the clear images of the heavenly reality became more like a wispy dream dancing at the corners of her consciousness.

She was sitting on some type of a bench, in the middle of a wooded area. A hard path ran in front of her. Her eyes opened wide. Her hands shot up to cover her mouth.

There are people on the path!

Walking, running, pushing carts containing smaller people. And noise!

So much noise. In the distance, a horn honked. It didn't sound like any heavenly musical instrument she'd ever heard.

Not too melodious.

"What a wonder," she gasped.

"Oh, child! You startled me! I didn't see you there."

Melissa looked to her right. Seated next to her was another human. "What a wonder!"

Something's different.

Melissa held out her arm to study. Then sliding closer, she placed it against the other woman's. *Hers is a little ... thicker.* There was something else, too. "We aren't the same color."

"Excuse me?" The woman glared over the top of her glasses.

"I said, we aren't the same color. I'm paler than you."

The old African-American's forehead wrinkled. "Are you okay?"

Melissa reached out and touched the woman's arm. "Oh! But you're so beautiful. What a pretty color!"

She smiled. "Thank you dear. Haven't you ever seen a black person before?"

Melissa's brow creased. "No ... Yes ... I don't know." *I sound foolish.* Could she have told the woman what color her own skin was before making this trip to Earth? It simply didn't seem to matter. She glanced back and forth between their arms.

The other woman pulled her glasses down lower on her nose. "You're not from around here, are you?"

Melissa hung her head. "No."

"Don't they have black people where you come from?"

"I ... never noticed."

After a pause, the woman gave a hearty laugh. "I suppose that's the way to be. Like Dr. King said, 'Judge a person by the content of his heart, and not the color of his skin.' Well, sweetheart, around here people come in all shapes and colors."

"Really?" Melissa pivoted on the bench to face her new friend. "I'd love to see a blue one."

"Blue?" The woman cocked her head. "What are you looking for? Smurfs?" Again, she laughed.

"Oh!" *How could I forget so quickly?* She grabbed the woman's arm, looked intently into her eyes. "The Lord loves you, and Jesus forgives you, too!" With a triumphant smile, she sat back, closed her eyes, and waited to be transported back to Heaven.

Mission Accomplished! That was easy!

Thirty heartbeats ticked by.

"Child?"

With her eyes tightly clenched, Melissa tipped her head to one side. *That didn't sound like Jesus.*

"Are you all right?"

She opened her eyes. She was still on the bench. *I don't understand. I gave the message.*

The old woman took her hand. "I said, are you all right?"

"Yes. It's just that ... I thought once my mission was done ..."

"Is there something I can do for you? You seem a bit out of sorts."

Why? Why am I still here? Oh! She glanced over at the woman. *She's not the one!*

Melissa hopped to her feet. People were hurrying by, busy with the day's activities. *One of them must be the one I'm supposed to talk to.*

Like a bee flitting from flower to flower, she scurried from person to person.

"The Lord loves you! Jesus forgives you," Melissa shouted to a young couple. They avoided eye contact and rushed away.

"The Lord loves you," she said to a woman jogging by.

"And I love Him, too," the woman called out.

A group of older teenage boys and young men were coming her way, walking with a collective swagger.

A young mother, pushing her child in a stroller, pulled to the side and waited for them to pass. One of the young men, whose shaved head revealed a tattoo of a human skull with a knife stabbed through one of its eyes, stopped and leaned over the stroller. He reached a hand toward the child. The mother tensed. The man gave a scornful laugh and continued on his way.

Melissa walked toward him to share God's message.

"Child," the black woman's voice rang out. "Come back here!"

Melissa glanced toward the bench.

The woman gave a frightened look beyond Melissa, down the path. The group of men were laughing as they grew closer.

I'll just share God's message with these people before I go see what she wants.

She picked something off the bench and waved it in the air. "You forgot your envelope."

"My envelope?"

The woman continued the frantic waving.

"My envelope?" She strolled back to the bench. "I don't—"

"Sit down. Now!"

Melissa tipped her head to the side and sank down in the seat.

The woman leaned in and whispered, "It's wonderful that you want to tell everyone about God's love, but ..." She paused as the group walked by, their gaze lingering on the two ladies.

"Why are they looking at us?"

Her new friend waited until the group had traveled out of earshot before answering. "They're not looking at us, they're looking at you. You're a pretty young woman. You've got to be careful!"

"You're pretty, too."

The older woman smiled. "What's your name?"

"Melissa."

The lady reached out. Melissa took hold of her hand, and the two shook. "That's a nice name. And it suits you, too. Melissa. My name is Harriet. Harriet Simmons."

"Nice to meet you, Harriet Simmons."

Harriet held out the envelope. "This is yours."

Melissa shrugged. "I don't think so."

"It must be yours. It has your name on it."

Melissa took the envelope. Her right eyebrow rose. Sure enough. There was her name, printed right across its front. And under it- "McCullen's Department Store- Tuesday at 2:30 PM."

Harriet was leaning closer, studying the writing. "Today is Tuesday."

McCullen's Department Store. That's where I need to go. That's where I must deliver God's message! She turned to Harriet. "Where is that?"

"McCullen's? On the far side of the park." Harriet pointed. Then looking at her watch she added, "It's two now. If you're going to make it there by two-thirty, you'd better hurry."

Melissa jumped up, grabbed Harriet's hand, and gave it a hearty shake. "Thank you. And don't forget, the Lord loves you!" She ran off. Looking back over her shoulder she hollered out, "He forgives you, too!"

"I know He does, child," Harriet yelled after the girl. She raised her hands. "Every day, I thank Him for that."

Melissa ran down the sidewalk, talking to everyone she passed. Being beyond Harriet's hearing range, the older woman could only assume Melissa was telling them all about God's love.

"He loves you too, child. He loves you too," Harriet whispered.

Once Melissa was out of sight, Harriet picked up her knitting and resumed the sweater she'd been making for a friend's baby. After a couple of minutes, she held it out to examine her progress. "Not bad. A couple more hours and I'll be done."

She lowered the sweater as a man strolled by. He acknowledged her presence with a polite smile. Harriet smiled back.

For no apparent reason, the man came to an abrupt halt right in front of her. He lifted his face to the wind and sniffed. His eyebrows rose. "Something ..." A grin slowly stretched across his face. He continued on his way.

Harriet sniffed at the air, but found nothing out of the ordinary. No harsh odors, just the everyday smells of the park. She shrugged her shoulders and resumed her knitting.

• *Three* •

"McCullen ... McCullen." Melissa chanted the name with each step. The park was alive with people. People of all shapes and sizes; many shades and colors, just like Harriet had said. But she hadn't come across a blue one yet.

Along the way, she took every opportunity to tell people, "God loves you and Jesus forgives you, too!"

She received a marked variety of responses.

She crossed over the path that bordered the outside edge of the park. How would she know where this McCullen's Department Store was? Across a busy street was a large building. Big red letters on its outside announced, McCullen's Department Store.

There it is. Easy enough.

Melissa's heart raced. Her mission was almost complete. Who knows? If she was successful at this one, God might be willing to send her out again. And her friends in Heaven would be so excited to hear all about her adventures.

She dodged speeding cars to cross the road. Then, taking a deep breath, she burst into the shop. With a swoosh, the automatic doors closed behind her. The noise from the busy street cut off, replaced with subdued strains of music.

No heavenly choir. That's for sure.

She stood still. Rows and aisles, filled with clothing and cooking pots, toys and canned food, stretched off into the store. People mulled about, taking things off the shelves and placing them in carts.

Melissa frowned. No one was paying attention to her. But then again, what did she expect? Someone to race up and say 'Welcome'? Someone to cry out to her, 'Tell me God's message'?

Where do I start? Where do I find the right one?

Over to the right, a young man with curly red hair and a pimply face was slumped over a counter, flipping through a book. Melissa marched over to him. "The Lord loves you, and Jesus forgives you!"

He paused from his reading to give Melissa a slow, dull look. "Register's closed. You'll have to go to the one over there."

"You don't understand. I have a message to deliver."

The boy sighed and, with exaggerated difficulty, pushed his tall, lanky frame into an upright position. He pointed at the envelope clutched in Melissa's hands. "Let's see."

She handed it over.

After a quick peek at the envelope's contents, he gave a vague nod down one of the aisles. Then he returned to his reading. "You want the office. Back of the store."

"Thank you." Melissa headed off through the less-than-crowded aisles. The office. That's where she'd be able to deliver her message. With every step, her pace quickened. *Won't the Lord be so pleased with me?*

There were large, swinging doors at the back of the store with the words 'Employees Only' printed on them.

Could this be the office? Only one way to find out.

She pushed through and stepped into a musty room lined with floor-to-ceiling metal shelves piled high with boxes and bags.

"Can I help you?" A middle-aged woman, dressed in a smock printed with the name McCullen's, approached Melissa. She pulled some type of a stick from a small package she was carrying and placed it in her mouth. It dangled precariously from her lips. Melissa waited for the stick to fall to the floor when she spoke. But it didn't.

"I'm looking for the office."

"That door over there." The woman swung her hand—the one that wasn't holding the package—across the room and pointed. There, nestled between pallets loaded with large cardboard boxes, was a door.

"Thank you." Melissa turned to leave, but stopped short. What was she thinking? She had forgotten her mission. "Wait!"

The woman, who'd begun walking toward a door marked 'Exit,' paused. She gave a deep sigh. "I only have ten minutes for my break. What now?"

Melissa smiled brightly. "The Lord loves you and forgives you!"

The woman turned with a harrumph and shuffled away, mumbling, "One of them, huh."

Odd. One of what?

No matter. Her goal was in sight. She walked to the door and pushed it open. Inside was a short hallway whose floor was covered with dulled linoleum tiles. The walls were a faded yellow. A couple of chairs sat against the wall to Melissa's right. On her left were two doors. One was marked 'Men,' the other marked 'Women.'

Straight ahead was another door. The top half was frosted glass, with three-inch-tall letters that read, 'Office.' That's the one she wanted. Melissa opened it and stepped in.

The room was small. Bulletins, notices, and posters were tacked on the walls, partially covering the cracked and faded paint. A large filing cabinet with a well-cared-for spider plant draped over its top was crammed next to a desk whose side pressed against the far wall. A woman sat behind it, holding some paperwork under the desk lamp. She didn't look up.

"Er ... Hello."

"Oh!" The woman jumped. Soft and friendly eyes met Melissa's. "May I help you?"

"Yes! I've come to—"

"You must be one of the new hires." She glanced at her watch. "Right on time. That's good. I have two more coming in after you." She pointed to a folding chair on the other side of the desk. "Have a seat."

Melissa obeyed.

"Honestly. I'm surprised that Mr. McCullen hired you." The woman covered her mouth. "Sorry. I hope I didn't offend you."

"No."

"I mean, not that he shouldn't have hired you. I'm not talking about you personally. I'm talking about all the new hires. I'm sure you're a wonderful worker. But, to be perfectly honest, the store is barely surviving." She shrugged and gave a weak smile. "Well, who am I to doubt Mr. McCullen's wisdom? He's the owner. By the way, I'm Ms. Lisa Gibbons, the store's Day Manager." She rolled her eyes. "Who am I kidding? I'm the only manager. But saying Day Manager seems more official." She leaned closer and whispered. "Mr. McCullen's idea."

She was older and slightly heavier than Melissa, with streaks of gray showing in her hair, and laugh lines around the eyes. All in all, she seemed a nice individual.

"Now, let's get started. What's your name?"

"Melissa."

"Melissa what?"

Melissa's brow wrinkled. "I don't understand."

"Your last name, dear. What's your last name?"

"Oh ..." *A last name?* It was like the conversation with Harriet about skin color all over again.

Ms. Gibbons waited for an answer.

Melissa chewed on a fingernail as she stared back at the woman.

"Let's see your papers. I'm sure all the information I need will be on them."

Melissa set the envelope on the desk. Ms. Gibbons reached across, took it, and pulled some papers out. She held them up to the desk lamp, moving them back and forth, closer and farther away from her eyes. Then she adjusted her reading glasses. "Having trouble making this out. Would you mind flipping on the overhead light?"

Melissa raised her eyebrows.

"The overhead." Ms. Gibbons pointed to the ceiling. "Could you flip it on?"

Melissa peered up at the fixture on the ceiling.

"The switch is on the wall."

A pretty, red switch on the wall behind Melissa was held in place by a cylinder of glass. "That switch?"

"Yes, please," Ms. Gibbons said without looking. "Could you flip it on?"

Melissa hopped up. The switch was encased in a red and white box of some type. She reached for it.

"No!"

Melissa jumped back. "But you said —"

"Not that switch, dear." Ms. Gibbons jumped from her seat and around the desk. "The other one."

About sixteen inches to the right of the red switch, was another one. Not as pretty and much smaller.

Ms. Gibbons flipped it upward. The overhead light sprang to life. "This one."

"Oh." Melissa reached over to the switch. *Can I touch it?* Her hand trembled. *A messenger of God needs courage.* She took a breath and flipped the switch down. Then up. Then down and up, faster and faster. Amazed, she gazed at the blinking light.

Ms. Gibbons gently took her hand off the switch. "Let's leave the light on. Shall we?"

"Okay."

The Day Manager spoke as she made her way around to the back of her desk. "It's a good thing you didn't pull the other switch."

"Why? It's so pretty."

Ms. Gibbons gaped. "That's the fire alarm. You'd have brought the fire department here in a matter of minutes. We'd have had to evacuate the whole store."

Melissa paused. "And that's not a good thing?"

Ms. Gibbons tipped her head and studied the girl. "No, dear. That's not a good thing."

Melissa hung her head. "I'm sorry."

"No, no. That's fine. I'm sure you won't make that mistake again, will you?" Ms. Gibbons smiled.

"No, ma'am. I won't."

The manager leaned back in her seat and narrowed her eyes. "Tell me something. Are you related to someone in the store? Maybe Mr. McCullen himself?"

"No."

With a shrug, Ms. Gibbons returned her attention to the paper in front of her. "That's better. I can see it clearly now. All filled out and ready to go."

She scanned the page. "Name ... Melissa ... That's all it says ... Melissa." Deep wrinkles formed between Ms. Gibbons' eyebrows as she studied the paper. "Well I guess you're like one of those rock stars. Like Cher or Prince. You go by one name?"

Melissa smiled. *What in the world is a rock star?*

"Age ... Twenty. Date of birth ... June ... 12th ..."

"Is something wrong?"

The manager's eyes were focused on the page. "No ... it's just ... I've never seen an application like this." She dropped the paper on the desk and turned to her computer. She clicked away at the keys and waited. "Here you are. Melissa ... date of birth June 12th. Looks like Mr. McCullen himself approved your application and already entered the information in the database. Very good." She focused back on Melissa. "When can you start?"

Melissa tipped her head. "Start what?"

"Work, of course."

Work? Was she supposed to work at this store? Was that part of God's great plan? It must be. Why else would there be a job application in her envelope? "I guess I can start right away."

"Good. Why don't you come back tomorrow at 9:00 am. We'll begin your training then."

"Tomorrow? What will I do until then?"

"I don't know. What do you usually do?"

I worship God, help out in the Temple. Play hide and seek with my angel, run through the fields of Heaven. She wanted to say all these things, but remained silent.

Ms. Gibbons reached across the desk and patted Melissa's hand. "Why don't you go home? Come back tomorrow."

"Home?" Home was Heaven. Home was being in the presence of her Lord.

"Why, yes." Ms. Gibbons face clouded. "You do have a home, don't you?" She looked down at the application and raised up her reading glasses to see. "Of course you do. It says right here. 421 Woodland Road, Apartment C."

Melissa clasped her hands to the sides of her face. "I have a home? Isn't God wonderful!"

"Er ... I suppose." The Day Manager gathered Melissa's papers into the envelope and handed them back. "See you tomorrow, dear."

Melissa stood. *Wait! I almost forgot again!* She reached across the table and grabbed the woman's hand. "The Lord loves you. He forgives you."

Ms. Gibbons pulled back, causing her seat, which was on wheels, to slap into the wall behind her. Then, giving a small cough to clear her throat, she smiled sweetly at Melissa. "That's nice, dear. I'm sure He does. Now you go do whatever it is you do during the day, and we'll see you tomorrow."

Melissa crossed to the door. As she opened it, Ms. Gibbons again cleared her throat. "Are you sure you're not related to someone in the store?"

"Not that I know of. Why?"

"Just wondering how you got ..." She paused. "Just wondering. That's all."

Melissa left the office. *What a nice woman Ms. Lisa Gibbons is.* She pulled the door closed and started down the hall. Two young men were sitting in the previously empty chairs. One of them had darker skin, like Harriet. He was jerking his head from side to side, and fidgeting with his tie. The other young man's dark eyes fixed on Melissa. She smiled at them and waved. The African-American smiled back. The other nodded in her direction ... no smile.

"Are you all right?" she asked the man with the tie.

"Huh?"

"You seem nervous."

The young man stuck his fingers inside his collar, pulling at his necktie. "No. I'm fine. I'm fine. It's my first job interview. That's all."

Melissa rested a hand on his shoulder. "Don't worry. Ms. Gibbons is a nice lady."

The young man gave a weak smile. "Thanks."

She smiled back at him. She also nodded and smiled at the other man, then headed into the store.

No sooner had the door closed behind Melissa, when Ms. Gibbons stepped out of her office. "Todd?"

The African-American boy hopped to his feet.

"I'll see you now." She held the door open, allowing Todd to pass through. "Jonathan." She turned to the other young man seated in the hallway. "I'll be with you in a few minutes."

Jonathan didn't respond.

Lisa Gibbons shrugged. She walked into her office and let the door close behind her.

Jonathan sat perfectly still, his eyes riveted on the door leading to the store, to where Melissa had just exited. He stared intently, as if he could see through it, to where she was standing on the other side.

· *Four* ·

Melissa meandered around the different departments in the store to see everything, experience everything, learn everything. Clothing, shoes, sporting goods, and pet supplies. Finally, she headed out to go find her new home.

She was on Earth! A mission. She had assumed it would be accomplished right away. Obviously, God had something else in mind. But what?

Apparently, I have plenty of time to figure it out.

Melissa took a deep breath, sucking in the thrill of adventure. She had to find 421 Woodland Road, Apartment C. On the busy sidewalk, people scurried in all directions, not paying even a lick of attention to each other. Bumper-to-bumper traffic chugged down the street.

She looked at the paper Ms. Gibbons had given back to her. There it was. Her name was Melissa. She lived at 421 Woodland Road, Apartment C. She was twenty years old. Born on June 12th. Melissa smiled. June 12th sounded like such a nice date.

She hurried down the sidewalk.

I have to find my apartment.

Her speed decreased. Her steps became shorter, until finally she came to a complete stop. She'd barely gone ten feet from the store's door.

How do I do that?

"Hey. How ya doing?"

Melissa turned. The young African-American man who'd been seated outside Ms. Gibbons' office was emerging from the building. He gave her a friendly smile as he approached. "You starting work here, too?"

"Yes. I am."

"I'm Todd." He stuck his hand out.

He's a giant.

Todd stood a good eight to ten inches taller than Melissa. Of course, judging by the people she'd met so far, she was on the short side; somewhere just north of five feet. He looked to be about the same age as her ... maybe a couple of years younger. Clean face, bright brown eyes, and a wiry frame.

"Hi. I'm Melissa. I start tomorrow."

"Me, too."

"Oh, Todd. I must tell you — The Lord loves you and Jesus forgives you, too!"

"Amen to that, sister!" With half a smile, Todd shook his head. "Not everyone gets the message, if you know what I mean."

Melissa's brow puckered. "No. I don't know what you mean."

"Not everybody believes."

"Believes what?"

"Believes in God." Todd laughed. "What'd you think I meant? Believes in the tooth fairy?"

"Really?" Melissa's eyes widened. How could anybody not believe in God? She squared her shoulders. "It's a good thing I'm here then."

Todd's attention shifted to the doors of the store. The other young man who'd been sitting outside of the Day Manager's office was exiting. Todd called out, "How'd it go? You get the job?"

Somber faced, the man nodded.

"Good for you." Todd gave a thumbs up. "Starting tomorrow?"

The newcomer's gaze passed between Melissa and Todd. An expressionless stare. He gave another quick nod, then turned and walked away.

That was creepy.

Todd hesitated. "Okay then. Nice talking to you, brother."

"He's ... interesting."

Todd scratched the back of his head. "That's one way to put it. The whole time we sat outside the office, he never spoke. Just stared."

Melissa looked toward the departing figure, who'd walked about a hundred feet away and stopped. Then, he turned to come back. His gaze quickly went back and forth from Melissa to Todd. In an awkward move, he scooted to a storefront and peered through the window, casting a furtive glance Melissa's way.

"Maybe he's shy." Melissa shrugged.

"Maybe." Todd shook his head. "But that's a conversation for another time. Right now you look like you could use some help."

"Yes. I'm trying to find ..." Melissa hesitated. Admitting to not knowing where her apartment was would make her sound crazy. "Do you know the fastest way to get here?" She pointed to the address on the paper.

"Sure. That's just a couple of blocks from where I live. Come on. I'll show you." The two strolled off through the afternoon's hustle and bustle. "You can either take the Main Street bus," Todd pointed at one that was passing by, "which gets you pretty close, or you can walk."

"A bus?" She watched the large vehicle chug down the busy street. Her heart pounded at the prospect of getting inside one. "Let's take the bus!"

Todd pulled his pockets inside out. "Got no money today. Maybe we'll do a bus some other time."

They continued along the sidewalk.

"So Melissa, huh? Not a bad name." He kicked at a discarded can. "But I think you need a nickname."

"Nickname?"

"Sure. Melissa's three syllables. We gotta shorten it." He stroked his chin. "How about Millie?"

"No thank you."

"Lizzy?"

Melissa stuck out her tongue.

"How about Spike?"

"Spike?"

The two laughed.

"You have to help me here, Melissa. I'm doing the best I can." His eyebrows furrowed for a second. "I know. How about Mel? It's unique."

Hmmm. Mel. "Do you think Mel's a good nickname?"

"Sure. Short. Easy to remember. Besides," he gave a broad smile, "I like it."

"Then Mel it is. What about you? What's your nickname?"

"Don't need one." He tapped his chest. "Todd is short enough."

As they walked on, Todd carried the weight of the conversation. He prattled on about his life, telling her how he lived with his grandmother; this was his first job; how excited he was, but nervous, too. Occasionally he'd ask Melissa about her life. She tried to skirt these questions, not knowing what to say.

After about ten minutes, he asked, "Have you lived around —" His words cut off abruptly.

Melissa looked at her new friend. The young man had stopped walking. He stood rigid, biting on his bottom lip, staring up at the building to their right. His head was slowly shaking.

What is wrong?

Melissa glanced over at the brick building. It looked like all the others in the area, set about thirty feet back from the road. A cement walkway cut through a well-manicured lawn, leading up to the front door. 'Southside Women's Health Center' the sign over the door read. A banner tacked under it declared, 'Now Open.'

"Are you all right, Todd?"

He nodded. "Sure, I'm fine."

He wasn't though. As they continued on their way, he'd stopped talking. When Melissa asked him questions, the answers he gave were short. "That's great. That's great," he'd mutter to whatever she'd say, while staring at the ground.

Did I do something wrong?

They came to a busy intersection with a green street sign. "Woodland Road," she read. "Is this it?"

"What?" He looked up. "Oh ... Sure. Woodland Road."

"Thank you for showing me the way."

Todd gave a weak smile "No problem, Mel. Do you think you can make it on your own from here? I'm late for supper.

Gram goes all postal on me when I'm late. She's afraid I'm getting involved in a gang or something."

Todd had the strangest way of talking. Postal? Gang? She nodded and smiled. "Oh yes. I should be fine from here. Thank you so much."

"Okay. See you tomorrow at work." Todd hurried away.

Melissa stood at the intersection of Main and Woodland, gazing up and down the street.

Which way?

She squared her shoulders and trekked off to her left. Eventually she realized the building numbers were going in the wrong direction. She turned around. Finally, a red, three-story tenement loomed in front of her. The number on the outside said 421.

This must be it. She headed up the five cement steps and through the front door. Inside, she faced a set of stairs that led to the second floor. A hallway ran along its side. There was a door to the right of her with the letter A on it. Down the hallway was another door, but it didn't have a letter. Melissa reexamined the paper in her hand. She was looking for C. She raised one eyebrow. There wasn't a C visible. What should she do? At that moment, the A door flew open and a heavy-set woman stepped out, accompanied by the most heavenly aromas.

"Can I help you?" The woman dried some water and soapsuds off her hands with a dishcloth.

"I'm looking for C."

"C?"

"Yes." Melissa looked down at the paper in her hand to make sure she had the correct letter. "421 Woodland Road. Apartment C."

"Oh!" The woman said, throwing up her arms for extra emphasis. "You must be the new tenant. Yes? Yes. I'm the landlord, Mrs. Parsioni." Mrs. Parsioni grabbed hold of Melissa's hands, engulfing them in both of hers. She pumped her arms up and down. "So good to meet you! Hold on. Hold on."

She scurried back into apartment A. Like a kite on a string, Melissa was pulled in with her. They were standing in a large eat-in kitchen, the source of the delicious aromas. "Sorry about the mess. I've been cooking up some tomato sauce. Do you like tomato sauce? Of course you do! Everybody likes tomato sauce."

The woman crossed to a stove covered with bubbling pots, scooped up a spoonful of sauce and brought it up to Melissa's lips. "Here. Taste. Taste. It's good?"

She stopped talking and stood staring at Melissa, waiting for her opinion of the sauce.

Melissa obliged. How could she not? As the sauce went over her taste buds, Melissa's eyes widened in utter delight. "Yes. It's good. It's delicious."

Mrs. Parsioni beamed. "All from scratch. No store bought garbage comes out of my kitchen!"

The woman flittered around the room, searching through a cluttered tabletop, tossing the papers in every direction. Then she ferreted about a counter and a couple of bookcases.

"Now where did Mr. Parsioni put that key? Honestly, I love the man, but if his head weren't attached ..." She pretended to take her head off and toss it to the side. "He'd lose it. God didn't give him the common sense he gave a hamster."

Melissa stared. *Why would God leave common sense out of someone's makeup? And how much does He give to hamsters?*

The woman shouted, "Aha!"

Melissa flinched.

"Here it is! Here it is! On top of the refrigerator." Mrs. Parsioni snatched up a key and hurried the two of them out of the apartment. "Honestly! Men! You know what I mean?" Without waiting for an answer, Mrs. Parsioni headed up the staircase. Melissa paused. From her perch at the top, Mrs. Parsioni looked down at her. "Come dear. Follow me."

Before Melissa reached the top of the steps, Mrs. Parsioni had already bustled down the hall toward the front of the building and inserted the key in a door with a big C on it. "Your boxes came. I hope you don't mind, but I hung some of your clothes in the bedroom closet."

My boxes? "No. That's okay."

"Funny way to rent an apartment, sight unseen. But Mr. Parsioni said you had good references." The woman gave Melissa the quick once over. "You look like a nice girl to me." She wagged a finger in her face. "Are you a nice girl?"

Wide eyed, Melissa nodded. "I think so."

"Good. We want only nice tenants." She pushed the door open and led Melissa in. "It's nothing fancy, but it's clean. And you have good neighbors. Mr. Parsioni and I are down below you. Mrs. Stanley lives in apartment B, down the hall. A widow. Nice lady. And up on the third floor, in apartment D, is a young couple. Newlyweds. We don't see much of them, if you know what I mean." She gave Melissa a sly wink. "He works for some medical supply company. She works at a hair salon down the street. Nice couple."

They'd entered a small kitchen area. Melissa's head pivoted from side to side so she could take in all the wonders of her apartment. She brushed her fingers along the countertop and stove. Crossing the room, she stepped through an archway into a living room furnished with an overstuffed love seat and armchair.

Mrs. Parsioni followed after Melissa as she walked into the bedroom, located off the living room. "Like I said, I hope you don't mind I hung up some of your clothes." She gestured toward the closet.

Melissa rushed over and opened the sliding door, revealing about two dozen dresses of various colors, all hung and arranged neatly. She ran her hand over them. If only she could try on each and every one right then and there. "No. That was nice of you."

"So, I'll let you get settled in. Remember rent is due the first of the month. If you need anything, we're right down stairs. Oh, by the way, you got some mail. I put it on the kitchen table."

"Thank you."

Mrs. Parsioni had exited the apartment and was pulling the door closed when Melissa slapped her forehead. Being overwhelmed by all these new things was no excuse for forgetting why she was here. "Mrs. Parsioni!"

The woman stuck her head inside. "Yes?"

"God loves you, and He forgives you, too."

"Thank you, dear. I know He loves me. But what He has to forgive me for, I don't know. Unless it's me wanting to hit Mr. Parsioni over the head with a rolling pin every once in a while. That man can be so aggravating! Sometimes—" She pulled the door closed. The murmurs of the landlord continuing her conversation with herself seeped through the walls as she headed down the stairs.

Melissa chuckled. She returned to the kitchen table. Sitting next to the door key, was a single envelope addressed to Melissa.

So that's mail. She ripped it open. A wide grin stretched across her face as she read the simple letter.

Dear Melissa, Remember — I am with you always!

It wasn't signed, but it didn't have to be.

Melissa glided into the living room and fell back on the couch. She stared up at the ceiling, took a deep breath, and let it out slowly. God was good. Even here, He was taking care of her.

But, with a job and an apartment, what's His plan?

With a burst of energy, she hopped up and raced across the floor. Standing in the bedroom doorway, she gazed around. The full-sized bed filled the majority of the room, covered with a flowery, pink spread and a variety of frilly throw pillows. Across from the foot of the bed was a low dresser. A big mirror hung on the wall above it. The room wasn't fancy or large by any stretch of the imagination. Nonetheless, a huge smile spread across Melissa's face. *It's mine.*

She spent the rest of the early evening exploring her tiny apartment. It may have seemed small, but to someone who had never had one before there were tons of things to investigate. In the bathroom, she frowned as she studied the sink and ... other fixtures. In the kitchen, she found something called frozen pizza in the freezer. It took her a while, but she deciphered the cooking instructions. Once done, she sat at her kitchen table and took her first mouthful.

"Hmmm." She gazed at the pizza. "This is wonderful."

Night came on too quickly. There was so much more to investigate, but she was yawning every few minutes. Melissa stood in front of the open bedroom window as she changed into a nightgown, watching the street below. The evening breeze was cool and refreshing.

She crawled between the sheets. The soft mattress felt so good as it caressed her tired body. And it had a slight scent of daisies. As she drifted off, Melissa gave a satisfied smile.

God was correct in choosing me. I'll show Him. This mission is going to be easy.

The night air was chilly for late spring. He stood motionless, half hidden in the alley's shadows for the better part of the evening. The cold didn't bother him, though.

At first, the traffic had been heavy as people headed home from work or out for a bite to eat. But as the evening progressed, things slowed down. An occasional car or a stray person went by, their day's tasks completed. No one noticed him.

He remained, eyes not blinking, not wavering.

He watched.

He waited.

The figure stood silent, staring up at the second floor front window of 421 Woodland Rd.

• *Five* •

Pressure. Pushing against the side of her head. A gnawing, drilling pressure. It grew and grew, until it became unbearable.

Overwhelming.

Unyielding.

Melissa begged for it to stop, to be over.

She grabbed the spot. She pulled at it, clawed at it, but nothing helped.

The pressure erupted into a stinging pain.

Suddenly, the air was filled with BUZZ BUZZ BUZZ BUZZ. Melissa's eyes snapped open just as the floor rushed up to meet her. She stretched out her hands to soften the blow, and thudded against the braided rug. The bed loomed large next to her. The sheet was a massive jumble, half tucked in the edge of the bed, half wrapped around her. As she lay there, the first thing she did was to cover her ears.

What's that awful sound?

A minute passed as she struggled to clear the fog from her head and get her bearings. Pulling herself up, she traced the buzzing to the clock sitting on the nightstand. She grabbed at it, which only seemed to get it angrier. She fiddled with its buttons and knobs until finally ... Relief! It fell silent. The pain in her head was gone, too.

Melissa sat on the bed and examined the sides of her head. Where in the world had the pressure and pain come from?

Probably from that annoying buzzing noise.

She stretched, rubbed the sleep out of her eyes, shook it from her brain, and pushed loose strands of hair back over the top of her head.

Earth. My mission.
The now-silent clock read seven forty-five.
Uh-oh.
She was supposed to be at work at nine.
In a whirlwind, she washed, dressed, and ate some leftover pizza, all this accomplished in half an hour. "A miracle!" She added, with a smile, "Kinda."
She descended the outside steps of her building at eight twenty-five. If she hurried she'd get to the store in plenty of time. And hurrying should be no problem at all. *I have a job, here on Earth!*
Her whole body tingled as she sprinted down the sidewalk. When the store came into sight, her pace quickened.
My first full day at work!
She approached the front doors and burst onto the scene.
No one noticed.
The store looked much the same as it did the day before. The same bored-looking boy was leaning against the same counter at the same register.
Melissa raced over to him. "Hello again."
"Hello," he said in a drone-like voice.
"This is my first official day."
"Uh-huh." With great effort, he turned the page of the book in front of him. "Probably should head to the office."
"Thank you."
Melissa's day began with the tedious task of filling out some paperwork. When that was done she got to tag along with seasoned workers, participating in thrilling activities like hanging clothes on racks, restocking footwear, and learning the basics of the cash register. All the while, she made sure that everyone knew, "The Lord loves you and forgives you, too."
Things were going well, for the most part. Of course, when she was hanging up woman's clothing, she had wanted to try everything on. And when she was working the register, Ms. Gibbons had to come over and gently persuade her to stop scanning extra items.
"But I like the sound it makes," she argued.
"I know, sweetheart," Ms. Gibbons said with the same patience she'd been showing Melissa all day. "But the customers don't want to pay for extra items." The Day Manager gave an

apologetic smile to a male shopper who was standing at the register glaring at a receipt for forty-nine packs of gum while gripping one pack in his hand. It all got worked out though, and Ms. Gibbons told Melissa, "What you lack in work-smarts you make up for in enthusiasm."

Throughout the morning, Melissa was introduced to a couple dozen other workers. There was Danny and Susan, and Marcus and Josh, Mabel, Juan, ... too many for her to remember all the names. She'd also seen Todd and that other boy who was sitting with him outside Ms. Gibbons' office. His name was Jonathan. He never smiled, but he stared a lot. As a matter of fact, that would be a good nickname for him — The Starer.

Part way through the day, when she was coming out of the bathroom, he was walking down the hallway. The moment their eyes met, he jerked, accidentally hitting the water cooler and almost knocking it over.

"Hi," Melissa said.

Jonathan made a clumsy grab at the cooler and steadied it. "Oh, hi. I ... I was just getting a drink of water."

"I don't think I've spoken to you before. Did you know the Lord loves you and Jesus forgives you?"

"No. I mean, yes ... I mean ..." He stammered and stuttered, fidgeting to his left and then his right. He almost walked into the women's bathroom. Finally, spinning on his heels, he announced, "I have to get going." He then ran off.

"I'll see you around." Melissa called after him. Odd. Really odd. With a shrug of her shoulders, she too headed back to work.

· *Six* ·

"Come on, Melissa." Mabel, a coworker who appeared to be about her age, had been teaching Melissa how to use a cash register. "It's time for lunch break."

"Really?" Melissa smiled. "Where's the time gone? I've been having such fun."

Mabel snickered while chewing on a wad of gum. "Yeah. That's life at McCullen's!" She waved a hand in front of her, as if following words on a sign. "The place where work and fun meet."

Mabel led the way to the break room.

"You know, Mabel—"

Mabel rolled her eyes. "I know. I know. God loves me and all that stuff." She twirled a finger through a lock of her curly brown hair.

"Oh." Melissa's face got hot. "I already told you."

"Only a hundred times. Come and sit with me."

The room was fairly large, and could seat many more people than were presently employed by the company. About ten small round tables were scattered about. One whole wall was lined with box-covered steel shelving.

Mabel headed for a table far off in the corner of the room. She explained her choice of seats. "This way we're not near the vending machines." She pointed to the candy, drinks, chips, and snacks displayed in the glass-fronted units across the room as she tossed a small paper bag on the table. "My mother nags me to brown bag it. Says I'll save money." She sat down and fished through the sack, pulling out a sandwich. "Says I spend my whole pay check on junk food." She bit off a chunk of the sandwich and chewed.

Melissa's stomach growled loud enough to be heard over their conversation. She grabbed hold of it and looked down, eyes wide.

"Wow, Melissa. You must really be hungry."

"I guess I am."

"So what did you bring to eat?"

"I ... I didn't bring anything." Her face flushed. "I forgot."

Mabel paused. Then she tore her sandwich in two pieces and handed one over. "Here. It's peanut butter and jelly."

"Oh, I couldn't take your food."

"I insist. Besides, it gives me a reason to buy a pack of those chocolate cupcakes." She gazed at one of the vending machines. "It's been calling to me since I came into the room."

"Really?" *Hmmm, I don't hear anything.*

"I'll be right back." Mabel hopped up and made a beeline to the cupcakes while rummaging through her pocketbook.

As Melissa watched her friend go, she took a bite of the sandwich. Her eyes popped open. She took another bite and chewed. Then another, and another, rolling the delicious concoction around with her tongue, savoring every bit of it.

"What's wrong?" Mabel had come back to the table and was ripping open the twin pack of cupcakes.

"Wrong?" Melissa mumbled, her mouth still filled with peanut butter. "Nothing. This is incredible! Why it might be even tastier than ... frozen pizza!"

Mabel raised an eyebrow. "Haven't you ever had peanut butter and jelly before?"

"Not that I can remember."

Mabel grinned. "If you think that's good," she slid one of the cupcakes across the table, "try this."

Melissa held the chocolate pastry in her hand, slowly spinning and examining it. She shrugged. How could this possibly beat peanut butter and jelly? Then she took her first bite. *Wow!*

"Well?" Mabel leaned forward. "What do you think?"

Through a cupcake-stuffed mouth, Melissa proclaimed, "It's wonderful. And look." She pointed to the portion that remained in her hand. "There's white stuff in the center."

"That's the cream filling." Mabel smiled. "My favorite part."

For the next fifteen minutes, Mabel had Melissa sampling a variety of vending machine delicacies, everything from potato sticks to cola. Most were delicious, except the barbecue potato chips and cola.

As Melissa did her sampling, she studied the people around her who were busily engaged in their lunchtime rituals. They seemed to be enjoying a wide variety of activities—gabbing, playing cards, punching buttons on cell phones—all manner of things, while cramming food into their mouths.

Which one of these people is my mission? I've already told a zillion of them God's message. Why am I still here?

She scanned the crowd. Todd sat by the far wall, having a conversation with a much older man. He had his back to Melissa and the older man was facing her. He was nicely dressed, all prim and proper, with a full head of white hair and a broad smile. The man talked non-stop. When he caught sight of Melissa staring at him, he leaned in close to Todd and whispered something. Todd turned and looked. Then he said something back to the man. They shared a knowing smile, got up and approached.

"Hey, Mel," Todd greeted. "So today's it. First day of work." The dark cloud that had covered Todd on yesterday's walk home seemed to have lifted and his happy-go-lucky attitude had reemerged.

The white haired gentleman, who was much shorter than Todd, was peeking around from behind him.

The door to the break room opened and Jonathan walked in. True to form, the Starer slowly perused the room. When his gaze passed over Melissa's table, he stopped.

Oh no. She slumped down in her seat. *He's looking at me.*

At a quick pace, Jonathan made his way through the tables toward her. But when he caught sight of Todd and the other fellow, he pulled up short. For a full fifteen seconds, conflicting emotions played out on his face. It looked like he was torn as to whether he should move forward or turn to the side. Then, he pushed forward.

The table next to Melissa's was empty.

"Please don't sit there. Please don't sit there. Please don't sit there," Melissa mumbled.

He sat there. Then he rummaged through a lunch bag while staring at Melissa's table.

"Anyway," Todd said, while watching Jonathan out of the corner of his eye. "This is Martin." He waved in the direction of the white haired gentleman. "Martin, this is Melissa."

Melissa hopped to her feet. "Martin. The Lord loves you. He forgives you, too."

"See," Todd beamed. "I told you she'd say that. She says that to everybody."

Why is this such a big thing, telling people about God's love? In Heaven, everyone knows the Lord loves them. What is so different here?

"Interesting way to start a conversation." Martin bowed slightly. There was a twinkle in his eye and a hint of admiration in his tone. "Yes, yes," he went on in a high-pitched voice. "Isn't it wonderful to think of how much God loves! Yes indeed."

At least this man seemed to appreciate her message.

"But," Martin waved a finger in the air, "does He love everyone the same?"

Before Melissa could answer, Martin prattled on ... and on and on, bringing up every subject from the weather to nuclear war.

Eventually, he got back to his comment about God's love. "I guess that's the question, isn't it? That's the question philosophers and theologians have debated for hundreds of years. You see some of the terrible things in this world and you wonder about God's love. I mean, I don't wonder. Oh, no. Not me. I know He loves me. But, people who have been in terrible tragedies. They have to doubt, I think. We are so fortunate. But, what about those who aren't? I wonder if they question God's love. I wonder ..." He stopped speaking abruptly. His eyes went from person to person. "I've been rambling. Haven't I? Sorry about that."

"No problem," Todd answered. "We all have our little quirks. You ramble. Melissa tells everyone God loves them."

"Ah, yes." Martin giggled. "But you see, my quirk can be annoying."

"No." Todd shook his head. He turned and spoke to Melissa and Mabel. "Martin's been teaching me the ropes over in Sporting Goods. I can attest to the fact that he likes to talk." A smile stretched across Todd's face.

Everyone laughed.

"But it doesn't bother me," Todd added.

"You're too kind to an old man." Martin patted Todd's arm. "As I was saying, there are those who find my philosophizing annoying, but our friend Melissa here is simply showing great courage."

"Thank you." *I like this fellow, squeaky voice and all.* Then she tipped her head to the side. "Courage? Why courage?"

"Well, my dear. You put your whole self out there. You don't care what people think or say about you."

Melissa grew quiet. She shrunk down in her seat. "Are people saying things about me?"

Todd shrugged. "Nothing you have to be worried about. Who cares what some people think?"

"Yeah," Mabel was shoving the last bite of a chocolate cupcake into her mouth as she spoke. "You be you."

Melissa pursed her lips and glanced around the room. She'd just met all these people. Were some of them saying terrible things about her? She swallowed hard. Were all of them saying terrible things about her?

A group of boys was sitting over in the corner. It included the one who had directed her to the office yesterday morning, along with three others. They had their heads close together and were chuckling and laughing.

Could they be laughing at me?

"Our friend Todd is right," Martin said. "Who cares what others say." He pumped his slim, pale fist in the air. "Commitment to the cause. That's what's important. If people laugh and giggle because you push them to think outside of their comfort zone, then more power to you."

Melissa opened her mouth to answer, but closed it again. Why would anyone find God's message of love and forgiveness something to scoff at?

Martin leaned his hands on the table. "If you'd like my advice—"

Suddenly, there was a grating noise, worse than a cat's claws on a blackboard. Martin jumped. His hands clasped the sides of his head. The four of them turned toward the source of the sound.

There sat Jonathan, fidgeting with his table and chair, scraping them along the cement floor. He went on for a full minute. Then, he gave an awkward look and muttered, "Sorry. Chair's wobbly. Trying to find the right spot." He continued his scraping for another few seconds then went back to his lunch.

Before Martin could continue with the conversation, Todd spoke up. "Hey, Melissa, Mabel's right. You be you. Besides, it's a great message. More people need to hear it. Okay?"

Melissa sat taller in her seat. "Okay."

Martin raised his hand, as if to offer some sage advice, but Todd, looking at the wall clock, interrupted him. "Whoops. Look at the time. Come on, old man. You can philosophize all you want while we're restocking tennis balls."

Martin laughed. "It's your first day and already you're a task master." He turned to the girls and gave a slight bow. "A true pleasure. I wish I could stay and chat, but duty calls. Busy, busy. That's how the store keeps us. I'm sure our paths will cross again."

"Nice meeting you, Martin," Melissa waved.

Martin nodded at her and Mabel. Then he scurried away.

"Funny old bird." Mabel shook her head.

"He seems sweet enough. Certainly gave me something to think about. I'd have never thought anyone would laugh at my message." She turned to the table in the corner. The boys were picking up their lunch trash and getting ready to head back to work.

"Ah-hem ..."

Mabel and Melissa turned to Jonathan who was sheepishly looking their way.

"I um ... I think ... your message is great."

"Do you?" *Considering his earlier reaction, outside of the bathrooms, that's kinda hard to believe.*

"Oh yes." He pushed himself away from the table and stood up. "You're doing a good job. Keep it up." With that said, he ran off.

"You know what?" Mabel said. "If Martin is a funny old bird, then Jonathan is a funnier young bird." She cocked her head to the side. "I'm not sure if funnier is the right word, though."

The Starer. Jonathan exited the room. *Funny young bird.*

• *Seven* •

Dr. Henry Winters was following his morning routine—a quick jog before breakfast, which always consisted of toast, poached eggs, and a glass of orange juice. Then he'd sit in his study and go through yesterday's mail. Most people would come home after a hard day's work and take care of this chore right way, but not him. Once he left the Center, he liked to put all work behind him and devote a couple of hours to his wife.

"Bill, bill, junk ..." He flipped through the stack, separating it into piles of important, not important, and throw right out. One envelope was addressed with big block letters. No return label. That would usually place it in the junk pile. But his address was handwritten. He gave it a wary look. It might contain a white powder.

All those post-9/11 stories of poisoned mail.

Finally, using a small letter opener, he gingerly sliced through the seal. He took a deep breath. Dangling the envelope at arm's length, he peered inside for any hazardous or dangerous material. Nothing. He held the envelope on end and shook. A letter fell to the desk. He unfolded it. The words were written in the same big block lettering as the address on the envelope. As he read, his jaw tightened. "Murderer. I'm watching you. You will pay for your crimes."

He shrugged. *Just some nut job blowing off steam. Nothing to worry about.*

In his line of work, he got hate mail all the time. Crazies and ultra-conservatives all had a vendetta against him, but it never amounted to anything more than an occasional letter and dirty looks.

He picked up the envelope to crumple and trash, and a 3X5 photo fell out.

How'd I miss that?

He scooped it off the floor. His eyebrows rose. It was a picture of him and his wife, relaxing in the backyard by their pool. The particular day the picture was taken was oppressively hot and they'd decided on what he had laughingly called 'alternative beach apparel', which basically meant skinny dipping. He blushed slightly. He'd assumed they were safe from prying eyes. Two adults, enjoying a relaxing afternoon in their own backyard. Then the lines between his eyebrows deepened. He clenched his teeth. *Someone was watching us. How dare they invade our privacy?*

He scrutinized the picture. "How did someone ..."

The backyard was surrounded by tall hedges. Impossible for anyone with a telescopic lens to take this picture from a far distance.

Whoever did this had to be in one of the neighbor's yards. Yet, the only one close enough to get this shot belonged to a retired judge. Not the kind of person to risk incarceration on charges of being a Peeping Tom. Besides, the man was well into his eighties.

Don't think he's up to the task.

Doctor Winters smirked at the image of the octogenarian battling through the privacy hedges with a machete.

"What are you looking at?"

He jumped at his wife's voice. The tall blonde entered the room, walked over to the window and opened the blinds. The brilliance of the sunlight outlined her shapely body.

"Nothing." He tried to sound nonchalant. "Just some mail." He slid open the top drawer of his desk and swept the envelope and its contents inside.

His wife walked behind him and kissed the top of his head. "Don't take too long. You don't want to be late for work." She strolled out the study.

After a few seconds, Dr. Winters pulled the picture back out. Something else on it caught his eye, or more appropriately, his fingers. A smudge or stain of some kind. He held the photo close and squinted. A reddish-brown line was drawn across both their faces.

"Reddish-brown. Like dried ..." The muscles in his neck tensed.

Maybe this is more than a harmless crackpot.

· *Eight* ·

Melissa finished her second week of work. She was getting the opportunity to investigate Earth, but when would her mission be completed? Why was it taking so long? She shrugged her shoulders. *Oh well.* Until her time on earth was done, she'd enjoy this life with her new friends Todd, Martin, and Mabel. Even Ms. Gibbons seemed more like a friend than a boss. At home, she'd struck up some nice conversations with Mrs. Parsioni. Melissa smirked. *Though, keeping up with that woman is extremely difficult.*

Melissa exited the store and looked up at the gray sky. Dark, cold, and wet. Another rainy day.

This had been the weather for the past forty-eight hours. She huddled under the store's canvas awning as little streams flowed over its edge, drizzling onto the pavement below. The rain picked up. Wind-driven sheets blew across the sidewalk. It was as if it knew she had come out of the store and was thumbing its nose at her, daring her to step out into the deluge.

How am I going to get home without getting soaked? She glanced down the sidewalk. *Should I run to the bus stop?*

A car rolled to the curb in front of her. The driver lowered the passenger window and called across the sidewalk to her. "Hi there, do you need a ride?"

Melissa peered into the darkened interior at the man seated behind the steering wheel. He had brown hair with graying temples, and was well dressed with a tie hanging loosely around his neck. *Do I know him?*

His pearly white teeth flashed a smile in her direction. "Don't you recognize me? I come in the store all the time. You sold me some socks today."

"Oh yes."

"Kind of wet out there." The rain was pelting against the hood of the car, causing such a loud ruckus that it was hard to hear him. He raised his voice above the din. "But if you don't mind me saying, you wear the water well." His eyes ran up and down her form.

Melissa nodded. *Was that a compliment?*

"It's a lot drier in here. Maybe I could give you a ride." He leaned over and smiled. "Maybe go have some fun. I hear you like to have fun."

"I like fun." She smiled back at him.

He reached across and opened the door, his grin stretching from ear to ear. "Get in."

She obeyed. "It's so nice of you to offer me a ride, Mr ...."

"Parker. Parker Stevens. Think nothing of it." He touched her shoulder. "I'm sure we can think of some way for you to thank me."

Danger! Run! A small voice at the back of her head was nagging at her. But as she settled into the seat, the warm air from the vent blew on her face, drying her wet skin. Parker seemed like a happy person.

What danger could I possibly be in?

"How about if we go for a drive?"

"Sure." Her eyes danced about as she gripped the door handle. Not only was she out of the wet rain, she was going for a ride in a car, something she hadn't done in her time here. She looked back at the people trying to stay dry under the awning. *Lucky me. Safe, out of the rain.*

The engine revved and they sped away.

The scenery flashed by as the car raced down the road. Colors zipped passed, faster and faster, just like when her angel would take her flying around in Heaven. Buildings, trees, people. So wonderful.

Parker engaged in small talk, nothing of any consequence.

As they hurried along, the buildings appeared less frequently. Less city and more countryside.

After a while, Parker pulled the vehicle onto the deep shoulder of the road, under a clump of trees.

Melissa looked all around, out the front window and out the back. Nothing but trees. Dark trees. The rain was banging against the roof of the car. "Where are we?"

"Oh ... I thought we'd take a break." His voice took on a sing-songy quality. "Enjoy each other's company. If you know what I mean."

Melissa's forehead wrinkled. *Huh?*

Parker reached over and with one finger drew circles on Melissa's shoulder.

Adrenaline coursed through her veins and her heart pounded wildly. "What–what are you doing?"

"Like I said, we're going to have a little fun. I was told you like to have fun." He moved closer to her.

Her back stiffened. "Who told you that?"

He flitted his hand through the air. "Word gets around." He brushed the back of his hand against her cheek. "You're such a pretty young thing."

She pulled away. "I–I don't understand."

"Oh come now." He undid his seatbelt, turned to face her, and moved as close as the bucket seats would allow. His hand rested on her knee. "Don't be a tease."

Melissa's heart beat faster. Parker's breath was hot as he pressed closer. His hand began a slow ascent up her leg.

Like a small bird cornered by a wild cat, she froze. There was nowhere for her to go. She opened her mouth to speak, but nothing came out. *This is wrong. This is so wrong.* Finally, she blurted in a shrill voice, "The Lord ... loves you. He forgives you!"

Parker sat straight up, his head almost hitting the car's ceiling. He recovered and smiled at her, raising his left eyebrow. "Where did that come from? Are you trying to ruin the mood?"

"Mood?"

"Don't be a cold fish. My wife's a cold fish."

"You're married?" Melissa's mouth dropped open.

"Yes, but not to anything as sweet as you. Besides," He put on sad puppy dog eyes, "she doesn't understand me. Come on sweetheart." He tried to kiss her.

She turned her face away from him and pressed it against the rain-streaked window.

"Oh, playing hard to get?" He put his hand around her head and forced her to turn back. His fingers pulled at her hair, digging into her skin. "Come on. You know you want it."

"No!" She screamed and tried to slap his face, but he caught her hand short of its mark.

"Naughty, naughty."

She squirmed, kicking and punching, trying to break free, but Parker held her firmly.

"Fight all you want. I like a feisty woman." He got up on his knees and pinned her against the door. The shoulder of her dress ripped. "Don't you worry your pretty little head over that. You be good to me and I'll buy you a new dress. Heck, I'll buy you a closet full!"

He pressed his body into hers, his lips and teeth against her neck. His hot breath on her skin.

Melissa's stomach churned. She closed her eyes, clenching them so tightly that tears squeezed out. She turned her head as far away from him as she could and screamed, "God, help me!"

Parker gave a sadistic chuckle. "No one's going to hear you."

Melissa looked up at this animal holding her prisoner, and her heart sank to her feet. *He's right. No one will hear.*

But then, something ... a figure moved outside the driver's window.

Parker turned his head. He lifted himself off her. "What's that?"

Melissa was free from the weight of his body. She gulped in a lung-full of air.

The driver's door burst open. Two hands grabbed Parker and tore him out of the car. In a blink, he was lying on the ground in a puddle.

Melissa pulled herself up in her seat. Who was her rescuer? His back was to her, his head above the doorframe.

Whoever it was had to be an improvement over Parker.

"Who do you think you are?" Parker pushed himself off the muddy pavement and headed toward the vehicle. A scowl erupted through his dirt-streaked face. "You're interrupting us."

The newcomer stood guard, blocking the car door. "I don't think so."

Melissa cocked her head to the side. *That voice ... it sounds familiar. But it's so hard to hear through this pelting rain.*

Parker stepped forward, standing chest to chest with the stranger. "Leave me and the lady alone."

"The young lady is mine." The voice spoke with a calm authority. "You will not touch her again."

Melissa froze. Had she heard right?

Parker's face twisted. "I gave you a chance." He drew out his right hand from behind his back, revealing a rock he'd picked off the ground, and swung it at his assailant's head. The stranger didn't even flinch. He merely lifted his hand and blocked the attack. Then he gave Parker a backhanded slap, again knocking him to the ground.

Parker got up and wiped the blood from his lip. His chest heaving, he glared at the stranger. "Who cares? She's not worth it." He then turned, as if to give up and walk away. But, in an instant, he swung back at the other man. His scream filled the air, more animal than human. Melissa huddled against the passenger door as Parker threw himself at the stranger.

The stranger sidestepped the attack, grabbed ahold of Parker as he passed and flung him into the side of the car, slamming his head into the roof. Then, grasping the collar of Parker's shirt, the stranger flung him at least ten feet in the air before he hit the ground once again.

Battered and beaten, Parker slowly rose to his feet. His expensive suit was ruined, ripped and covered with mud. He waved his hands in surrender. "All right. You win."

The stranger's back was still toward Melissa. His hands were curled into tight fists. "Start walking." He pointed down the road.

Parker gave him a puzzled look. He spoke, almost pleading. "But this is my car."

"It will be waiting for you back at your house."

"But—"

"Walk!"

Parker glared at the other man. But the fury and fight were gone from him. He turned and disappeared into the rain.

Then Melissa's rescuer climbed in the driver's seat.

A lump formed in her throat. She was having trouble catching her breath. "Jonathan ... What are you doing here?"

"Melissa." Jonathan's black eyes looked out between rain soaked strands of hair. "Are you okay?"

Melissa's heart raced.

The Starer sat motionless. Only his eyes moved, scanning her. When he spotted the rip in her dress, by her shoulder, his face darkened.

Melissa fumbled with the two pieces of the tear, trying to pull them back together again. Had she been rescued from one attacker only to be placed in the hands of another? She forced herself to look away from him, focusing instead on her hands, fidgeting in her lap.

"I ... I heard you tell Parker that ... I was yours." She swallowed hard.

Jonathan smiled. "You are."

Melissa fumbled for the door handle.

"We have to talk," he said.

"I think I'll walk home." She fell out of the car onto the muddy ground. She had to get away. She got up and walked, she trotted, she ran. Anything to put distance between her and the car.

"Melissa, stop!"

The driver's door slammed shut. Glancing over her shoulder, Melissa gasped. Jonathan was marching at her, the rain pelting off his large muscular frame. Why had God given her such a small body and made these men so big? So strong? What could she do?

"Melissa!" He picked up his pace.

A knot formed in the pit of her stomach.

I could die out here. Out in the middle of nowhere. No one around. No one to care. No one to know.

She ran down the road, driven by the footsteps pressing after her, slapping against the wet pavement. She tried to run faster.

"Melissa, stop! I have to talk to you."

Maybe there's a house up ahead.

She ran harder.

Or maybe another car will come by.

Melissa's foot caught on a crack in the road and she tumbled forward, slamming into the pavement, face first. Her vision filled with stars. She tasted blood in her mouth. She winced when her finger probed the cut lip and abrasions on her cheek. She lay there, face down, her hands clawing against the dirt and pebbles under her. Raindrops splashed in the puddles around her.

She began to weep.

The footsteps grew closer ... closer.

Then they stopped.

It was too late. She couldn't get away, couldn't hide. She turned her head and looked up. The rain stung as it hit her bruises. Jonathan stood over her, staring down. She turned back toward the road. Pebbles and bits of dirt ground into her forehead.

"No. Please don't." She curled into a fetal position and covered her face with her arm.

Oh, God. Help me.

"He is. And He did." Jonathan whispered.

She gazed up at him. *Did he hear my prayer? Had I said the words out loud? Can he read my mind?*

"Melissa," he said softly.

"No." She blindly swung her arm out. Maybe she could get one good hit in. "No. Leave me alone."

"Melissa!"

"Please." She rolled on her side and sobbed. "Don't hurt me."

"Child." Jonathan spoke with such softness, such tenderness, in a way she had heard many times before. That voice. It was so familiar. Muddied and bruised, she faced the man. The rain streamed down her forehead and carried bits of dirt into her eyes. She tried to blink them away, and through blurry vision gave him a questioning look.

He stretched out his hand. "Touch me."

"What?"

"You heard me. Take my hand!" He didn't wait for her to respond, but reached down and pulled her to her feet. As soon as their hands touched, her eyes were opened. Not physically, but spiritually. Jonathan transformed. His stature, his size, grew right before her. His wings swept out from his back, arching high above, covering her from the beating rain.

She stood, trembling and shivering. *I can't believe what I'm seeing.* After a moment, she threw herself into him. "Angel! My angel!"

He wrapped his arms around her and enfolded her with his wings, pulling her in as a mother hen would pull in her baby chicks. "Yes. Your angel. You're safe now."

Then he scooped her up in his arms and took her back to the car.

• *Nine* •

Melissa sat in the passenger seat, drenched and shivering. The car's heater was taking a while to warm her chilled skin. Jonathan had returned to human form and was digging around in the car's trunk. Soon he returned to the driver's seat, a blanket in hand. It scratched her chin as he tucked it around her shoulders. He put the car in gear and aimed it back toward the city.

My angel.

It was so odd, seeing him in this tiny human form.

Their last encounter in Heaven seemed so long ago.

Melissa was crawling through the tall grass, the blades sweeping against her face. Her heart pumped, her palms sweated. *There it is!* A large oak tree in the middle of the clearing.

Not far now. Keep calm. Keep calm.

She took long, deep breaths, and glanced around. Nothing to the left ... nothing to the right ... nothing up above. All appeared to be clear, but caution was the key to success.

I've been fooled before.

She held her breath and reached for the soft cool grass of the open expanse. One hand touched down. Then another. Finally, she inched into the clearing. Vulnerable now, out in the open. Slowly, her head pivoted from left to right.

"Please, oh please let me make it," she whispered.

As she crept closer to the tree, her whole body trembled. It was as if the branches were beckoning to her—Run! Run! Should she leap up and make a mad dash for it? Victory was only a few feet away. Finally, she bolted.

Yes. Oh yes! There it was. She could almost touch it. Her neck tingled, her muscles tensed.

A shadow crossed over her, blocking the light, blocking the warmth.

Like a rock, she fell to the ground. *Lay still! Maybe he didn't see you. Blend with the field. Look like a mound of dirt. Or a stone.*

After an eternity of seconds, she slowly turned her head and looked skyward. A figure was gliding high overhead. His eyes were scanning. His wings glistened in the light as he circled closer ... closer.

Her stomach churned. Her heart sank. Had he seen her? Maybe not. Now the oak tree looked miles away.

But wait!

She smiled. A small elm lay between her and the oak. About half the distance. Maybe she could get there, find safety beneath its branches. She had to risk it, risk moving. Staying down on the ground, she rolled toward the tree.

Go! Faster!

As she moved forward the ground beneath her changed. More hard dirt. Less soft grass. She rolled over a tree root. *Made it!* She pushed onto her knees and scurried for the trunk. Clinging to the rough bark, she held her breath. Her mouth went dry.

Look up. See if he's still there. No, he might see me. Might sense me looking at him. With her eyes squeezed closed, she remained motionless. *Fly away. Fly away!*

Five heartbeats ... Ten. When at least forty-five heartbeats passed, she dared to look. For the first time since hugging the tree, she exhaled. The sky was empty. He was gone. She relaxed her hold on the tree and smirked. "He thinks he's so smart."

"Not smart. I just have good eye sight."

She startled and spun around. A big hand reached out to grab hold of her. She tried to duck, but it was too late. He caught her by the shoulder. "Gotcha!" A toothy smile crossed her captor's broad face.

"No you don't!" She was so close to her goal, closer than she'd ever been before. Too close to give up. With a mighty burst, she pushed out of his clutches and launched herself the last twenty feet. She reached out her hand, stretching her arm as far as she could, grasping for her goal. "Yes! Victory!"

"Not this time." An iron grip clamped onto her leg. He lifted her like a rag doll and dangled her upside down. She crossed her arms and gave him a defiant stare. "Good try, though," he said.

She wriggled and squirmed. The angel released his grip and she fell. As soon as she hit the ground, she scampered to the large oak. Touching its base, she proclaimed, "I made it! I win!"

"Oh, no. I caught you fair and square."

"Okay, okay." She raised her hands in surrender and laughed.

"I think that was the farthest you've gotten."

Her face beamed. "Really? You're not just saying that?"

Out of all the angels, this particular one was her favorite. He wasn't the most important angel, nor was he the biggest, though he towered above her. What he was, was her angel. That's how she would usually refer to him — My angel.

She inhaled deeply, fell backwards into the grassy field and gazed up at the sky. "Doesn't the air smell sweet today?"

The angel sniffed and wrinkled his nose. "I've never thought of the air as sweet. I simply think of it as ... air. But if you say it's sweet, then it's sweet." He tipped his head to the side. "You have a unique way of looking at things."

"Thank you."

They were on a hillside, surrounded by a forest of brightly colored trees and flowers. It was as if God had taken from His palette all the tints and hues of creation and brushed them throughout Heaven, to be a visual feast for its inhabitants to enjoy.

She gazed beyond the forest to the roofs and spires of the celestial city in the distance. *There's only one thing that would make me happier.*

The angel approached and sat beside her, his massive form dwarfing hers. "You look deep in thought."

She nestled deeper into the forest floor. The garden of wild flowers tickled the sides of her face. "Let's talk."

"What about?"

She hesitated. "Earth?"

"Earth?" His voice had a 'not that again' tone to it. "Why?"

"Well, you say that's where I'm from. I'd like to know all about it."

"I've told you everything I can." He shrugged his massive shoulders. "I don't know what else to say."

She sat up and scratched her head. "I wish I could remember something ... anything. I have no memories of Earth. What's it like there?"

Her angel stood and paced. A deep scowl covered his face. He shook his head. "Well. It's different. Very different."

"How so?"

He huffed and turned his back to her. "Why are you asking so many questions about Earth?"

She looked down at the flowers and hunched her shoulders. "It's just ... other people remember." A tinge of frustration crept into her tone. She pulled a daisy out of the ground and proceeded to pluck its petals, one by one. "Earlier, I was talking with my friends, Susan and Jeffrey. They shared memories of their time on Earth."

"That's not important. All that matters is God loves you." His tone softened. "You like being here, don't you?"

"Yes! It's only ..."

The angel sank down beside her and placed a hand on her shoulder. "Sometimes remembering is not a good thing. Sometimes we don't remember because it's too painful."

She tipped her head to the side. "Painful? What is painful?"

The angel thought. "It is a hurting ... an emptiness. Physical, but it can be emotional, too." Each word he spoke brought a deeper crease in Melissa's brow. He ran a finger along her cheek. "How would you feel if you were separated from the Lord?"

Melissa took in a sharp breath. "I can't even imagine such a thing."

The angel grunted. "That, child, is why I'm having trouble explaining pain. It's hard for you to understand what you've never experienced."

Jonathan steered the car into a parking space outside Melissa's apartment.

Now I know what pain is.

His eyes burrowed into her. "Are you sure you're all right?"

"Yes," she sniffed. "Thanks to you." She lowered her head.

The angel sighed. "You've got to be more careful. This isn't Heaven."

"But he offered me a ride home."

Jonathan grunted and shook his head. "Humans can be so deceitful."

Melissa used the edge of the blanket to wipe the rain and mud off her face. "What are you doing here, anyway?"

He shrugged. "I'm an angel. I go where the Lord sends me. I deliver His messages."

"Jonathan?"

"What?"

"No. I mean ... Jonathan ... the name you're using. How did you choose it?"

"In the Old Testament, he was a good friend to David, willing to risk all to help him."

She smiled. *So am I your David?* "It fits."

Jonathan sighed. "How could you get yourself in such a predicament?"

"Sorry." She hung her head.

"Thankfully, the Lord arranged for us both to work at the store. I've been keeping an eye on you."

"I know."

"What's that supposed to mean?"

"Well," she hesitated. Her lips curled in a small smirk. "You're kind of creepy, the way you watch me. Todd and I call you the Starer. You've really got to work on those people skills."

Jonathan grumbled. Melissa continued to look at her long-time friend. "Look who's staring now," he said. "What's wrong?"

"Nothing. It's just ... different, seeing you like this." She shook her head. "So different ... so small."

He glared out the front window, steely-eyed. "Be prepared to see a lot of ... different things. The Earth is filled with them."

"Jonathan. Why didn't you tell me?"

"Tell you what?"

"Who you were? Why didn't you let me know right away?"

"Would you have done anything different?"

"No." She hesitated. "I don't think so."

He shrugged. "God has sent me on a mission. You have yours. I have mine."

"Does anyone else know?"

"Do you mean do other people know I'm an angel?" He shook his head. "No, they don't."

"Why not?"

"Melissa." His voice grew grimmer. "This is very important. You can't tell anyone I'm an angel. Do you understand?"

"But wouldn't it make your job easier?"

"No." There was no negotiation in his tone. "No one. That means Todd, Ms. Gibbons, Mabel ... no one. In fact, no one should know the truth about you, either. You can't tell anyone. Do you understand?"

She shuffled her feet. "If it's so important, how come the Lord didn't tell me this?"

"He did." Jonathan practically shouted. "You weren't listening." A small grumbling sound came from deep in his throat. "You were too excited about coming to Earth."

She winced. *Maybe I missed a few things He said.* "I won't tell anyone," she mumbled. With her head hung low, she pulled the blanket up, covering her face. "You don't have to yell at me."

Jonathan sighed. He reached over and pulled the blanket down. "I didn't mean to get you upset. I'm simply impressing on you the importance of secrecy. It's vital to my mission. It's vital to your mission. It's what God wants. Do you understand?"

Finally, she nodded. "Okay." Her face brightened. *I always have trouble staying mad at my angel.* "It will be our secret." She opened the car door.

"Would you like me to come up with you?"

She shook her head. "I promised Mrs. Parsioni that I wouldn't entertain gentlemen callers." She hopped out of the car and closed the door. The rain had slowed to a small trickle and the evening sun was beginning to peek out through the clouds.

Jonathan rolled down the window. "I'll see you tomorrow at work."

What a funny thing to hear my angel say.

She turned to leave, but hesitated. "Jonathan." She peered back into the car window. "What about Parker?"

"He'll be all right. The walk will do him good." Jonathan's face darkened. "The Lord and I will take care of him."

The smoldering anger in his voice chilled Melissa. *I've never seen him like this before.*

"Oh, by the way." Jonathan glanced across the street to an alley. Then he looked up at her window. "At night, pull the shades down before you get undressed."

Melissa looked up at the window. Her face warmed. "Okay."

She headed up the steps of her building and gave her friend one final wave as she closed the front door. It clicked shut. Melissa was cut off from her angel. Cut off from the world. The hallway was so empty, so desolate. Specks of dust floated in the stream of sunlight that came through the rain-streaked window above the door. Melissa started up the stairs. The first step creaked. As did the second ... and the third. *Did they always creak?* Before she stepped onto the top landing, she peered over the banister and down the long hall that led to her apartment. *It looks empty.*

She took that final step onto the second floor. A loud clunk sounded from below. She jumped. Then she looked over the rail. No one. Nothing. She shook her head. *Probably the house settling.*

Melissa unlocked her door. She pushed it open until it hit the inside wall. Again, she jumped. "Silly." She caught her breath. "It's only your door."

She stood still on the threshold, peering into the darkened kitchen. It wasn't the pitch black of night, but the shadowy darkness that comes when the sun is getting lower in the sky. Long shadows stretched across the room.

No way of knowing what's lurking in those shadows. Goose bumps prickled as if Parker's cold hand crept up her leg that instant. Her hands brushed against her thighs over and over.

From the security of the hallway, she slid her hand along the inside wall of the apartment, searching for the light switch. Her eyes closed and she gave a quick prayer of thanks when she found it and flipped it on. The kitchen was bathed with a warm glow, chasing the shadows away.

Melissa's brow creased. Even when the light was turned off, her apartment wasn't dark. She could see everything. *So how come that single light bulb makes me feel so much better, so much safer?* She hurried inside and pushed the door shut. Then her shaking hands fumbled with the deadbolt.

Her eyes darted around the small kitchen, making sure she was all alone.

Foolish! Of course I'm alone. She gave a thankful glance at the floor. *But not too alone. Mrs. Parsioni is right downstairs.*

She quickstepped to the living room, all the while looking over her shoulder to make sure no one was reaching out to grab her. She sat on the couch, not moving, barely breathing ... just listening. Not for anything in particular, but for everything. For any sound that meant trouble. There were plenty of them. Creaking floorboards from the apartment upstairs, traffic sounds from outside, something moving in the wall. Probably just a mouse. They were common noises, but now they took on a new meaning. Now she jumped at each creak, whether or not it was coming from inside her apartment.

Her heart pounded in her ears. She ran into the kitchen, rummaged through a drawer, and pulled out a steak knife. She grunted and gave a dismissive shake of her head. *I don't think I could stab someone.* Searching the drawer again, she pulled out a spatula. Then she crept from room to room, holding this weapon in front of her for protection. She peeked around every corner, waved the spatula like a sword through every shadow. Her palms were sweating. She found no one.

Then why am I still afraid?

Melissa sank on the edge of the bed and frowned into the dresser's mirror. Her face was streaked with tears, dried blood, and dirt. Her hair was matted and soaked. She took a deep breath and puffed it out through her nose. *Fear or no fear, I have to get cleaned up.*

The shower's warm water splashed on the tub's floor. Melissa climbed in and let it flow over her face.

What was that?

She pulled the shower curtain back to look into the bathroom, wrapping it around herself for protection. *I'm sure I heard a noise.* Her eyes narrowed. Nothing. With her hands clutching the curtain, she did another slow scan of the room.

No one's here. Get a hold of yourself.

The door was locked. The apartment was empty. She was all alone. Still, over the water beating against the tub and curtain, there was a noise. Not a constant one. It seemed to happen only when her guard was lowering, when she was beginning to relax just a bit.

During the shower, she jerked back the curtain several times, half expecting to see Parker's sadistic smile.

Stop it!

But she didn't. She kept looking.

She gripped the soap in her hands and rubbed it on her skin. Over and over she scrubbed. The water streamed through her hair and down her face. The dirt and mud ran into the drain.

When she was done, she stood in the center of the bathroom, pressing the towel on her face, crying. She moped into the bedroom, plunked down on the edge of the bed, and gazed into the mirror. This time, the image that stared back had a different appearance. Bruised yet clean. She frowned. Not clean. Something's still wrong. Something on the inside. An aching. A con- stant desire to weep. With wide-eyed astonishment, she looked at her reflection. *I'm ... I'm afraid.*

Melissa had gazed into the ugliest face of humanity and she had found fear. She cringed.

She pulled on her clothes and opened the window to let in some air. Then she crossed the room and fell onto the bed. "Oh Lord. How do they do it? How do these people exist in this world?" She beat her fists on her forehead. "It's so hard. I miss Heaven, Lord. You said You'd be with me. Where are You? I feel so alone." Melissa closed her eyes. A tear rolled down the side of her face. Then she turned onto her side and gazed at the blank wall. All alone.

The sounds of the street came through the open bedroom window. Cars zooming by, horns blowing, people's conversations as they strolled along the sidewalk.

Then the noise muffled. Over the dampened sound, music floated in on the evening breeze. "Amazing Grace. How sweet the sound, that saved a wretch like me ..."

Melissa bolted upright.

"I once was lost ..."

The angel choir?

She bounded across her room and leaned so far out the window, she almost fell through. She searched the sky for a group of hovering angels.

Where is that singing coming from? Her eyes locked on a large stone building at the corner.

There! That's it!

Melissa rushed through her apartment door, out of the building, and down the street.

· Ten ·

With each step she took toward the corner building, the singing grew louder.

That isn't the angelic choir.

There weren't the depths of harmonies, the quality of sound, the perfection of Heaven. But there was something else, something that made Melissa's heart jump in her chest. There was a joy, a passion. Oh, yes, the angels had passion. But somehow, this was different.

The sign above the door read, 'The Joy of the Lord Tabernacle.' She paused on the sidewalk, gazing up at the big glass doors. The music was so loud now, so clear. Every chord, every tone, every note. Even the ones that were a bit off key. Melissa smiled. It was wonderful.

She stood there, chewing on her fingernails. *Can I go in?* What right did she have? She didn't even know these people. Then with a deep breath, she tossed away those thoughts, like a person would toss off a heavy winter coat, and headed into the building.

She was at the back of a large room. Rows of long, wooden pews all faced the front where a group of about thirty people stood, singing praises to the Lord. Colored windows lined the walls. She tipped her head and squinted. *Hmmm. Something's familiar.* She walked over and examined one of the windows more closely. It showed two people. One standing and the other kneeling. The standing man had placed his hand on the kneeler's head. The inscription read, 'Jesus heals the blind man.' *Not bad.* She frowned. *But they didn't quite get Jesus right.*

As pretty as the windows were, it was the music that had drawn her. She sank into one of the pews at the back of the room, closed her eyes, and listened.

"When we've been there ten thousand years ..."

Beautiful!

Like a cleansing spring, the music flowed over her. Several minutes passed.

"Sweetheart. What are you doing here?"

Melissa opened her eyes. She beamed. It was the woman she'd met on the park bench. What was her name? She'd been introduced to so many people since then. Her face scrunched up.

"Harriet," the woman prompted.

"Yes! Harriet."

"And you are Melissa. I never forget a name. Besides, who could forget such a lovely young lady like you? But, what are you doing here?"

"I wanted to listen to the music."

"You listen all you want, child." Harriet patted Melissa's shoulder. "Right now, I have to get up there. I'm late." She bustled up the aisle and took her place amongst the crowd. A woman handed her a folder of music and Harriet lifted her voice in joyful sound, all the while smiling at Melissa.

The music engulfed Melissa and carried her beyond the day's cares—helping, healing, freeing, encouraging. It was wonderful. Eventually, it stopped.

"Okey-dokey," said a man standing before the group. "That's it for the night. We'll see you all here on Sunday. Don't forget to be early. A rehearsal before church never hurt anybody." He pointed at someone and said in a joking tone, "That means you too, George! Don't be late. No stopping for doughnuts on the way."

Everyone laughed as they began milling about the front of the room, breaking into smaller groups and chatting. Melissa rose from her seat and ambled around, checking out the bright and colorful windows. Right now they were illuminated by the streetlights and neon signs of the nearby businesses.

Imagine how beautiful they'd look in sunlight.

One window depicted a group of people gathered around one man. The inscription read, 'Jesus and His Apostles.'

Melissa tipped her head to one side, scrutinizing the image. Jesus' arms were out to the sides, His palms up, showing holes in their centers.

Well, at least they got that part right.

Reaching up, she ran her fingers along the glass hands. As she gazed at the window, the corners of her mouth drew up.

The cool meadow grass tickled her bare feet. Melissa sank down on a large rock and slid forward until her toes submerged beneath the water's surface. She lobbed a stone into the lake and watched the circles ripple out. The warm air caressed her.

"Hello Melissa," a voice called from across the lake, where a small group of people were picnicking on the shore. A young girl was waving at her.

With great enthusiasm, she waved back. "See you at worship!"

"I'll save a seat for you!"

Melissa nodded. Then she went back to her game of tossing stones. Small waves licked against the shore.

"Having fun?"

Like sunshine bursting through rainclouds, Melissa's grin spread across her face. Jesus was standing beside her. "Yes."

He reached down and picked up a stone. "Have you tried skipping them?"

Her head cocked to the side. "Skipping?"

"Yes. Many children on Earth find great pleasure in skipping stones across ponds and lakes."

Her nose wrinkled. *Did I skip stones on Earth?* She tried to think back, but couldn't get beyond her memories of Heaven.

"Here. Let me show you." With a sidearm throw, Jesus skipped a stone across the water's surface. It skidded for some forty feet before sinking.

Melissa laughed. "That was wonderful." She picked up a stone and tried to mimic the Master's actions. It hit the surface and immediately dropped to the bottom.

She frowned.

"Try again," Jesus encouraged.

She did, with the same results. "Something must be wrong with my stones."

"Let me help you." Jesus placed a stone in her hand, forming her fingers to hold it in the proper way. Then moving around behind her, He took hold of her arm and gently guided it in the throwing motion. "Like this." Then stepping back, He said, "Now give it a try."

Melissa's tongue stuck out the side of her mouth as her arm moved back and forth. At the proper moment, she released the stone. It skidded across the surface. "Yes!" She squeezed Jesus' hands and jumped up and down. "I did it! I did it!"

"Yes, you did." Jesus' eyes sparkled.

After a moment of celebration, she released her grip on Him. Her hands slid over His until her fingers touched something ... something different. She turned His palms over for a closer look. At the base of each hand was a scar-encircled hole. She traced them with her finger.

"What's this?"

"That, my child, is a sign of my love."

She gave a quizzical look.

"Redemption," He said.

Redemption? She shrugged. "What's that?" "Humans on Earth don't always do what they should." "That's silly."

"They disobey me."

"But you're the Lord. You created them."

"I know."

She looked over to where the small group was picnicking. "If they disobeyed ... how can they be here with us?" Her eyes swept around, taking in all the wonder, glory, beauty and joy that is Heaven. "How can they be here?"

Jesus placed His hand on the side of her face. The scar scratched her cheek. He spoke as a loving father to a small child. "Sacrifice."

Was there a small change in His manner? When He spoke the word, was there something? Around the corners of His eyes had there been a twinge of something Melissa hadn't ever seen before?

"Sacrifice? I don't understand."

The Lord nodded. "When sin is committed, there must be payment. The great sin of mankind was more than they could pay for. It called for a perfect life. A perfect sacrifice."

"So where did they get one?"

"I died for them." He spoke the words quietly, and with great love. "I was the sacrifice."

"Died?" *Why? How does God die?* It didn't make any sense. "Did it ... did it hurt?"

"Yes." Jesus looked out at the people across the lake. "But the greater pain would have been to lose my love. My people."

She ran her finger along the nail-scarred hand. Then announced in a confident voice, "I would never sin. Never disobey you."

Jesus lowered His head and closed His eyes. He remained silent.

"Did you enjoy the music?"

Melissa jumped. Harriet was standing beside her, along with a tall, thin man. "Oh yes. It was wonderful."

"You think so?" The older woman chuckled. "We're no angelic choir, but—"

"Oh no! You are much more." Melissa's eyes widened. "They don't sing with the same joy."

Harriet and the man shared a puzzled look.

"This is a wonderful place, too." Melissa continued, as she walked back to the pew. "Do you sing here often?"

"Every Sunday morning," Harriet said.

"Really?" Melissa beamed. "Can I come and listen?"

"Of course," Harriet said. "You can sit with my grandson. He's always complaining about sitting alone. Oh, by the way, Melissa," Harriet turned to the man standing with her. "I'd like you to meet Pastor Tom Reading. Pastor Tom, this is Melissa. She's the young lady I was telling you about."

Melissa's eyebrows knit together. *Telling him about? Parker said he'd heard things about me, too. Heard I was the kind of girl who liked to ... have fun.*

The man extended his right hand. Melissa drew in a sharp breath and stepped back. She pulled her hand to her chest. Then, her face flushed. *Oh boy. My experience with Parker must have affected me more than I thought.* "I ... I'm sorry. I didn't mean —"

"It's all right. He doesn't bite," Harriet joked.

Melissa gave a bashful grin and they shook hands.

"I was telling the Pastor about the message you shared with me the other day."

"Oh yes!" She straightened up. "The Lord loves you, and He forgives you."

"And He loves you, too." The pastor smiled.

Melissa gave a vigorous nod. *He has a nice smile ... and kind eyes, too.* But still, Jonathan told her to be wary of everyone. *Then again, Jonathan is a bit overprotective.*

Harriet's eyes narrowed as she peered at Melissa's face. "I didn't see that before. What happened? Are you all right?"

Melissa covered the bruise. Her mind raced. *What should I say? If I tell the whole story, how do I explain Jonathan?* In a somewhat halting voice, she answered, "It's nothing. I fell."

Harriet looked skeptical. "Really?"

"Yes." She avoided Harriet's stare. "But God protected me."

"Thank you, Lord." Harriet raised a hand to the sky. "For watching over us."

"Amen," the Pastor added.

"Over here!" Harriet looked passed Melissa, to the back of the church. A smile formed on the older woman's lips, quickly replaced with a half-hearted frown. "It's about time you got here. Come over here. I want you to meet someone."

"Yes, ma'am."

"This is Melissa," Harriet said. "Melissa, this is my grandson."

Melissa turned to greet the newcomer. "Todd?"

"Mel?"

"You two know each other?" Harriet raised an eyebrow.

"Sure," Todd said. "I told you about the new friend I'd made."

With her mouth half opened, Harriet looked from Todd to Melissa. "This is Mel?"

Melissa grinned. "It's a nickname. Todd gave it to me."

Harriet shook her head and mumbled, "It figures. He meets a pretty girl with a pretty name like Melissa and he has to nickname her Mel."

"Todd's so considerate," Melissa said. "Sometimes he walks home with me."

"Isn't that nice," Harriet beamed. "He walks home with me, too." She leaned over to Melissa and in a loud whisper said, "He doesn't think I can make it there on my own. Too old and fragile!"

"Gramma!" Todd rolled his eyes. "You know that's not the truth. The streets aren't always safe at night. I'd rather be there to protect you. Just in case."

Melissa giggled. *Todd sounds just like Jonathan.*

"Some protection," Harriet folded her arms and grumbled. "You're late."

Todd lowered his head. "Sorry. But, I'm here now. You ready to go?"

"I suppose. How about you Melissa?" She looked at Todd when she said this, stressing the word Melissa. "You need walking home?"

"Might as well," Todd added. "She'll never let me live it down if I make you walk home all alone."

Melissa agreed and the three headed out the door.

• *Eleven* •

That next afternoon, Melissa stepped out of the store. Unlike the day before, the sun was shining. There was no need to race through the rain, no need for umbrellas. The sky was a bright and beautiful blue. Yet Melissa pulled the collar of her shirt closed, as if she'd been hit by a cold wind. The notion of walking home alone made her stomach churn. Her eyes darted up and down the busy street, looking for a car. Parker's car.

It's stupid! It's irrational. Parker won't bother you anymore. She gave a hesitant nod. That's what Jonathan said. She wrung her hands. *There's nothing to be afraid of.* But something in the pit of her stomach kept saying, 'Yes there is. Don't walk home alone.'

Todd emerged from the store. Melissa raced up to him, a big smile on her face. "Hi."

Todd gave a slight start.

"I didn't mean to frighten you," Melissa said.

"I'm okay. Didn't see you. What do you want?" He clutched a paper bag in his hands.

"Do I have to want something to say hi?"

"Sorry." He hurried away while calling back, "See ya."

Huh? How unlike him. She quickened her pace to reach his side. "Can I walk with you?"

"Sorta busy." He twisted the top of the bag in his hands, curling the paper tighter and tighter.

"Are you heading home?" Walking with Todd part of the way was better than nothing. "Do you mind if I tag along?"

Todd's heel scraped the sidewalk as he came to an abrupt stop. "You might not want to be with me today."

She hung her head. "I just wanted someone to walk home with. That's all."

"Tell you what." Todd's tone softened a bit. "You can go part way with me. But when I tell you to go on without me, you've got to listen. Okay?"

Melissa gave a half-hearted nod. As they started off, she struggled to keep up with her friend's longer stride, taking two steps for every one of his. "So, are you going anywhere special?"

"What's that supposed to mean?" Todd snapped.

"Nothing. You look like you're in a rush. That's all."

He mumbled an incoherent response.

"What's in the bag?"

He pulled the bag even closer to him. "Boy! You're sure asking a lot of questions."

Melissa slowed her pace, falling behind. "If you don't want to walk with me ... If I've insulted you somehow ..."

Todd stopped a few feet in front of her. He breathed a deep sigh. His shoulders slouched. Slowly, he turned to face her. "I'm sorry. I've got something on my mind. That's all. Something I got to take care of. You want to walk with me, that's fine. But you gotta promise—"

Melissa gave a quick nod. "I know. When you tell me to leave, I have to listen."

Todd forced a smile. "Come on, Mel. Let's go."

Melissa skipped merrily up and the two continued.

She carried the bulk of the conversation, going on and on about the day's work and all she was learning. Meanwhile, Todd kept glancing around the street.

"Todd, are you listening to me?"

"Huh?"

She sighed. "Where's your mind today?"

"Sorry." He shrugged.

A few more minutes passed. Todd's pace slowed to the point that Melissa found herself a few steps ahead of him. She frowned. *This is the same spot where he slowed down that first day.*

Todd glared ahead.

"Anyway," Melissa said, keeping a watchful eye on her friend. "It was a good day ... I guess. Everybody is so nice to me."

Todd opened the paper bag and peered inside.

"Even Miss Gibbons seems to like me, but she keeps giving me the oddest looks." Melissa gave a nervous laugh.

Todd halted. His back went rigid.

"But I guess everyone gives me odd looks," she said as she followed Todd's line of sight to where two people, a man and a woman, had just emerged from a building. It was that woman's health center. The couple stood on the stoop, chatting amiably.

"Melissa." His eyes remained fixed on the two people. "You had better walk on without me."

"Where are you going?"

He took a ball cap out of his back pocket and pulled it down over his head. "You said you'd listen. Leave me." He gave her a quick, but intense look. "Now!"

Then he put on a pair of dark sunglasses and marched forward.

"But—"

Todd was about half way between her and the couple when he reached into the paper sack, pulled something out, then dropped the sack on the ground.

The two people were busy in their conversation. The man had his back to Todd. The woman was facing him. Todd was almost on top of them before the woman reacted. "Doctor Winters!"

The man swung around. "What in the—" He raised his arms up in front of him. But it was too late. Todd slammed whatever he had taken from the bag against the man's chest. A loud thud echoed in the air and a red substance exploded in all directions. The man stumbled backwards.

The woman screamed.

Todd pointed a finger at the man. "Murderer! Murderer!"

The woman pulled open the door to the building and hollered, "George! Help!"

Melissa raced toward Todd.

Dr. Winters clutched at his chest.

A large man burst through the doorway, stepping out into the chaos. He looked at Dr. Winters and his mouth dropped open. "Doc!"

Todd stood there, the red substance dripping from his hand.

The man's eyes narrowed. "What did you do?"

The doctor staggered, and the woman grabbed his elbow to help steady him.

Todd sprinted off, screaming out, "Murderer! Murderer!"

Melissa stopped a few feet from the stoop and stared after Todd, her jaw slack.

George took two steps after Todd, but then hesitated and glanced the doctor's way. "Are you all right, Dr. Winters?"

The doctor was rocking back and forth on his heels, staring at the red gunk dripping off him.

"You should sit down," the woman said.

The two flanked the doctor, holding his arms. With a grunt, he shook both of them off and took a step away. He did a quick examination of his chest. "No pain ... No gushing wound." Then he ran his finger across his chest and cautiously raised it to his nose. His right eyebrow rose. "Ketchup. It's just ketchup. Stupid kid."

Melissa stood there, confused, shaking her head.

The woman pointed at her. "She's one of them. I saw her with that creep."

George moved forward, arms outstretched.

Melissa backed away. "But ... but ..." What could she say? Only one thing came to mind. "The Lord loves you ... He forgives you, too ..."

The man grabbed Melissa by the upper arm, squeezing so tightly that she winced.

"I'll call the police." The woman turned back to the building.

The doctor dabbed at the ketchup with a handkerchief he'd pulled from his pocket. With each touch, his face contorted as if he was handling cow manure. "When will you right wingers understand? What I do is totally legal." He shook his head. "I provide a service."

Melissa pulled at the man's hold on her arm. His hand tightened. "I ... I don't understand." She looked around. *Where's Todd?*

"No, you don't understand, young lady," the doctor said. "You don't understand at all. I will not allow people like you to stop me from doing what I do. Is that clear?"

Off in the distance, a siren wailed. Melissa's heart sank.

Oh no.

· *Twelve* ·

What *is that awful smell?*

Melissa covered her nose. *I've smelled some foul things — The stuff they clean the counters with at the store, or the dead skunk that was on the road outside my apartment, or wet cats.* She flapped a hand in the air, trying to push the odor away. *Nothing smells as revolting as this jail cell.*

A silver-colored toilet sat in the corner. *Kind of pretty, but I pray I never have to use it.* She grimaced. Was that where the smell was coming from?

There were two other people in the holding cell. Two too many. The walls were closing in, crushing her. She struggled to catch her breath.

Across the cell, a woman dressed in shabby, filthy clothes sat on a bench, her back up against the wall. Matted hair escaped from under an old ball cap. Her head bobbed up and down, as she drifted in and out of sleep.

She needs God's message, too.

Melissa took three quick steps toward the woman and stopped. She slapped her hand over her mouth and nose, and fought the urge to vomit. The woman was the source of the stench.

Melissa retreated, choking down the bile rising in her throat. With her back now pressed against the bars, she stared at the huddled pile of human rags sleeping on the bench. *This is a creation of God. She deserves to hear His message, too.* She pushed herself forward. "Excuse me?"

The woman's head remained bowed down to her chest.

"Excuse me," Melissa spoke a little louder, fighting to remove her hand from her mouth.

The woman stirred. Her head swung from side to side until she had awakened enough to gain full mastery over it. Then blurry and bloodshot eyes looked up at Melissa.

"The Lord loves you, and He forgives you," Melissa blurted out. Not waiting for a response, she backed away.

"Well ain't you the sweet thing?" A dry laugh sounded from the cell's other occupant, a woman who had spent this entire time leaning on the door. "Telling that pile of trash about God's love. Kind of sweet."

"He does love her. And he loves you, too." Melissa smiled. It wasn't easy. The looks the woman gave her were more scorn-filled than pleasant, the smile more angry than happy. Melissa hadn't come across many people dressed this way, either. A skirt made of some kind of animal material, so short and tight that it was almost nonexistent, clung to the woman's body, hugging and pulling at her form. A low cut black blouse, high boots, and fishnet stockings completed her ensemble.

I wonder how old she is? Usually there were clues to a person's age like hair color, facial wrinkles, things like that. But this woman had hidden all of her own colors, lines, wrinkles, and everything else, under a coat of makeup.

Eyes highlighted with black mascara and blotches of blue gave Melissa a once over. "Honey." Her voice was raspy. "You want to talk about love? I'll tell you about love." She stepped closer.

Melissa backed up.

"I'll teach you, as a matter of fact," the woman said. "You're a pretty young thing. I bet you'd turn a good trick in a night's work. Whadaya think?"

"No thank you. I already have a job."

"Not like this, you don't." The woman started to giggle, but ended in a coughing fit.

"Leave her alone, Flower." A female officer approached the cell. "She doesn't want any of what you're selling." The door clanked open and the officer stepped in. She stopped and made a sour face. Her hand went up to her nose. "What is that smell?" She cast a wary eye at the toilet. "Someone forget to flush?"

"Er ... Officer Ramarez." Melissa pointed at the sleeping figure. "I think it's her."

"Ohh," the officer moaned. She hollered out of the cell, "Hey, Warren! We got a situation in here!"

"Cleanup on aisle ten!" Flower laughed.

"You be quiet!" Officer Ramarez barked. Then she turned to Melissa. "You come with me." She led the way out of the cell and down the hall.

"Where are we going?" Melissa asked.

"You're being sprung."

The soles of Melissa's shoes squeaked against the floor as she skidded to a stop. "Is ... is that bad?"

Officer Ramarez laughed. "No. That's not bad. You're free to go."

The security door opened up. Officer Ramarez guided Melissa to the main desk. Another officer, a large man, whose neck was too thick for his collar, was sitting there.

"I'm being sprung," Melissa announced to him.

"That's right," he answered, a jovial smile on his face. "Got no reason to hold you." He handed Melissa her pocketbook. "Here you go. Please check the contents to make sure that everything is there. Then, please sign this." He slid a sheet of paper across the desk. Melissa finished checking through her purse and signed the paper.

After making sure everything was in order, the officer said, "You're free to go." He added with just a hint of sarcasm, "I hope your stay with us was a pleasant one."

Melissa's face lit up. "Oh thank you! Thank you. But I have to say, that cell was not the nicest place to be." She leaned over the desk and spoke in a confidential tone. "It stunk."

"Stunk?" His eyebrows knit together as he looked to Officer Ramarez for an explanation.

The officer winced. "It's being taken care of."

Melissa leaned in and whispered, "I think it was one of the other women ... the one who wasn't wearing the short skirt."

The officer smirked. "Thank you for bringing it to our attention."

Melissa turned from the desk.

Harriet Simmons was seated on a bench by the door, clutching her pocketbook. She hopped up as Melissa approached. "Oh child, I am so sorry."

"Harriet. Are you the one that sprung me?"

"Sprung you?"

"Yes. It means—"

"I know what it means. I'm just surprised you know what it means."

"You can learn a lot in prison. I actually had a woman named Flower offer me a job." As the two headed out the door, into the fading sunlight, Melissa explained about the offer.

"You don't want that job," Harriet insisted.

"I know. I already have a job. The one God gave me. How did you know I was in prison?"

"Todd." Harriet said the name with a grimness in her voice. As they walked down the sidewalk, she kept her eyes focused straight ahead. "Todd told me."

"That's what I figured." Except for the people at the Women's Health Center and the police, Todd was the only one who knew what had happened. "Why was I brought to jail? Why in the world did Todd throw ketchup at that man? Why did he run away and leave me?" Her stomach growled.

"Are you hungry?" Harriet asked. "There's a nice place to eat, up ahead. How about I get you some food and we can talk?"

· *Thirteen* ·

"Let's sit by the front window," Harriet suggested as they entered Sid's Diner.

The aroma of fresh-brewed coffee permeated the air. *Much better than the jail cell.* The two walked past the counter. A man seated there, munching on a burger, smiled at Melissa, revealing a piece of lettuce stuck between his front teeth.

She smiled back.

The diner was alive with new sounds—silverware clinking against china plates, food sizzling on the grill, low conversations from the other customers, and country western music drifting from a radio set on a high refrigerator chest.

The two women chose a small booth by the windows. Melissa ordered a hot dog and fries. Harriet decided on the chicken potpie. She suggested, "Why don't we eat first. Then we'll talk."

While they waited for their food, Harriet seemed preoccupied, sneaking glances outside, strumming impatiently against the tabletop.

The last bite of her hotdog was barely chewed and swallowed before Melissa launched right in. "Why did Todd throw ketchup at that man?"

Harriet sighed and rubbed the bridge of her noise. "I hope you won't judge him too harshly. Todd's heart is in the right place, but his brain goes in a whole different direction."

"Who was that man? The one Todd attacked?"

"Dr. Henry Winters." A coldness crept into Harriet's voice. "He runs the clinic."

"Clinic?"

"Yes. The Southside Woman's Health Center."

"Oh. That's the building that gets Todd upset."

Harriet chuckled. "Either you're very perceptive or Todd isn't good at masking his feelings. The papers announced the Center's opening a few months ago. Some people tried to stop it. I guess Todd just assumed they'd succeeded. The other day, when he saw the sign, he nearly went ballistic. He's been fuming ever since ... Swinging in and out of foul moods."

"But why?"

Harriet took a sip of her coffee. "Todd is adamantly opposed to abortion."

"To what?"

"Abortion."

Silence.

The older woman tipped her head to the side. "You know what an abortion is, don't you?"

Melissa's face warmed and she looked away. *If Harriet thinks I should know what this thing is, it must be pretty important.*

"Where have you been living? Under a rock? Honestly child. How can you not have heard of abortion?" Harriet gave a quick shake to her head. Then she explained, "An abortion is when a pregnant woman decides, for one reason or another, that she does not want to give birth to the baby she's carrying. She goes to a doctor or clinic and they ... remove the baby."

"Oh, I see." Melissa nodded, staring with wide-eyed innocence. "Then does someone else get the child?"

"No ... the child dies."

"Dies?" Melissa's face contorted. "They kill the baby?"

Harriet touched her hand. "I'm sorry. I didn't mean to upset you by blurting it out the way I did."

Melissa pulled away. "It's terrible."

Harriet nodded. "A crime against our unborn."

"And against God," Melissa chimed in, loud enough that others in the diner turned to look at her.

"Yes. And against God."

"Why doesn't someone report this to the police?"

"Why? It's legal." Harriet studied Melissa, intently. "You really must live under a rock."

Melissa's mouth hung open. Her hands trembled. Tears pooled in her eyes.

"Calm down. Please, Melissa."

"But, babies ..."

"I know." Harriet shook her head.

Melissa white-knuckled the edge of the table and clenched her teeth. "At first I felt foolish that I didn't know what abortion was. Now I'm more embarrassed, more ashamed to know. No one should know. No one should have ever heard ... ever thought of such a thing."

Harriet hung her head, her voice hushed to a whisper. "I know."

"Why would someone do such a thing?"

No answers came.

Melissa stared at Harriet. A knot formed in the pit of her stomach. All at once, as if a switch flipped in her brain, something inside her changed. The belief that there must be some good in man died. "What a horrible world."

"Yes, it is. I often wonder why God even bothers with us."

"He loves you," Melissa said, quietly. Then she added, in a thoughtful manner. "He ... He forgives you."

Harriet sighed. "He does, doesn't He. It's a wonder. While we were yet sinners, Christ died for us."

Melissa nodded. "It's a wonder."

Harriet forced a smile. "There is hope. Plenty of people oppose abortion. Politicians, doctors, regular folks. People trying to change the law, educate others. Unfortunately, there's much misinformation out there." She sighed. "Anyway, Todd threw a baggy filled with ketchup at the doctor today as his way of protesting. You know ... the ketchup symbolic of the blood on the doctor's hands."

Harriet gave a low chuckle. "Ketchup. A poor man's substitute for blood. Todd'd probably faint if it was a baggy of real blood. The dummy." She shook her head and groaned. "I am so sorry that my grandson got you in such trouble."

"That's all right. I'm fine."

The waitress came by and the two fell silent. She refilled Harriet's coffee. Once she walked away, Harriet said, "I suppose it's all in how you look at it."

"How's Todd?"

"See for yourself." She nodded toward the window. "The lunkhead is across the street."

Melissa peeked out and searched for her friend.

Harriet picked up her cup, and blew across the top of the hot liquid. "He's the dummy trying to hide behind that telephone pole on the corner."

There he was. Hands shoved deep in his pockets, head hung, half hidden behind the pole.

"He's been following me since I headed to the police station. Wanted to make sure I was safe. Don't wave at him!" Harriet chastised.

Melissa quickly lowered her arm.

"Let him suffer a little for abandoning you like he did. He came running home, all upset. Didn't know what to do. Thankfully, he confided in me." Harriet's face softened. "He's a good boy."

Melissa bit her top lip. "I'm concerned for him. He's so ..." She searched for the right word.

"Angry?" Harriet suggested.

"Yes. Angry."

"Well, dear. He feels he has a right to be angry." She slowly shook her head. "It's an old wound. Old wounds run deep."

Melissa paused. "What old wound?"

Harriet peered over the top of her glasses, looking up at the ceiling. "O Lord. O Lord." She sighed.

"I'm sorry. I didn't mean to cause you pain."

"No, child. It's just ... It's a story not many people know. Me ... the Pastor ... a couple of other relatives. Not many."

"You don't have to tell me."

Harriet gazed at Melissa, curiously, as if seeing her for the first time. She half smiled. "What is it about you?"

"Pardon?"

She reached across the table and patted Melissa's hand. "Child. You are not like anyone else I've ever met. Filled with happiness. You seem unsullied by the world, almost like you've stepped out of a different time. You see everything through new eyes. I hardly know you, yet for some reason, I want to tell you my life story. I don't know. Maybe it's the Lord."

Melissa beamed. "Maybe it is."

Harriet chuckled. "Where did you come from anyway?"

The girl shrugged, remembering her promise to Jonathan. *I doubt you'd believe me, even if I told you.* She focused on the subject at hand. "Could you tell me about Todd?"

"Why are you so interested?"

It was a good question. Why was she so interested? Was it simply that Todd was her friend or was it something else? "I'm not sure ... I guess I want to help him. That's all."

Harriet's eyes narrowed. "I think you have the right to know. After all, that lunkhead got you arrested."

"Actually, I didn't get arrested ... just taken to the police station for a while. Besides, if I'd had the mind to run when he did, I wouldn't have been caught."

Harriet wagged a finger in Melissa's face. "Never do anything you have to run away from out of shame." She leaned back in the booth. Her eyes gazed out the window. "Now where to start ... It happened several years ago. I was a nurse, by the way, before I retired." She paused and took a deep breath. "I worked in a place similar to the Southside Women's Health Center." She looked down into her coffee.

The waitress walked over. "Dessert?"

"Apple pie?" Harriet glanced at Melissa, who answered with a nod. "Two pieces of apple pie, please." The waitress walked away and Harriet continued. "That was twenty years ago. I'd like to blame it on the foolishness of youth, but let's be serious." She chuckled. "I wasn't young even twenty years ago. I guess I believed all the hype about 'products of conception' and 'fetal tissue'." She hung her head.

"Were you a believer then?"

Harriet nodded. "Don't forget sweetheart. Christians aren't perfect. Just forgiven. I mostly worked the front desk. Checked girls in. Prepared them. Answered their questions. Things like that. The doctor took care of most of the procedure himself. Besides, when I did help, I'd never see ..." She hesitated. Her bottom lip quivered.

"It must have been difficult for you."

"You can't fool me," the older woman said. "You're trying to be supportive, but I can see it in your eyes. The thought of me being involved in something like this sickens you. But you have to understand, I truly convinced myself that I was performing a service for lower income girls, keeping them out of back alley shops where coat hangers were used. That's what they always said the past was like, before they legalized abortion."

Melissa asked, "What does this have to do with Todd?"

"One day. I remember it like it was yesterday." Harriet's eyes focused on a spot somewhere in the space in front of Melissa.

It was early spring ... A slow day at our clinic. We were ready to close up shop. The doctor was in his office, filling out some government paper work. I was in the back room, sterilizing instruments, when the door opened. I went to see who it was. A young girl walked in. Blonde hair, blue eyes ... hardly looked old enough to be out of high school. I could see by the wide eyes and nervous fidgeting that she was frightened, very frightened. That's nothing new, though. Many of the girls who came in were frightened.

"May I help you?" I asked.

A nervous voice answered, "I'd like to see a doctor. I think I'm pregnant." Her hands pressed against her stomach. She wasn't showing too much, but with these young girls it's hard to judge how far along they are. I've seen some come to full term and hardly show, while others look like they have a beach ball under their shirt.

"When was your last period?" I asked.

"Two months ago ... maybe three. I don't remember."

I could tell she was lying. She was having trouble making eye contact with me and was shifting her weight from one foot to the other. Something else was going on here, but before I could ask any more questions, the doctor walked in and took over the conversation. He believed everything she said. Believed her when she said how far along she was ... how old she was. All the time she spoke, she was holding that stomach, giving an occasional grimace of pain.

"I'm sure we can help you," he said to her. "Everything is going to be all right." He directed her to the examining room, where she could change into a hospital gown, and closed the door to give her some privacy.

That's when I grabbed his arm and pulled him aside. "You can't be serious," I whispered. "There is no way that child is telling us the truth."

"Does it matter?" He stared, steely-eyed.

"Of course it does. Besides, she doesn't look too healthy. I think she's sick."

"Relax, Harriet," he answered in a smug voice. "I know what I'm doing."

But he didn't, as time would tell. When she had changed, I followed the doctor into the room. Something told me he was going to need my help with this one. He assisted the young girl onto the table. Then he sat on a stool next to her. "This isn't going to hurt at all," he assured her.

The doctor realized something was wrong as soon as he began his examination. I could see it on his face.

"Miss, you're bleeding." He turned white. "Did your water break?" He already knew the answer. "You're in labor, aren't you? How long have you been in labor?"

She lay on the table, breathing rapidly, clutching at her abdomen. Glassy eyed, she stared up at the ceiling.

"Sweetheart," I asked, while caressing her hair. "How far along are you, really?"

The girl clenched her teeth and screamed. She was in the middle of a major contraction. "Please no. Stop it. I was wrong. Please stop."

Stop what? The abortion? The pain? The delivery? It was too late. The baby was coming.

"It hurts," she cried.

There was nothing we could do about it. She was giving birth, right then and there. As my granddad used to say, 'When the apple is ripe, it'll drop.' I give the doctor credit. Even though we were not the best equipped for delivery — especially when it was happening as fast as this one was — we did our best. Before we knew it, a tiny premature baby was born. A little boy. A little black boy.

After the delivery, things didn't go well at all. The poor girl. Who knows how long she'd been bleeding before she came to see us. The doctor couldn't stop it. Something was wrong with the pregnancy. That's why she was delivering so soon. In a matter of minutes, she died.

Harriet closed her eyes and hung her head.

"Why did she lie about how far along she was?" Melissa asked.

Harriet shrugged. "Who knows. Maybe the poor thing was afraid of having a child. Maybe the baby's father abandoned her, or her parents put pressure on her. There are a hundred different reasons I've come up with over the years." She wiped a tear from her eye. "Once the labor pains started, I figure she panicked. Didn't expect them ... not yet at least. We were probably the closest place for her to get to. At that moment in time, all I knew was I had a dead girl and a live baby."

"What did you do?"

"It's what the doctor didn't want to do that mattered. He didn't want to give that child any help. Said if the mother wanted an abortion, then he was obliged to push aside the cart the baby was lying on and let the child die. No food ... no love ..."

Melissa shivered. "That's horrible."

"I thought so too. I marched right over to that beautiful baby boy and picked him up. The doctor watched in shock as I began to clean and tend to him."

"What do you think you're doing?" the doctor asked.

I have to tell you, I was afraid. You have to understand, I remember a day when black folks were put in their place. Here I was standing up to a white doctor, a big man at that.

"Put that thing back where it was," the doctor ordered.

Funny how he called it a thing. Couldn't bring himself to call it a child.

I stood my ground. Shoulders thrust back, chest out and head held high, I announced, "No sir! I will not!"

"I order you —"

"No sir!"

"You have no right!"

"You had no right to do what you just did!" My eyes shot over to the lifeless girl.

He stumbled back, like I'd hit him in the chest with my fist. You have to understand, it wasn't as if he'd killed her. I'm sure if he'd known she was in labor, he'd have shipped her over to a hospital, to receive the needed care. He should have listened to me. Should have known that something was wrong.

Harriet shook her head. "Maybe I shamed him into it, but he allowed me to tend to the child. To be honest, without that doctor's connections, I wouldn't have been able to pull it off. The neonatal care ... birth certificate ... everything." Harriet gazed across the street. "That's how Todd came into my life."

Melissa tipped her head to the side. "But he's your grandchild."

"No. That's what I told him when he was younger. It wasn't until he was a teenager, just a couple of years ago, that he found out the truth. He had difficulty accepting it, but finally, he settled down. That is, until that Women's Health Center moved into town. Now he's become obsessed. Can't get it out of his head. Honestly! He's like two different people. Most of the time, he's my easy going grandson, but when he thinks about that place ..." Harriet shuddered. "It's like the devil takes over! To him, they represent where his mother died ... Where he almost died. Blames them all. I think he lies awake at night hatching plots to destroy it."

"Did you ever find out who the girl was?"

Harriet shook her head. "No. Not for want of trying, though. She had no ID on her. Over the next few months, I checked the papers, looking for missing persons. Checked the police department. From what I understand, the body was buried as a Jane Doe. I never did find out who she was, or if Todd had any living relatives."

Melissa peered out the window at the young man standing by the telephone pole, looking sad and forlorn, kicking at the dirt.

So young.

The word fit. Young. When Todd wasn't obsessing over the Women's Center, he had an innocent quality. Kind of like a puppy dog. He tried so hard at work, always willing to do whatever job Ms. Gibbons gave him, always wanting to please. The first to volunteer. "He really is a nice boy."

"I think so."

"Like a younger brother to me." Melissa smiled. "You've done a wonderful job of raising him."

Harriet's eyes misted over. "I've tried. Lord knows I've tried."

Melissa fixed her gaze on Todd. "It mustn't be easy, raising children today." She spoke in a voice which sounded much older than her own.

Harriet shook her head. "If he could only get past some things."

Suddenly, Todd stiffened. He was staring directly at the restaurant's window.

"I think he sees you staring at him," Harriet said.

He bolted behind the too thin telephone pole. His shoulders stuck out on both sides.

Harriet chuckled. "Like that's going to work."

He darted from side to side.

Melissa smiled and waved.

"What are you doing?" Harriet asked.

"I'm signaling for him to come join us." She gestured to the door.

Todd pointed at himself, as if to ask, 'Who me?'

Melissa nodded, and he made his way across the street. *Poor Todd. He really needs help.* As he walked in the front door, she gazed at him as if seeing him for the first time. A triumphant smile spread across her face. *Todd's my mission. Yes. That must be it.* She'd told a million people God's message. No one had responded. Here was this troubled young man. *The Lord has sent me here to help Todd!*

He shuffled up to the table, looking like a small boy waiting to be scolded. Harriet glared at him and said in a stern voice. "Do you have anything to say to Melissa?"

He stood there, head hanging low, chin hitting against his chest. "I'm sorry, Mel. I didn't mean to get you arrested. Is everything okay between us? I mean are we gonna be all right?"

"Yes, Todd." She smiled up at him. "I think everything is going to be all right."

· *Fourteen* ·

Melissa awoke with renewed energy. A new direction. *I'm here to help Todd. I don't know when or how, but if I stick close to him, the opportunity will arise.*

It was Sunday morning. *The day Harriet sings in the church.* She hurried to get ready.

She was one of about a hundred or so worshipers. A music group was up front, leading in some choruses. From her seat, Melissa kept an eye out for Todd. When he appeared at the back door, she waved.

"Good morning," he said as he sank into the seat next to her.

"Good morning."

Glancing over, his brow creased.

"What?" she asked.

"You got this funny look on your face. If my gramma was here, she'd say you look like the cat who swallowed the canary."

"Sorry. It's nothing. I'm happy to be here, that's all. Did you know that God loves you and forgives you?"

Todd smirked. "So I've heard."

A voice shouted out from the front of the sanctuary, "This is the day the Lord has made. We will rejoice and be glad in it!"

A few 'Amens' and 'Hallelujahs' rang out from around the church. Then several rousing choruses were sung.

Todd has a nice voice.

When they finished, the congregation settled in their seats. The choir sang an inspiring medley. Then Pastor Tom came to the pulpit. "It's time for prayer. Any special needs this week?"

A few hands went up around the congregation. He called on an elderly woman seated near the front. But before she could speak, Todd jumped up. "I got one."

The Pastor nodded. "Yes, Todd."

"I want to pray for that abortion clinic."

A wave of grumbles rippled through the room.

Todd glanced around.

"Okay." The Pastor said, and he turned back to the elderly woman, who was now standing up, raising her hand to be seen.

Todd pushed on. "I want to pray that it closes." Anger was creeping into his voice.

The elderly woman sat back down. Harriet, who was seated with the choir, shot warning looks Todd's way.

"I want us ... want Christians to take a stand." He spoke even louder now. His words echoed through the large sanctuary. "To be more active in the battle against that evil place."

A couple of 'Amens' sang out.

This seemed to encourage Todd. He continued. "They're murdering babies. What do we do about it?" He paused and looked up at the pulpit, at the Pastor, and waited for a response.

"Thank you, Todd," the Pastor said, showing no signs of impatience. If anything, the look in his eyes showed more sympathy and compassion than impatience. "With that in mind, I believe we should also keep the pro-life ministries in our prayers. The ones who assist pregnant women in having their babies. After all, they offer an alternative to abortion."

"Harrumph," a voice sounded from the pew behind Melissa, where a middle-aged woman fidgeted in her seat. Her face had the sour look of someone who's perpetually sucking on a lemon. "Fat lot of good those places do," she groused in a voice so low only those closest to her could hear. "Welfare cases go there ... foreigners! Just for the free baby food and clothing. I hear girls get pregnant, knowing those places will pay for the delivery."

"Anything else?" The pastor asked Todd.

"Nope," Todd said. "That's it. I just want us to do something. Anything!" He sat down.

The elderly woman toward the front, popped back up. "Is it my turn?"

Laughter rang out.

Todd stiffened, then shot a disdainful look at the people around him. He went to stand up again, but Melissa placed a hand on his shoulder and pulled him back down.

"It's okay," she whispered in a soothing voice. "Let it go."

Slowly, and with a grumble, he settled in his seat.

The pastor fielded several more prayer requests before saying, "Let's go to the Lord in prayer." As the congregation bowed their heads, Melissa caught sight of Harriet. The older woman was smiling at her. She mouthed the words, 'Thank you.'

Through the rest of the service, Melissa kept a concerned eye on her friend, who looked like a pot on a low flame. Ready to come to a boil.

· Fifteen ·

"Boy, you beat the band." Harriet loomed over her grandson's seat. Service was over. Most people had already left, but some were still chatting, greeting one another. Todd and Melissa hadn't had a chance to move. As soon as the last 'Amen' was said, Harriet had barreled down the aisle and cornered them.

"What did I do?" Todd asked, looking up at her.

"You used prayer time as an opportunity to wage war."

"I don't think he meant to," Melissa defended.

"It's how I feel," Todd said.

"You basically attacked your own church. Made it sound like we don't care."

"Maybe you don't," he hollered at his grandmother.

The church became dead quiet. The few people who were still there focused on the small group. Some stopped to listen, waiting to hear more. Others, whether out of fear or the belief that it was none of their concern, gave the area a wide berth.

Melissa, half expecting a bomb to hit, slid down the pew, separating herself from Todd.

"How dare you!" Harriet pointed at her grandson's face, her finger trembling.

Pastor Tom made his way to the source of the commotion. He stood on one side of Melissa, with Todd on her other. "Good morning," he said, keeping a peaceful smile on his face. "Is there a problem here?"

"Yes," Todd snapped.

The Pastor asked, "Is there anything I can do to help?"

"Yes, there is!" Todd jumped to his feet. He stepped toward Pastor Tom, making the Melissa sandwich even tighter.

Oh boy!

"You can do something. Anything!" His scornful look went from Harriet to the Pastor. "Because right now, you're doing nothing."

"I take it you're talking about the Southside Women's Health Center."

"The abortion clinic," Todd said. "Why don't you call it what it is?

The Pastor kept his voice calm, his tone sympathetic. "Todd, you know we take a stand against abortion."

"What do you do about it?" Todd's voice was laced with accusation. As he spoke, he pushed against Melissa, knocking her into the pastor.

"We are actively involved in supporting our local pro-life ministries," Pastor Tom answered. "They educate young women on abortion alternatives. We donate to a home for un-wed mothers, where they can go and receive the support they need to have healthy babies."

"But what are you doing *against* the Southside Women's Health Center?"

Harriet wagged a finger at Todd. "Do not take that tone with the Pastor."

"I don't think he means any disrespect," Melissa interject-ed. Todd needed to hear her and remember she was there, be-ing squeezed between the two men.

"Nothing! You're doing nothing!" Red faced, Todd shoved past Melissa and Pastor Tom, pushing them into the pew, and stormed out of the church.

"What am I going to do with that boy?" Harriet asked as she watched him leave.

"Let me try and talk to him," Melissa said. She rushed through the church and out the front door.

Todd was half way down the block.

"Todd," she called out. He didn't respond, just kept moving away from her. "Todd," she yelled louder. Melissa shook her head as Todd disappeared around a corner. Her heart sank. *Not a good beginning for my mission. That's for sure.*

• *Sixteen* •

McCullen's employee lunch break was divided into two different times so that there would always be sales associates available for shoppers. The first lunchtime, the one Melissa was assigned that day, was finishing up. People were clearing their trash and heading back to work.

Melissa hurried to the far cor- ner of the room where the ladies' room was located, hidden behind a tall shelving unit covered in boxes. She didn't want to get in trouble for being late getting back out on the floor. Today, she was working in girl's fashions. She smiled. *I love working in girl's fashions.*

A few minutes later, she was exiting the restroom and walking along the back of the shelves, when a sound from the lunchroom caught her attention. Peeking between two boxes, she spotted Jonathan seated at a table. *What's he still doing here?*

He sat perfectly rigid, his sight fixed straight ahead. *Something isn't right.* His demeanor was just like the enormous Doberman Pincer Melissa passed on her walk home from work. The dog always stood motionless by the gate of the fenced yard, watching her. Not a movement, not a sound. As if challenging her to come closer.

What's he looking at? Her brow puckered. *Curious.* There sat the old man, Martin, three tables away, sipping on a cup of coffee. Except for Melissa, the two of them were the only ones in the lunchroom. Martin's chair creaked as he rose to his feet. "Well, I suppose it's time to get back to work," he said in his high-pitched voice.

Jonathan sat in silence.

"Another day, another dollar. That's what they say." Martin moved toward the trash bin, passing behind Jonathan as he did. He dumped his coffee.

If it were at all possible, Jonathan grew even more rigid.

Martin chuckled. "Of course, I'd never work for a dollar a day. Can't get much for a dollar these days, can you? No indeedy."

Melissa stifled a laugh. Martin had a way of going on about absolutely nothing. It was quite endearing. Jonathan didn't look amused, though. Martin walked up behind him and rested his hand on Jonathan's shoulder. "Well, my friend. Would you like to walk back with—"

Jonathan jumped out of his seat. He grabbed the older man's hand and twisted it behind his back.

Martin squirmed, a look of terror on his face. "What are you doing?"

Jonathan gave the old man a hard shove, driving him into the trash can. His frail body fell in a heap against the wall.

"Do not touch me," Jonathan growled, his face twisted in rage. He was bearing his teeth like a wild animal.

Melissa covered her mouth. *What's gotten into my angel?*

She looked over at Martin, expecting to see a bruised and battered body struggling to lift himself off the floor. Instead, Martin spryly hopped to his feet. A sly smile crossed his lips as he brushed off his shirt. "So, the jig's up, as they say. Better this way, I suppose."

Jonathan waved a hand at the break room door, which was open just a crack. It slammed shut. The lock clicked in place.

"Reveal yourself," Jonathan ordered.

Reveal yourself? What's he—

Melissa's breath caught in her throat. Jonathan transformed. It wasn't like the transformation outside of Parker's car. That one happened slowly, a calm and casual pace. Now, Jonathan's angelic form burst forth with a mighty explosion, as if God had brought a star to life out of the darkness. The angel stood before her. Magnificent wings unfurled, his frame stretched upward to his full height. His head towered toward the lunchroom ceiling, his eyes ablaze with a brilliance not seen this side of Heaven.

How can he change like that in front of Martin? Melissa looked back at the old man and her heart stopped. Martin too was transforming, but not like Jonathan had. Martin's beautiful head of white hair shriveled back into his skull, facial features turned ashen. His cheekbones shrank into hollowed holes. Eyes red as fire, blackened wing-structure covered with cobwebs of decaying gray flesh. Claws stretched out where dainty, white hands had been. The room reeked of death.

"Demon!" Jonathan exclaimed. "What is your business here?"

Melissa shrank to the floor. *What in the world? A demon.* Her angel and the Lord had always kept her safe from them. Now to have one standing right here. Her palms sweat. Her stomach churned.

"Well, well. So we meet again." Martin's voice had changed, too. No longer the sweet, nervous voice of an older man. Now, words rasped forth from a dry throat. Metal on metal grated with every syllable.

"Answer," Jonathan barked. He was circling around the demon now, tense, ready to strike. "Why are you here?"

Martin sat against a table. He laughed—a hoarse, grotesque laugh. "Isn't it obvious? Can you angels be so dimwitted? I've come for the girl."

Melissa cowered behind a box.

"She's already mine." The demon said it plain and simple. He sneered. "Has been since our first encounter."

Jonathan hung his head and turned away.

"Tell me." The demon's tone dripped with a feigned ignorance. "I'm having trouble remembering. How did that first meeting go?"

Jonathan clenched and unclenched his fists.

"Oh yes." Martin's voice sang with perverted pleasure. "I remember now. I won. You lost."

"This time will be different."

"I don't think so. The girl is mine. Has been since ... Well, you know." Martin's lips curled up into a sinister smile.

"She's not yours. The Lord says all humans have the right to choose. She will make her own choice."

Martin sighed and shook his head. He sauntered toward Jonathan as if approaching an old friend. Jonathan raised his arm to strike.

"Wait. Wait." Martin curled his wings back in a submissive manner. "I just want to talk. I promise."

Jonathan laughed. "Means a lot coming from the likes of you."

"More than you may think." Martin ventured another small, cautious step forward. "Yes, I'm here for the girl. But the unholy one, as you like to call him, has given me a sub-mission, so to speak." He walked right up to Jonathan's side, leaned in close and whispered, "It's you."

Jonathan stiffened.

The demon seemed pleased with the effect this had on the angel. He strolled around him. "You know I was once like you." Martin pointed an annoyed finger toward the ceiling. "Oh, yes. Doing His work. But what did it ever get me? Have you ever wondered if maybe you're on the wrong side?"

Jonathan grumbled. "Why would I want to be on the losing side?"

The room filled with the demon's laughter. He slowly spun, waving his hands in the air, dramatically. "Have you looked around? Does it look like we're losing?"

"In the end Satan and his followers will be thrown into the lake of fire. Eternal damnation."

"Where did you hear that?"

"In the Word."

"And," Martin said, sounding like a court lawyer, interrogating a witness, "Who wrote the Word?"

"That's a stupid question."

"Ah-hah!" The demon stabbed a finger in Jonathan's face. "Is it? *He* wrote the Word. *He* wrote that He'd win ... But what if *He's* wrong?"

Jonathan gasped.

"Oh come on now. You've never considered that He may be wrong?"

"Never!" Johnathan folded his arms and gave his back to the demon.

"Fine." Martin threw up his arms. "Follow blindly if you must. But our side has some benefits you haven't thought of."

He slithered up next to Jonathan. "These humans have such wonderful pleasures. We are allowed to taste of them, if you know what I mean."

"No. I don't."

Martin rolled his eyes. "You are so naïve." He took a couple of steps away from Jonathan. "Take for instance ... the women. There is definite pleasure there."

Jonathan's gaze slowly turned toward the demon.

"Oh yes, indeed." He started a slow walk back to Jonathan's side. "As a matter of fact, there's one cute little number working right here that I noticed you eyeing." Martin leaned in close to Jonathan's ear. "What's her name? Melissa ... isn't that it?"

Death seemed to clutch at Melissa's throat when her name spewed out of the demon's mouth.

"Yesss ... Melissa." Martin's eyes burned brightly. "She could be yours, to do with whatever you wanted ... Whatever you desired. A tasty plaything. Join us!"

An aching pain rose from Melissa's stomach. *What if Jonathan feels that way about me? Would he yield to this demon's temptation?*

Jonathan burst into a heavenly brightness. Fire shot from his hands, slamming into the demon's chest and knocking him across the room. "Mind your tongue!" He spoke with a commanding voice that Melissa hadn't heard since leaving Heaven. "I am not to be trifled with. I am a messenger sent from God Almighty. I do His bidding. His will! I've seen Him create stars, transform planets. I've praised Him as He has given sight to the blind and life to the lifeless. You, and those like you, will cower and tremble at His Glory. At His power!"

And Martin did cower, huddled behind a table as Jonathan's angelic presence shone forth. "Okay. Okay." He waved a weak hand. "I get it." He fumbled to his feet. "You can't blame me for trying, but ..." He shook his head. "This changes nothing about the girl!"

Jonathan opened his mouth to answer, but was interrupted by a loud rapping on the door.

Someone yelled out, "Why won't this stupid door open? Come on. I want to eat my lunch."

A host of voices in the hallway joined in. The two beings transformed back into their human personas.

Martin scurried over and swung the door wide open. "Oh my. It must have been stuck." The nervous, high-pitched voice was back. "So sorry."

He stepped aside and about twenty-five people pushed their way to the tables. Pulling out their sandwiches, salads, and yogurts, they began their lunchtime rituals, ignorant of the supernatural events that had just transpired.

"Enjoy your lunches. Enjoy your lunches," Martin squealed. Before he left, he gave Jonathan one last look. For an instant, the face of the dear old man was replaced with the demon's sneer. Then he turned and walked away.

Jonathan followed.

Melissa waited until both men were gone before coming out of her hiding place. She shivered as she walked between the crowded tables.

The girl is mine. She was having trouble catching her breath and had to grab the back of one of the metal chairs for support. *The girl is mine.* Her bottom lip trembled. Slowly, she shook her head. She clenched her teeth. "Never!"

• *Seventeen* •

That night, Melissa lay in bed, Martin's words chasing sleep away. *Why was he so sure I was his?* When did he and Jonathan battle before? Most importantly, had Jonathan really lost?

Sweat beaded up on the small of Melissa's back. She rolled over, trying to catch any whisper of a breeze that might come through the window. The blinds and curtains hung straight and still. No good. No movement. It was hot. Too hot to sleep in a room without a fan or air conditioning. *Note to self. Tomorrow buy a fan.* The damp sheets peeled off her as she rolled on her side.

The clock read 11:30 PM. With a deep sigh, she climbed out of bed, crossed the room, and knelt in front of her open window. *Not going to sleep tonight.*

She stuck her arm outside and a slight breeze swept across it. A bit cooler than in the room. She decided to dress and go for a short stroll.

Jonathan won't approve. He'd be worried about her safety that late at night. She could just hear him, lecturing. 'You don't know how dangerous it is out there. You've got to be careful!'

She tiptoed down the stairs. *I'll be careful. I'll keep to well-lit streets, far away from any dark alleys* ... She paused. *And any stranger's cars.*

The door loomed in front of her, like a portal to another world. She chewed on her bottom lip. Is it a safe world, or is it a world filled with danger? She stiffened her back, turned the knob, and marched out. A cool breeze blew across her face and she tilted her head back so the air could caress her neck.

She wandered. How different the world seemed now. Less traffic, less people. An occasional car sped by, or a person passed her on the sidewalk, enjoying a night stroll. The air was quiet. Calm. *Like the whole world's asleep.*

Eventually she found herself right in front of the Southside Women's Health Center. Except for a light illumining the sign on the front lawn, it stood in total darkness. With an eyebrow raised, Melissa studied the building. It didn't look any different than any other one on the street.

And yet it evokes such a strong reaction in poor Todd.

She turned to leave when a small noise halted her. It only lasted a second, but there was no mistaking it—the sound of glass breaking.

An alley stretched off into the pitch dark along the side of the Southside Women's Health Center. That's where the noise came from. Melissa stood motionless, waiting. She tipped her head, listening. Nothing. No more noise. *Just my imagination.*

Then, something scraped. Along the ground? Along the side of the building? No way of telling.

She peered down the alley. Everything was swallowed by the black of the night. *What if someone is hurt?* She took a very small step in that direction.

No. Jonathan would not be happy with me. She could just picture his face. She'd never hear the end of it. Her eyes swept over the space between the two buildings. Definitely a dark alley.

Without warning, a circle of light danced along the outside of the building next to the clinic. Melissa gasped. The light was coming from one of the clinic's side windows.

Melissa took another small step. She leaned forward and squinted.

The light disappeared.

I could see better from the front lawn. After all, Jonathan never said anything against walking on a lawn.

She crept forward. A shadow flickered across a venetian blind in one of the front windows. Someone was in there. A lump formed in Melissa's throat. This was not good. This was the kind of situation Jonathan had told her to avoid.

She was about to leave, run to a telephone and call the police. *They seemed like nice people.* But as she turned to go, there was more movement at the front window. She froze. Maybe whoever was in there hadn't spotted her. Just then someone pulled down on one of the slats and peeked out. Todd. It looked like Todd.

What's he doing in there?

The face disappeared behind the blinds.

Should I run away or should I investigate?

Melissa backed up a few steps until her feet were on the hard sidewalk. *It's probably best if I leave. That's what Jonathan would want me to do.* She hesitated, gazing at the window. Then, she marched down the alley. Jonathan would understand.

Behind the building was a square, concrete yard enclosed by the backs of several neighboring buildings. A security light, high up on a utility pole, cast a large yellow circle whose edges crept up the buildings. The yard was empty, save for a Dumpster with some old furniture piled around it.

Melissa scanned the first floor of the clinic for a way in. There it was. A broken window. A beat-up upholstered chair was pushed under it. In the sand and dirt on the concrete, scrape marks led from the chair to the Dumpster.

And that accounts for the scraping noise.

Melissa climbed on the chair and hoisted herself through the window, careful to avoid the jagged edges of the broken glass. She tumbled into the building and onto the floor. Light streaked in through the window, across the floor and up the wall, revealing a number of medical diplomas. A doctor's office. A thick pile rug muffled her footsteps as she crossed to the door. She cracked it open and peeked out. A long hallway stretched from left to right, lined with doors.

Which room is Todd in?

A light flashed across the hall from the last door on the right.

"Todd?" She called out in a hushed tone.

The light went out.

"I know you're in here."

Silence.

Melissa held her breath. What if it's somebody else? She backed into the doctor's office. *Then again, maybe it's Todd and he's simply afraid of getting caught.*

She swallowed hard. "It's me. Melissa."

Someone groaned and a voice called through the darkness. "Mel. What are you doing here?"

Melissa began to breathe again. "I saw your light through the window. Thought I'd come and see what you're up to."

Todd emerged from the room. His eyebrows knit together. "I'll have to be more careful."

Melissa shielded her eyes from the flashlight Todd was shining in her face. "What are you doing here?"

Todd grimaced. "This is the place. The belly of the beast. Follow me." He disappeared back into the room, and Melissa followed. When they were both inside, Todd closed the door and flipped on the overhead lights. Melissa squinted. They were standing in some type of examining room. A metal table was in the center. Along one wall were glass-door cabinets, filled with medicine bottles. Various pieces of shiny medical equipment lined the walls.

"Aren't you afraid of someone seeing us?" Melissa pointed to the ceiling light.

Todd approached the only window in the room and pulled back the blind, revealing a brick wall mere inches away. "Nothing out there but the next building. No one's gonna see through that."

Melissa's mouth went dry. She forced herself to swallow. *What's he planning on doing?*

He walked around the room, running his hand over the equipment. "I knew this was my last chance."

"Last chance for what?"

"On the way home from work today, I saw two guys standing next to an alarm company's truck parked out front. I overheard what they were talking about. The alarm in this building is on the fritz and they won't be able to fix it until tomorrow morning. I figured God's giving me an opportunity."

"To do what?"

Todd pulled a small hammer out of his back pocket. "Some damage."

Melissa shook her head. "No Todd. This is wrong."

"Wrong?" He slammed the hammer down into the metal table. The room reverberated with so loud a noise that Melissa and Todd both jumped. "Look around you. This is wrong." He grabbed hold of a metal stirrup sticking up from the end of a table. "Having a girl's legs strapped in here while they rip out living babies is wrong."

He stared deep into Melissa's eyes. "Telling young teenage girls that no one gets hurt is wrong!"

He spun around and smashed the hammer against one of the glass-enclosed cabinets. Shards flew in all directions. "Not giving a baby the right to choose whether they live or die is wrong!"

He stood in the center of the room, his chest heaving.

Lord, please. Help him control this anger.

"Wrong?" Todd clenched his teeth. "No, it's not. It's retribution. Revenge!" He held the hammer up and glared at it. "For all the innocents. For the millions they've murdered."

"Please Todd. Would God really want you to do this?"

"Yes," he said without hesitation. "You know what, Melissa? You're always talking about how much God loves us. Doesn't He love the little children? The unborn babies?"

"Of course He does."

"Who does He love more? The unborn babies or the people who kill them?"

"That's not a fair question."

"Really?" Todd reached into the pocket of his hoodie and produced a rolled up stack of papers. He peeled off a couple, and thrust them at her. "Look!"

Melissa examined the top one. It was a brochure from a place that specialized in terminating pregnancies, filled with phrases like 'fetal tissue' and 'product of conception.' Procedures called Dilation and Curettage (D&C), Dilation & Evacuation (D&E), and Intact Dilation and Extraction (IDX).

Todd slapped another paper into Melissa's hand. "Here. Look at this one."

She gasped. "What's this?"

"This," Todd answered, a grimness in his tone, "is the handy-work of places like this."

Spread across the page were images of the remains of aborted babies, laid out on a white sheet. Dismembered arms and legs, tiny fingers and toes pointing up at her. Melissa dropped the paper on the floor and turned away, her stomach heaving.

"What's the matter?" Todd sneered. "A little hard to take? Not as sterile-sounding as the other brochure made it out to be, is it? I got this picture off the internet. Nobody ever sees this stuff. Nobody ever hears. On the nightly news they can show the horrors of war ... but not of the horrors of abortion clinics." He picked up the paper, moved to face her and stabbed at the images. "So who does God love more ... unborn babies or the people who do this?"

"What are you going to do with those, Todd?"

"Post them on the walls," he growled. "Show these people that some of us know. Some of us care. We know what they're doing in here. We are standing against them and we're gonna stop them!" He crumpled one of the papers and chucked it at the wall.

"I understand. I know you're angry, but—"

"You understand?" Todd stepped forward, causing Melissa to back up. "No. You don't understand. You don't know what it's like. I see places like this and I wonder." He tilted his head back and looked at the ceiling. "I try to control it. Really, I do. But, then the big question keeps popping up in my mind. Why? Why did my mother come to a place like this?"

His bottom lip quivered and a stream of tears flowed from his eyes. "Why didn't she want to have me? Why wasn't I loved? Why wasn't I wanted? That's me. The unloved ... unwanted. Look at these two papers." He held one in each hand. "One shows a nice, clean, sterile side of abortion, with terms, facts and statistics so shiny and bright for everyone to see."

Grim-faced, he looked at the picture of the dismembered children. "The other shows the truth. The dirty secret. Abortion leaves a trail of death and broken people." His voiced hushed to a whisper. "That's me."

"Todd. Your grandmother wants you. She loves you."

"Why not my mother?"

"You don't know—"

"Don't tell me what I don't know," he yelled. "You have no idea what it's like to not know where you came from ... Who your parents are."

Melissa pursed her lips. *If you only knew ...*

"Maybe you should leave," he said. "If I get caught, there's no reason for you to go down with me. After all, I already got you in trouble one time." He took her by the arm and pulled her out of the room.

"But Todd—"

"No buts." He dragged her along the hall.

How can I stop him from doing something stupid?

Her face lit up. There! What she needed was right in front of her. She dragged her feet. "Not so fast. You're hurting me."

"Sorry." He loosened his grip just a bit. "I'm not trying to. Honest. I'm only trying to protect you."

And I'm only trying to protect you. Just a couple of more steps

...

There it was, on the wall up ahead. *But is it what I think it is?* It was so dark in the hallway. Todd's flashlight was swinging to and fro, the light flitting about. As they drew closer, she got a better look.

Yes!

A switch! A red and white switch, just like the one in Ms. Gibbons' office. Melissa casually reached up and pulled it as she walked by.

WAAAA WAAAA WAAAA!

Melissa pressed her hands against her ears.

Todd released his hold on her arm, pushing her aside, and flattened himself against the wall. His eyes darted in all directions. After a moment, he grabbed her by both shoulders, pulled her close enough so that she could hear over the din, and hollered, "What did you do?"

She shook her head as she glanced over at the red switch. "Sorry. I must have hit it by accident. What does it mean?"

"It means in about five minutes, the fire and police departments are gonna be crawling all over this place."

"Oh. Then we'd better get out of here."

Todd paced back and forth. Finally, he threw the roll of papers down, scattering them all over the floor. Then he pulled Melissa to the office with the broken window.

They climbed out into the alley and made their escape. When they'd put about three blocks between themselves and the clinic, they stopped running.

A fire engine screamed by.

Standing under a streetlight, Todd leaned forward, resting his hands on his knees and breathing heavily. "That was close."

"Yes," Melissa held her chest. Her heart was racing. "You almost did something you'd have come to regret."

"That's not what I meant." He scowled at her. "If I didn't know better, I'd swear you pulled that alarm on purpose."

Melissa struggled to maintain a look of wide-eyed innocence. "I don't know what you mean."

Another fire engine and a police car sped by.

She glanced at the ground and backed away from her friend. "It's late. I'd better get home."

Todd shook his head. "Chasing me out of there tonight doesn't change the way I feel."

"I'm only trying to help you—"

"I don't need your help!"

"But—"

"No," he barked.

"But Todd, the Lord loves you and—"

"I know. I know." Todd raised his hands in exasperation. "I don't understand you. You keep saying that to me as if I'm too stupid to have heard you the first time."

Melissa shrank back. "I didn't mean—"

"You try to act like you're so much older and more mature than me. But you're not." He turned away, shaking his head. "Maybe Martin was right about you."

"Martin?" She bristled. A knot tightened in her stomach. How could she explain the truth about Martin without telling Todd who she was? And she'd promised Jonathan she wouldn't share that information with anyone. But Todd was listening to this demon and she couldn't let that happen.

"Todd," she began cautiously. "There are things about Martin you don't know."

"Don't go off against Martin now. He's a nice old guy. Gives me some good advice."

"Todd—"

He raised a hand to silence her. "Here's the deal. I know God loves me. I know that. I don't need you constantly telling me. I don't need you following me around. I don't need you messing up my plans." He looked straight into her eyes. "I don't need you at all."

He stormed away.

· *Eighteen* ·

Mrs. Heather Winters eyed the steps to the city bus as if they were a bed of hot coals. She climbed up anyway and made her way down the aisle, the shopping bags looped over her arm brushing against each seat. She held her wallet like a squirrel clutching the last acorn on Earth.

Thankfully, it's not too crowded. She curled her lip at a grayish stain on the back of an empty seat. *Do I really want to subject myself to this?*

The bus lurched forward. She was caught off balance and fell into the seat and against the stain. "Wonderful," she moaned.

Just a bit ago, things were going so well. She'd had a wonderful morning of shopping, had found quite a few good deals. Then she was ready to head home. That's when things took a turn for the worse.

At first, she rather enjoyed the notion of a bus ride. But now, as Heather turned a suspicious eye on the other passengers, any joy faded away. Oh yes, some would say she was a bigot ... a bit pretentious.

Look at them. Frankly, there was nothing to distinguish these people apart from each other. Workers, young mothers, old women, street people. They were all the same. And they certainly weren't doctor's wives.

Not that I'm a snob or anything. But Henry and I do come from a different social class than these people.

The skin on Heather's neck began to crawl. She was being watched.

Nonsense.

She glanced around. A couple of rows ahead of her sat a young mother struggling to keep control of two toddlers. One of the children was lounging over the back of the seat, drooling on the headrest and staring at her. *Maybe I got the feeling from him.*

Across the aisle to her right, an older man was staring at her legs. He averted his eyes when she caught him. She grinned. Her personal trainer had told her on many occasions that she was hot. It was good to see all of her hard work was paying off.

Stop being paranoid. This is simply the result of not being used to taking public transit.

But then it happened again. It was no one in front of her, nor to her sides, so that left only one other option. She spun to face whatever danger lurked behind her.

There he is. A young African-American man, seated way in the back. The bus jostled and bumped about, but his eyes never wavered. They stared straight at her.

Do I know him?

Young ... Maybe from the health club. *No, doesn't look like he could afford the membership fee.* She faced forward. *Whoever he is, let him stare. I'll be getting off soon enough.*

For several awkward minutes, Heather sat rigid. Then her stop appeared in the bus's front window. She jumped out of her seat and raced forward.

"Ma'am," the bus driver said, "You gotta stay seated until we come to a full stop."

"Sorry." She darted a glance to the back of the bus. "That's my stop coming up."

"Uh-huh," he added in a bored tone.

The bus swerved to the curb. The doors swished open and Heather bounded down the steps and out onto the sidewalk. The bus pulled away.

What a relief that's over.

Turning to walk away, she collided with the young man who must have exited from the rear side door of the bus. She gasped.

"Sorry," he mumbled.

Their eyes met for the briefest of instants. Heather shivered. Cold eyes. She struggled to catch her breath.

He walked away, glancing over his shoulder as he did, staring at her.

Was this man stalking her? Was her life in danger?

Thankfully, the Women's Health Center wasn't too far away. Her eyes darted about. *And there are plenty of people on the street. I should be safe.* She fled, keeping a constant watch. At almost every turn, she swore she spotted him, skulking around a corner. *Is it my imagination or is he getting closer?* At last, she arrived at the Center and raced through the front doors.

The receptionist, a large, redheaded woman, gasped and jumped to her feet. "Are you all right, Mrs. Winter?"

"Where's my husband, Stacy?" She peered out the front window.

"In his office."

"Could you get him for me?" Mrs. Winters didn't take her eyes off the street. *I know you're out there.*

Stacy clomped down the hall. In no time at all, she was back with Dr. Henry Winters in tow.

"Heather?" Dr. Winters said.

Heather rushed to her husband and clung to him.

His brow wrinkled with concern. "What is it? What's happened?"

"I'll get her some coffee," Stacy called out as she headed off to the kitchen area.

Dr. Winters guided his wife to a seat. She set her shopping bags on the floor beside her.

"Oh, Henry. It's been a terrible morning. First I lost my pocketbook."

"Lost your pocketbook?"

She nodded. "I was shopping. At the register, I took my wallet out to pay, and placed the pocketbook on the counter next to me. When I went to pick it up, it was gone." She grunted in disgust. "Of course no one saw a thing. Luckily I had my wallet in my hand." She held the leather wallet up for her husband to see.

"How'd you get here?" Henry Winters sat on the edge of the seat next to his wife.

Heather puffed out her chest with pride. "I took a bus."

Dr. Winters, wide eyed, exclaimed, "A bus? You took a bus?"

"Don't sound so surprised."

He grinned. "Honey, let's face it. I love you, but I can't picture you on public transportation."

With her eyes closed, she rubbed her forehead. "What an awful experience."

Stacy returned with a cup of coffee and handed it over.

Heather took a sip. "It was filled with the most revolting things. Dirty seats ... offensive odors!" She glanced up at the receptionist. "Honestly, Stacy. How do you people do it?"

"It's a struggle. But people like me do our best." Stacy rolled her eyes, turned and walked back to her desk.

Heather grabbed her husband's arm and squeezed. "I think someone was stalking me. He ... he wouldn't stop gawking."

"Well," her husband smiled. "You are rather beautiful."

She ignored the compliment. "He got off the bus when I did. I think he followed me here."

Henry Winters jumped up and rushed to the front window. He scanned the street. "No one out there now. What did he look like?"

"A young man. Maybe eighteen ... twenty. African-American." Heather took another sip of coffee.

Dr. Winters shrugged. "I'm sure it was simply your imagination."

Heather spoke in an almost nonchalant tone, "I found the letter."

"Letter?"

She nodded. "And the picture ..."

He crossed to his wife. "I don't know what you're—"

"Henry!" She looked deep into his eyes. "I want the truth. I know you don't want me to worry. I know you hide things from me."

The man hung his head. "I didn't want you to get overly concerned."

"It's too late for that," she snorted. Then she took hold of her husband's hand. "Do you think we're in danger?"

Henry smiled. He patted the top of her hand, then let it go and headed back to the window. Pulling the blind, he peered out. "Don't be silly. Probably a coincidence. That's all."

Heather bit her bottom lip. *I wish I could believe you.*

• *Nineteen* •

It was a quiet day in the store. Most people preferred being outside, enjoying the beautiful weather, rather than being stuck in a stuffy old building. Even though it wasn't busy with customers, there were still jobs to accomplish, and Ms. Gibbons took the opportunity to get them done.

"All of these shelving units need to be emptied and broken down," she said. "We're going to move some outdoor furniture and grills over here."

Melissa, Todd, and Mabel stood before Ms. Gibbons as she issued general orders. Mabel was staring off into space, snapping her gum. Todd, sullen-faced, seemed to be occupied in a far distant world. Melissa watched him.

"We'll be moving these spring items off the shelves," Ms. Gibbons continued. "Packing some away, and relocating others to the bargain area. Also, these towels need folding." She waited for a response. Blank stares were all she got. "Okay then. Let's get busy. I'll check up on you in a while." She walked away.

They got started removing towels, folding them and placing them in a large plastic bin. Todd began dismantling a shelving unit.

"Do you need help with that?" Melissa asked eagerly.

Todd turned his back. "No."

There was a chill in the air.

Melissa hung her head. "I'm here ... if you need me." She walked over to a beaming and bright Mabel.

A lot different than Todd's cold shoulder.

"I cannot wait for today to be done," Mabel said. Then she added, bursting with excitement, "I can't wait for the week to be done. I've got big plans."

"Uh-huh." Melissa shoved another towel in the bin. Mabel liked to ramble on, especially about her weekend plans or the dates she'd have. Oh, yes. She'd talk and talk and talk.

How can she chew gum, breathe, and keep the chattering going, all at the same time?

Todd was using a hammer, smashing the bottom of shelves to dislodge them from their backing.

"Do you have to make so much noise?" Mabel complained.

Melissa agreed. Todd seemed to be whacking harder than was needed. She waited for him to respond to Mabel's question, but he said nothing, just continued taking angry wallops at the metal shelves.

"Some people," Mabel exclaimed. "Well, like I was saying, I have really great plans for Saturday night."

How long is Todd going remain angry with me?

"You should come with us ... Melissa?"

"Huh?"

Mabel was staring at her. "Honestly. Sometimes I don't think you listen to me."

"Sorry. My mind was somewhere else."

Mabel rolled her eyes. "I said you should come along on Saturday night. We could double date. What do you think?"

"Oh, I don't know ..."

"Sure! It'd be a kick." Mabel snapped her gum. "How about that weird guy? What's his name? Jonathan? He's always hanging around. I bet he'd go out with you."

Melissa tensed. "I don't think that would be a good idea."

"Okay then. How about Todd?" She leaned closer to Melissa and whispered, "He's kind of cute."

Todd came out of his sulk long enough to say, "Huh? You talking about me?"

A high-pitched laugh emanated from behind the group. "Todd, my boy, that's all girls talk about. Boys!" Martin walked up the aisle. "Oh, to be young again."

Melissa took a step backwards.

Martin peered at her. "Are you all right, my dear? You look a bit pale.

"I'm fine." Melissa's stomach did flip-flops. "Just a bit tired."

"Sorry to hear that," Martin answered. "But I think young Mabel here has a splendid idea. A double date. I can't tell you the number of times I and the late Mrs. Smith double dated with friends."He sighed. "Wonderful days. And you know, Melissa." He stepped closer to her. She had all she could do, not to turn and run away. "I think you should ask that young boy, Jonathan." He leaned in and whispered. "I hear he likes you." Martin's lips curled in a suggestive smile. "It would be fun. You like to have fun, don't you?"

Melissa's back stiffened. Parker had said those same words. 'I hear you like to have fun.' *Is this the source of the lie?* She gazed at Martin. *This demon is trying to cause havoc in as many lives as he can.*

"I'll—I'll think about it." Melissa turned away from the demon. "Right now, we need to get back to work."

"Right you are." Martin clicked his heels together. "Ms. Gibbons sent me over to see how you were doing." He gave a quick perusal of the scene. "Looks like everything is under control. You're doing a wonderful job."

Todd grunted.

"What's wrong, my friend? Are you all right?" Martin approached the young man and placed a concerned hand on his shoulder.

Melissa cringed.

Todd sighed. "It's ... I don't know ..."

"Tut, tut. I think I know. It's that ketchup incident the other day at the Woman's Health Center."

"How did you—" Todd gave Melissa an accusing look.

"Word gets around, my friend," Martin answered. "Word gets around."

Mabel had gone back to folding and storing the towels. She gave an occasional glance Todd and Martin's way.

"I didn't say anything," Melissa spoke up.

Todd gave her a cold stare.

"It doesn't matter how I heard," Martin said. "I know. That's all that matters." He wrapped an arm around Todd. "I'm concerned for you, my boy. I think of you as the son I never had."

Melissa's jaw clenched. *Watching this demon manipulate my friend is almost more than I can take.* Should she tell him the truth? Would it do any good? Would Todd believe her? Jonathan had said under no circumstances should she tell anyone.

"It's a terrible thing, this abortion problem." Martin shook his head. There was a tinge of deep regret in his voice. "A terrible thing."

Melissa's eyes narrowed to slits. *What's he up to?*

"A waste of the precious gift of God," Martin continued, his hand clenching tightly on Todd's upper arm. "When I think of the doctors who do these awful things, I ... I see red. But you've got to be careful, son. You could have gotten into quite a bit of trouble. Look what happened to Melissa. Jailed!"

Todd's face was a jumble of emotions.

"You can't take this issue so personally."

Todd tried to pull away from the demon. "You don't understand."

Martin held on to his arm, not allowing him to escape. He stared deep into his eyes. "But I do. I do."

Todd stood as if hypnotized. He slowly nodded.

Melissa shouted out, "Are you ready to get back to work?"

Her words were like a clap of thunder. Todd jumped, as if roused from a dream. "Sheesh! You don't have to yell."

"Was I yelling?" She asked, still in a voice two tones louder than it needed to be. "Sorry."

Martin's face, for a moment, showed disdain at being interrupted. Then the old man's gentle nature returned. "Quite right. Quite right. Your female taskmaster has cracked the whip!"

Martin flicked his wrist at Todd and made a snapping sound with his mouth. "Time to get back to work." He marched away. "I will tell our wonderful manager that you three are doing a splendid job. A splendid job indeed."

After he was out of earshot, Mabel said, "Kooky old man."

"He's not that bad," Todd answered. "He gives me some good advice."

Melissa shivered.

"What was all that talk about abortion?" Mabel asked.

"Nothing, really," Melissa answered, trying to change the subject. "So what do we do next?"

"That talk about life being a gift and all," Mabel continued. "What does he know? He's a guy. He'd never have to face an unwanted pregnancy."

Todd's whirled to face Mabel. "What's that supposed to mean?"

"He can't get pregnant," she answered in a matter-of-fact manner. "If you ask me, guys shouldn't have a say in something that doesn't affect them."

"Doesn't affect them?" Todd slammed the hammer into the shelf.

Uh-oh. Melissa wrung her hands.

"Does it affect the millions of baby boys who are aborted?" Todd asked.

Mabel sneered. "That's not what I meant. A girl carries the fetus."

Todd cringed. He stabbed the hammer at the young girl's face for emphasis. "Baby! It's a baby!"

Mabel rolled her eyes. "The girl's body is the issue here. It has nothing to do with the boy."

Todd shook his head. He shot around the far side of the display, away from Mabel, and got back to removing the shelves. As he knelt down to attack the bottom one, he muttered in a voice loud enough to be heard, "How anyone could kill a baby is beyond me."

"Knock it off, Mr. High and Mighty!" Mabel slammed a towel into the bin. "What do you know?"

His head popped up over the top of the unit. "I know what's right and I know what's wrong."

"Oh yeah? Have you ever considered there may be other reasons a girl would have an abortion? Legitimate reasons?"

Todd gave a contemptuous smile. "Millions of them. I'm sure. But they all boil down to one—the baby is in the way."

"You are so stupid." Mabel turned her back on him.

"Fine!" Todd marched up to her. "You give me one. One good reason to kill a baby."

Mabel turned back. Defiant eyes glared up at Todd. "A fetus!"

How quickly Melissa's carefree friends had become so angry! "Guys. Calm down."

Todd held a finger in the air. "One reason. Give me one reason."

Mabel paused for a moment. Then she said, "Here's one for you, Mr. Know-it-all. A girl is in high school. She comes from a poor family. Poor as dirt. She makes one mistake." Her face hardened. "The father-to-be, scum bag that he is, takes off. Doesn't want anything to do with her or the baby. Now, should the girl suffer for it? Should the baby suffer, being brought into a home that can barely feed the family living there already?"

"Should the child be killed instead of having the chance to live a normal life?"

"She did not kill a child." Mabel stamped a foot against the floor. "It was only a fetus!"

"Even a poor life is better than no life at all. Killing is killing."

Todd's and Mabel's volume had risen along with their tempers. Melissa stepped in between them. "Ummm, guys? Don't you think we should get back to work?"

But it was too late for calmer minds to prevail. Like a teakettle that reached its boiling point, Mabel exploded. "Shut up! You're an idiot! You have no idea what you're talking about. What kind of life could a poor teenage girl have offered a baby?"

"Instead she offered the child death," Todd flatly stated.

"What do you know? You're a boy." She pulled a towel out of the bin and tossed it at Todd. "You shouldn't even be in this conversation."

"Oh yeah!" Todd pulled a shelf off the backboard and smashed it to the floor. "I know enough not to kill. At least not innocent babies!"

"What is going on here?" Ms. Gibbons was fast approaching several customers, who were huddled in the aisle, gawking at this exchange. She stormed passed them, her usual mild-mannered expression replaced with one of controlled rage. "I could hear you from all the way in the front of the store."

She turned to the crowd and forced a smile. "Everything is fine here. Sorry if these employees have bothered you."

People broke off from the group, appearing sad that it was over, as if their morning entertainment had been interrupted.

Ms. Gibbons glared at the three workers.

Melissa was the first to speak. "Sorry."

"What were you fighting about?" Ms. Gibbons demanded.

"Nothing," Todd mumbled. He bent over and picked up a shelf.

"It didn't sound like nothing to me." Ms. Gibbons stood, hands on hips, waiting for a response.

Finally, Mabel blurted out, "Abortion. We were talking about abortion." She scowled at Todd. "A woman's right to choose what happens to her own body."

Todd's face reddened. His mouth trembled. He pointed at Mabel and started to speak.

She cut him off. "He thinks if a woman has an abortion she's a killer." Mabel lowered her head.

"Oh ..." Ms. Gibbons' stern demeanor melted. Her face went white. "I don't think that's proper talk for work hours. I suggest you change the subject." She turned to leave. "Todd. You come with me. I have another job for you."

Melissa sighed. *Smart move on Ms. Gibbons' part. Break up these two. Make sure that the battle is over.*

Todd followed the store manager down the aisle and out of sight.

The two girls returned to work. An uneasy quiet hung over them. Mabel wrestled with the towels, folding and unfolding them. Flapping them in the air with such ferocity that they gave a loud snap. Finally, she broke the silence.

"Todd doesn't get it. Sometimes a girl doesn't have a choice. Am I right?" She looked to Melissa, waiting for a response.

She's not going to like what I have to say.

"Melissa? What do you think? What else could a poor teenage girl do?"

Melissa swallowed hard. "Have the baby."

Mabel gawked. "Do you know what that would have done to ... her life?"

Melissa was silent.

"You're always saying God loves and forgives ... He forgives a girl whose had an abortion. Doesn't He?"

Melissa whispered, "Did the girl do something wrong?"

Without a second's thought, Mabel answered, "No."

"How can God forgive someone who's not seeking forgiveness? Who doesn't think they've done anything wrong?" Melissa turned and walked away.

From three aisles away, Martin peeked out from behind a rack of women's blouses. Watching the scene transpire, he gave a satisfied smirk and began humming to himself. Slowly the humming turned into quiet singing. "Pull a brick out here, pull a brick out there. The camel's back breaks, each straw placed with care ..."

"What are you up to?" Jonathan demanded as he walked up behind the demon.

"Oh!" Martin jumped. "You startled me." His hands clutched at his chest. "Be careful," he said with a sly grin. "I'm an old man, you know."

Jonathan repeated, more sternly, "What are you up to?"

Martin looked back toward the show. Todd was walking away with Ms. Gibbons. Melissa and Mabel were resuming their work. Everyone looked miserable. "Nothing. Just people watching. That's all."

After giving him a cold stare, Jonathan walked away.

Martin continued to sing, merrily. "One little crack on top of one little crack ..."

· *Twenty* ·

Usually Melissa took her lunch break with Todd or Mabel. But a chill had developed between them. Weather permitting, the city park across the street was a beautiful spot to eat lunch. And today, weather was permitting. Melissa found a nice bench and basked in the sunshine. As she munched on a peanut butter and jelly sandwich, she people watched.

"Fascinating, aren't they?" Jonathan strolled up from behind her, hopped over the back of the bench and sat down. Digging into a brown bag, he pulled out an apple. "Humans are interesting to watch."

Melissa nodded. A small group of preschoolers, like a gaggle of ducklings, were following after their teacher. Each child held tightly to a knot on a rope. Melissa giggled.

"What's so funny?" Jonathan asked.

"The children. They aren't tied to the rope, just holding on. Yet, because of it, they all obediently follow."

Jonathan nodded. "Humans are funny creatures. They're given such freedom, yet like children, are easily led, following after the leader, clinging onto whatever rope they're handed."

"I hadn't thought of it quite like that." With her sandwich finished, Melissa picked up her book and thumbed through the pages.

"What are you reading?"

"It's an atlas of the United States."

Jonathan laughed as he leaned over to get a better look. "Planning on a road trip?"

"No." Melissa went back to studying a map of Oregon. "I'm hoping it will trigger a memory of where I'm from. Maybe see the name of a town or city that will look familiar to me."

Jonathan groaned. "Melissa—"

"Of course I realize there are a lot of towns to search through."

"Do you think it's a good idea to—"

"And I'm assuming I'm from this country." Her eyes widened. "Maybe I'm from Europe. Maybe I'm from Asia." She turned to her friend. "What do you think?"

Jonathan sighed. "I think you need to remember why you're here."

At that moment, Ms. Gibbons came into view, strolling along the sidewalk.

I guess my idea of an outside lunch hour isn't unique.

Melissa was about to call out to her manager, asking if she wanted to join them, but the words caught in her throat when she saw who was with her.

"Well, dearie me. Look who we have here," Martin sang as he strolled along beside Ms. Gibbons. "A young couple enjoying the park. Spring is such a wonderful time."

Jonathan jumped up, looking rather nervous. "Would you two like to join us?"

Before Ms. Gibbons could speak, Martin answered, "We wouldn't think of imposing. We know what it's like with young people. You don't want old fuddy-duddies hanging about."

"Speak for yourself," Lisa Gibbons protested. "I don't think being thirty-six classifies me as an old fuddy-duddy."

"I stand corrected." Martin gave a slight bow. "Of course I was speaking only of myself."

Ms. Gibbons returned a curtsey. "How old are you, if you don't mind me asking."

"Not at all. I'm older than dirt, but not quite as old as time itself."

The two laughed.

Jonathan stood scowling.

Martin focused his attention back on Melissa and Jonathan, giving a toothy grin. "May I be so bold as to wonder ... is love in the air?"

Jonathan frowned. "No."

"Don't let him bother you." Ms. Gibbons slapped Martin gently on the shoulder. "It's just good natured kidding."

Sure it is. Melissa grimaced.

Jonathan took a step closer to the two, almost knocking into Ms. Gibbons. "Sorry. Would you ... err ... like us to ... uh, walk along with you? I mean, not that we have to or anything. Thought maybe you'd like the company."

How awkward. Melissa's face heated. *Jonathan has got to work on his social skills.*

"Tut, tut." Martin stepped between Ms. Gibbons and Jonathan. "You know what they say. 'Two's company. Three's a crowd.'" He took the woman by the arm and they went on their merry way, with Martin blabbering non-stop.

Jonathan watched them depart, standing rigid. His hand slowly tightened into a fist, until the apple he was holding was squished to a pulpy mess.

"Wow!" Melissa eyed him. "Were you planning on apple sauce?"

Jonathan tipped his head to the side. "What? Oh!" Sitting back down, he grabbed a napkin from his lunch bag and wiped the wet gunk off his hand. Then he gave an unconvincing smile. "Sorry. I know I shouldn't let what he says bother me. He's just an old man who likes to prattle on, but that's no rea-son—"

"I know," Melissa interrupted.

"Well, we all know. Martin likes to talk and tease—"

"No." She turned to face her friend. Looking him straight in the eye, she said, with extra emphasis on each word, "I KNOW."

Jonathan cocked his head to the side. "Know? Know what?"

"I know who Martin really is."

Jonathan shuffled his feet. "Is?"

"You don't do that too well. He does, though." She nodded in the direction of Martin and Ms. Gibbons.

"Does what?"

"Lie." She leaned in and whispered. "Of course, being a demon, his master is the father of lies."

"Shhh!" Jonathan looked down the path, to where the demon was still moving away. After a couple of seconds, he turned back to Melissa. "What makes you think that Martin is a demon?"

"I was in the break room." She recounted the whole story of her seeing the transformation that day. Jonathan sat still, eyes focused on her, occasionally warning her to keep her voice down. She ended the tale and asked, "So what can I do?"

"Do?"

"To help." She slid closer to Jonathan. "What can I do to help you?"

Jonathan's mouth dropped open. "Absolutely nothing! Do you hear me?"

Melissa went to protest.

"No!" He held a finger up in front of her face. "I mean it. You don't understand what you're getting yourself involved in. Stick to the mission God gave you."

"But I'm already involved, aren't I? Didn't he say that I belonged to him?"

Jonathan scowled. "Melissa. Stick to the mission. Thankfully, we were so focused on each other, neither one of us paid any attention to you. We don't want him to know who you are." Jonathan's eyes grew wide. He took in a quick breath. "He hasn't touched you, has he? I mean, you two haven't shaken hands? He hasn't placed a hand on your shoulder?"

Melissa crinkled her nose. "I don't know ... I don't think so. Ever since I found out what he is, I try to avoid him."

Jonathan sat back and gave a sigh of relief. "That's good."

"Why does that matter?"

He rubbed the back of his neck. "Angels, demons ... are spirit-sensitive. That's why I asked you to touch me the other day out on the road. If a supernatural being touches a supernatural being, they see with—for want of a better term—spirit sight. I knew once you saw me transformed, you'd believe."

Melissa scratched her ear. "As long as I don't touch him ..."

"We can also sense the presence of another spirit creature. Fortunately, I'm in the picture. He probably senses you, but assumes it's me. Remember. He cannot find out who you are."

"That's easy," Melissa slumped back and folded her arms across her chest. "Even I don't know who I am."

"You know what I'm talking about. He can't know you're on a mission from the Lord."

"Does he know who I was before ... before I went to Heaven?"

Exasperation rolled out with Jonathan's deep sigh. "Why is that so important to you? In Heaven, you have a wonderful life. Isn't that enough?"

Was it enough? *Before coming to Earth, I probably would have said yes. But now? Who am I? Who are my parents? Where do I come from?*

Jonathan continued. "Please child. Demons are more dangerous than you could imagine. Don't give him any more power by telling him who you are. He'll play on your weaknesses. Whisper temptations in your ear."

"He doesn't look that tough. Frankly, he doesn't look like a demon at all. He looks like a silly old man."

"That's their greatest weapon. Most humans picture demons as these cruel, twisted beings. Horned heads and hoofed feet. They forget that Satan is described as an angel of light. That's how they fool you into listening to them. They disguise themselves." He gave a nod in the direction Martin had just gone. "This one acts so innocent and helpless. He'll get your guard down, then WHAM!" Jonathan smashed his fist into the back of the bench. "He'll have you!"

"He won't have me. I'm smarter than that."

"Melissa!"

She sighed and rolled her eyes. "I'll be careful."

Jonathan gave a nod. "Good. And I'll be watching over you." He reached over and touched her shoulder.

Melissa stiffened.

"What's the matter?" He asked.

"Nothing."

"Obviously, something's wrong. What is it?"

Melissa slid down the bench, away from Jonathan. Her face grew warm and she looked down at the ground.

Jonathan leaned forward, to look up at her down-turned face. He spoke in a quiet voice. "Please, tell me."

She closed her eyes and took a deep breath. "It's just ... The other day, in the break room. He talked about me."

"Yes?"

"About you ... you and me. He tried to tempt you to ..." She risked a glance Jonathan's way.

As if the bench were on fire, Jonathan jumped up. "Stop right there. You don't think—"

"I don't know what to think. Were you ..." She hesitated.

Jonathan puffed out his chest. "I am an angel. God's messenger." He spoke with authority, with power. He said it in a way that stated, 'and that settles that.'

"So you would never—"

"Never!"

"But then, why did he try to tempt you? He said it was part of his mission. If there were no chance—"

"He's a liar. Remember that!" Jonathan's shoulders shuddered as he released a long breath. He settled back down on the bench next to Melissa. "Just as I am an angel, he is a demon. That's what he does. Tempts." Jonathan waved at the air. "He would tempt the breeze not to blow, tempt the sun not to rise. It's what he does."

A lump formed in Melissa's throat. *How could I have doubted my angel?*

Jonathan's hand rested on her shoulder. This time she didn't react. "Not only am I an angel. I am *your* angel."

She smiled.

"He has caused such havoc in your life without even talking to you. Imagine what would happen if he found out who you are. Promise me you won't tell him."

She reached up and touched her protector's hand. "I promise."

• *Twenty-One* •

Melissa rang up a woman's purchases at Cosmetics. When no other customers were in sight, she leaned against the counter and took a deep breath. The morning had given her quite a bit to think about.

Todd was still brimming with anger. How could she get through to him? She shook her head. Such a nice boy to have his life muddled like this.

I wonder where he is?

There were two main aisles of the store. One ran from the front door all the way to the back. The other went from left to right—from hardware to toys. The cosmetics area was right in the middle. Melissa turned her head in all directions. There was no sign of Todd.

She did catch sight of Jonathan, though, up at the front desk, standing beside Ms. Gibbons. They were deep in conversation. Ms. Gibbons smiled.

And she needs something to smile about. Ms. Gibbons had been appearing frazzled lately. This morning's situation with Todd hadn't helped.

Speaking of Todd ...

Again Melissa glanced around the store. He was nowhere in sight so she figured he must be busy doing something.

The speaker on the wall crackled as the store's PA system came to life. Its main components were in the back room—an ancient microphone for storewide announcements, and an old console containing an AM/FM radio and a slot marked 'Eight track tapes.' Whatever those were. Not state of the art, but it seemed to do the trick.

Usually music from some nondescript radio station played. One minute after a song ended, you couldn't remember what you'd just heard. 'Dentist Office Music', Mabel had called it.

But today, an angry voice bellowed, "I'd like to know what you think? Is it back-door politics? A bribe? Who's the whacko that let these murderers in? Should they be closed down?"

Everyone in the store looked up at the speakers in the ceiling tiles. Ms. Gibbons and Jonathan appeared just as confused as everyone else.

"This is the Claude Benning show. We're talking the issues of the day. The issues that matter the most to you. Nothing is too controversial. Nothing is taboo! Carol, on line one, what's your thoughts on this?"

"Hi Bob. I'm a first time caller ..."

Ms. Gibbons moved toward the back of the store, followed by Jonathan.

"So what do you think?" The radio talk show host said.

"It's a woman's right. Just because some people think we should go back to the dark ages doesn't mean we should. Would those same people want to do away with antibiotics and anti-depressants because they're new? Give me a break."

"Thanks for the call, Carol. But antibiotics aren't killing people, at least not that I know of."

Mabel wandered by, an amused smirk on her face. In the humdrum life of the store, any changes in the routine were a welcome distraction.

"Today we're talking about a woman's right to choose vs. right to life," the voice on the radio announced.

The smile disappeared from Mabel's face.

"More specifically, we're talking about the Southside Women's Health Center," the host continued. "Are they causing more harm than good?"

Ms. Gibbons quickened her pace and disappeared through the employee doorway to the back room.

"Yes, Dan. You're on the air."

"Hey Bob."

"Go ahead, caller."

"I just want to say that I think places like this should be closed down."

"Why is that?"

"Health Center my eye. All they do there is kill."

Mabel hung her head.

The caller continued. "I think that every doctor who does an abortion should be put on death row!"

"That's awfully strong." There was almost a note of glee in the DJ's voice. "Tell us how you really feel."

"I think any woman who has an abortion should be put on trial for mur—"

The PA system crackled and returned to some nameless and forgettable song from the past. A murmuring ran through the store, both from the workers and the customers.

Todd stormed out of the back room, followed closely by Ms. Gibbons, Jonathan, and Martin, all with disapproving looks on their faces. They stopped right in front of the Cosmetic counter.

"But I had nothing to do with it," Todd exclaimed. "I was using the bathroom. That's all. Why would I change the radio station?"

Mabel, who'd been standing there with tear-filled eyes since hearing the last caller's pronouncements, spoke out. "Todd. You're such a jerk!"

She spun and stomped away.

"Martin," Ms. Gibbons asked. "What were you doing back there?"

"The same thing as you. Hearing the crackling on the PA, I knew there was a problem and was going to see if there was anything I could do to fix it. I arrived right before you."

"Did you see Todd coming out of the bathroom?"

Todd looked to Martin.

Martin opened his mouth to speak, but hesitated.

"Well?"

Martin hung his head. "I honestly can't say that I did."

Todd gaped. "But—"

"However, I can't say I saw him by the PA system either."

"It's nice of you to try and defend him." Ms. Gibbons glared at Todd. "I don't know what I'm going to do with you."

"But I'm innocent."

"Did you know there are government regulations as to what we play on the radio? Did you know we have to pay for the right to play certain stations?"

"But I didn't—"

"I'm not finished. You were *not* hired for social commentary." Ms. Gibbons' face was turning beet red. "You were *not* hired to be the store's conscience. You were hired to work. Can you do that?"

Todd hung his head. "Yes ma'am."

"Good. Then get back to work," she practically screamed before heading off in the same direction Mabel had taken, with Jonathan chasing after her.

An uncomfortable silence covered the cosmetics counter area. Todd was trembling and blinking rapidly. Trying to fight back tears.

What can I say that will help?

Finally, Martin, in a sad, apologetic voice said, "I'm sorry, my boy. I wish I could say I saw you coming out of the bathroom, but I honestly can't."

Todd mumbled something under his breath.

"Best thing now is to put it behind you and get back to work."

When Todd remained silent, not moving, Martin retreated.

Anyone else would have doubted Todd. His track record showed that he did some pretty stupid things. However, there were two arguments on Todd's side. Number one, could anyone truly fake that miserable look on Todd's face? Secondly, Martin was back there with him. It was Martin, the demon in disguise, whose word Ms. Lisa Gibbons chose to take over Todd's. Melissa's heart ached at the torment on her friend's face. "I believe you," she said.

"Thanks."

Todd slinked away.

She shook her head. How could she help this boy?

Martin busied himself with the archery display, pretending to be straightening out the bows and organizing the arrows. All the while, he kept a watchful eye on the Ladies' room. Plotting and scheming, playing people like pieces in a chess game. That's what his existence was all about. And in regards to what was transpiring in the bathroom ... *If I could get the right pawns in play ...* He gave a wicked grin. It would be wonderful!

He laughed to himself. This was so much fun. *Enjoying one's work is half the battle.*

His grin turned into a frown. *Where does she think she's going?*

He kept a steady eye on Melissa as she made her way across the store toward the Ladies' room.

No! Don't go in there. Use the employee's room, you miserable ... He clenched his jaw. *Miserable whelp with your miserable message of God's love and forgiveness.*

Martin caressed the display he was working on. If only he could pick up one of these arrows and thrust it through Melissa's heart. He paused for a moment and licked his lips. Melissa's dead body, lying in a pool of her own blood. That would be amazing.

It would serve her right!

Melissa arrived at the door to the bathroom. Just before she opened it, she hesitated.

Yes! Turn around and leave.

She did turn around, but she didn't leave. Instead, she looked right at him. Martin blinked. But he quickly recovered, smiled and waved at the girl.

Witch! Parker should have raped you and killed you when he had the chance!

Melissa disappeared into the bathroom.

Martin went back to his work. *No matter. She can't do anything to stop my plan.*

· Twenty-Two ·

Melissa stood at the sink, washing her hands. *What was that?* She shut off the faucet. *Crying. Someone's crying.* A quick check revealed one of the stall doors had a pair of shoes showing from beneath it. But was it an employee or a customer?

"Hello," she called out in a soft voice. "Is everything all right? Can I help you?"

The sobbing stopped.

Getting no answer, she repeated, "Is everything all right?" Melissa stared at the closed door.

Again, no response.

With a shrug, she turned to leave. She grasped the door's handle and pulled it half way open. Then she paused.

What if whoever's in the stall needs help, but is embarrassed to ask? What if something is seriously wrong?

Melissa pulled the bathroom door all the way open and let it shut again with a loud thump. Then she stood motionless.

After a moment, the noise from the stall grew louder again. Someone tore toilet tissue off the roll. Then a nose blew. The toilet flushed. The door to the stall opened. And Mabel popped out, eyes red from crying.

"Oh," Mabel gasped. An awkward moment passed between the two. Then she quick-stepped to the sink and washed her hands. "I thought you'd left."

Mabel fidgeted in front of the mirror, splashing water on her face, dabbing her eyes with a tissue. Since Todd and Mabel's argument, Melissa had given the girl a wide berth.

"I must look awful," Mabel said, smiling weakly.

Melissa inched closer to her. "Are you all right?"

Mabel hung her head. "It's Todd. How could he do something like that? Is he intentionally trying to hurt me?"

"I don't understand."

Mabel burst into tears, raced back into the stall and sat down. She buried her head deep in her hands. "It's not fair!"

Melissa pulled the stall door open and crouched down in front of the girl. "What's wrong? Please tell me."

Her head shook violently. "Go back to work. Leave me alone."

"But Mabel—"

"Stupid radio show!" She spoke through clenched teeth. "Stupid Todd."

Melissa reached forward and touched her friend's shoulder. "Let me help you."

Mabel gave a bitter laugh. "Help me? Why should I let you help? You've already told me your God can't forgive. You're just like Todd. You think I'm a killer." With her lip quivering, she looked to the side wall of the stall, away from Melissa's stare.

Melissa gasped.

Mabel squirmed on her seat and avoided eye contact with her friend.

"Mabel? You?"

Her friend didn't answer. Instead she dug into her purse and pulled out a picture wallet. Flipping through the photos, she paused and gave one a particularly long look. "Here." She handed the picture to Melissa.

"What is this?" Melissa squinted and tipped the picture from side to side. It showed a gray and white, fuzzy, small figure, under some type of light. No details could really be seen.

"That," Mabel announced, a catch in her throat, "is my baby."

"You have a baby?"

Mabel nodded. "Up in Heaven. I was only sixteen ... still had a lot of growing up to do." The twenty year old snatched the ultrasound photo back from Melissa. She gave it a feeble smile as she affectionately ran her finger across it.

"You ..." Melissa caught herself. *I certainly can't say 'You killed your baby?'* "You had an abortion?"

Here was her friend, gazing at a photo with such love, one would have thought it was of her pride and joy. Yet, Mabel had willingly ended the child's life. There seemed a vast contradiction here.

Tears welled in Mabel's eye. "You don't understand. I had no choice. I hadn't finished high school yet. It was the only thing for me to do."

Melissa's brow knit in confusion. "I don't think I'll ever understand ..."

"Stop looking at me like I'm the devil or something."

Melissa's gaze fell to the floor. "I didn't mean—"

Amidst sobs, Mabel blurted out. "Why'd you have to push me to tell you? Why couldn't you let it be? Why does Todd have to bring it up?" She balled up her fist and drove it into her knee. "He gets me so angry."

"I don't think he means to."

Mabel sniffed deeply and shook her head. "You only know half the story. I was gonna try and have the baby." She cast a scornful look at Melissa. "Would that have made you happy? Me ... quitting school, struggling to make a life for us?"

Melissa remained silent.

"But the doctor said there were complications. Said there was greater than a sixty percent chance the baby would be born with some major issues. Birth defects. I was just a kid. What was I gonna do?" Mabel pulled off some toilet tissue and wiped her eyes. "Over the last four years, every time the subject of abortion comes up ... how do you think I feel?"

"Why don't you say that to Todd?"

"Stupid Todd." She blew her nose. "It's none of his business." She glared at Melissa. "It's none of your business. Right away he accuses all woman who've had abortions of murder. He doesn't deserve the truth." She fumbled through her purse. "Could you get me a cup of water?"

"Sure." Melissa crossed to the sink, pulled a disposable cup from the dispenser, filled it and brought it back to Mabel.

"Thanks." Mabel removed a bottle from her purse and shook a pill out of it. She popped it in her mouth and took a large gulp of water.

Melissa stared at the bottle. "Headache?"

Mabel rolled her eyes and grunted. "Depression, if it's any of your business."

Melissa knelt down in front of her. She spoke softly. "How many of those have you taken? How long have you —"

Mabel snapped. "Look. I know what you're thinking, and you're wrong. Dead wrong! I have no guilt about the abortion. I'm not depressed because of that!" She rolled her hands into fists and gently beat them against her forehead. "It's people like Todd. They're the problem. Judging me. Hurting me." She burst into tears. "It's not fair."

"What's going on in here?" A woman's voice echoed through the bathroom. "Shouldn't you be out on the floor?" Ms. Gibbons stood, poised in the bathroom's door, holding it wide open.

How long has she been there? How much had she heard?

"Sorry." Melissa hopped up. "I was just helping Mabel." She looked back in the stall, just in time to see her friend shove the bottle of pills into her purse.

Ms. Gibbons walked by the first two stalls and came to where Mabel sat. Her sternness melted away. "Are you okay?"

Mabel sniffed as she stood up, pushed her way passed the two other women, and crossed to the sink. She shook her head.

"Why don't you come with me to my office. We'll have a little chat. Melissa, you head back to work." She wrapped an arm around Mabel's shoulder and led her out of the bathroom.

Melissa rushed to catch the door before it closed. "Mabel," she called out.

The girl looked over her shoulder.

"Are we still friends?"

Mabel mouth turned up a bit. "Hey. I poured my heart out to you. We better be friends."

She and Ms. Gibbons disappeared down the aisle, and Melissa headed back to her department.

Should I tell Todd about Mabel? Would it change his opinion of her?

A crease formed in her forehead. Did it change her own opinion? Should birth defects matter? Does it make a difference?

The city hall was one of the oldest buildings in town, an architectural beauty of granite. High above the doors, seated on perches, holding up the roof, were a series of gargoyles. They were ever vigilant, ever watching over the affairs of state.

If a person were observant, and knew how many gargoyles there usually were, they'd get a surprise this evening. If they looked up, they'd see something strange— an extra statue.

Ah, darkness. Shadows. Martin did not need sleep. Instead, he wandered the night, causing mischief and mayhem. This night in particular, he had a special mission. He gazed at the digital clock on the bank across the street. 2:34 am.

It was time.

The breeze caught in his wings and pulled him aloft, off of city hall and up into the sky, into the darkness. But not too high. Not out of sight. Not that it mattered if he was seen. He laughed. *If a human caught sight of me, it would simply mean more fun.* Unlike those foolish angels who avoided detection by human eyes.

One quick mission for the evening. That was all. One quick phone call.

It didn't take long to reach his destination. On the street corner stood a telephone booth. An amazing thing. With the advent of the cellular age, there weren't many of those left. It was in the perfect location, too. Dark and desolate. Swooping down until his gray hooves rested on the asphalt, he changed back into the old man.

Not many people out and about this time of night. He chuckled. *Those who are, are usually up to no good.*

He fed quarters into the telephone and dialed.

One ring. Two rings. There was a click on the other end as someone answered. A female voice, groggy from sleep, said, "... Hello ..."

Martin spoke, but not with the old man's voice. This one was disguised. Muffled and low. "Murderer."

"W-what?" From the inflection of the word, it was apparent that the woman wasn't sure if she'd heard correctly.

"You are a murderer." Martin spoke the words crystal clear, in a tone that pronounced judgment as if he were standing in a court of law. "God will get you."

There was a long pause on the other end. "Who is this?"

Martin slammed the phone back in its cradle. A grin spread across his face. "Not bad ... not bad at all."

He was out of the phone booth and half way through the transformation back to demon, when he paused. *Hmmm.* He tapped a finger on the side of his nose. *Why not?* He transformed into the old man and reentered the phone booth.

He punched in a phone number.

A different voice answered this call. A man's voice with the same sleepy sounds, but with an added touch of annoyance, said, "Yes?"

"Murderer!"

"Who is this?"

"Killer!"

"Now you listen to me. You're not going to get away with —"

Martin's finger pulled down the switch, disconnecting the call. He beamed with joy as he flew off. *It's been a good night.*

Twenty-Three

Lunch time. Chocolate cupcakes! Melissa's mouth salivated. Though her relationship with Todd was still strained, at least she and Mabel had come to an understanding. A couple of days had passed since the radio incident. At first, conversation with Mabel was a little dicey, but they were back to enjoying their breaks together, and their lunchtimes with the delicacies from the vending machines.

Access to the break room was blocked by a small group of workers clustered in front of the bulletin board located on the wall outside its door. Many were cringing. Some were shaking their heads or turning away, disgusted looks on their faces.

"That is so gross," someone said.

"Inappropriate," another responded.

Melissa pushed through the crowd. Peeking over someone's shoulder, her mouth dropped open. Tacked up, right in the middle of the board, was a flyer with images of aborted babies on it. A scribbled heading read, 'Your Abortion Centers at Work.' The flyer was identical to the one Todd had shown her that night at the Women's Health Center.

An older woman, visibly shaking, asked, "Who would put that up there?"

A hand whipped passed Melissa's head, grabbed the flyer and ripped it down. A red-faced Ms. Gibbons tore the paper into tiny pieces. "There is no posting of flyers without my permission," she said, her voice shaking. "Get back to whatever you were doing. The show's over."

Todd appeared in the doorway from the sales floor. Everyone turned toward him. Some heads were shaking in sadness or anger. His steps slowed. He looked around at the crowd. "What? What did I do?"

Ms. Gibbons marched toward him. The crowd scattered. Melissa remained.

"Is this yours?" Ms. Gibbons held out the ripped and crumpled remains of the flyer.

Todd stared, bewildered. "I don't understand. What is it?"

"Don't give me that. You know what it is."

Melissa stepped in. "Todd, It's a flyer showing body parts from aborted babies. Someone posted it on the bulletin board."

Todd gave an incredulous look from Melissa to the pile of paper in Lisa Gibbons' hand. "And you think it was me?"

"What else should I think?" The store manager said.

He shook his head. His hands went up in surrender. "No! I didn't do it. You gotta believe me."

Ms. Gibbons stood, staring and speechless. Then she pushed passed him and toward her office. "You're treading on thin ice, young man. Thin ice."

"But, but—" Todd chased after her.

Melissa followed her friend, but came to an abrupt stop.

No. Let them talk this out. *I might get in the way. Besides, if forced to tell the truth, I'd have to admit I'd seen the flyer before.*

And when it came out where she'd seen it, it wouldn't look too good for Todd.

• *Twenty-Four* •

Melissa entered the lunchroom and headed for Mabel. The workers were caught up in their lunchtime routines, and so the bulletin board's flyer was simply one in a number of topics being whispered about at the various tables.

"You're late. Everything okay?" Mabel asked.

Melissa nodded and sat down. "Everything's ... fine."

"Look what I have." With a big grin, Mabel extended a cellophane wrapped package. "Jelly rolls! I'll admit, they don't have the addictive quality of chocolate, but I think you'll like them."

As the two dove into their vending machines treasures, Melissa kept glancing at the door. *I wonder how Todd is making out?*

"Mrs. Big Bags was here this morning," Mabel said, calling a customer by the nickname she'd been given. "You gotta keep an eye on her. She has a tendency to drop items in her large pocketbook as she strolls through the aisles." Mabel leaned forward and giggled. "Snot boy was in Sporting Goods."

"What an awful nickname." Melissa stifled a smirk.

"I didn't come up with it. Mark, over in shoes, did. Would you rather I call him mucous boy or constantly-wipes-his-nose-on-his-hand boy? Honestly! Has he ever heard of a tissue?"

The two laughed.

"Hey, kiddo! Over here. I saved a seat for you."

Melissa stiffened. She looked over her shoulder. Martin was sitting at the table directly behind her. He was waving his hand

and calling out to a grim-faced Todd, who'd just entered the room.

Melissa cringed. She traced back through her conversation with Mabel. Had she said something she shouldn't? Something Martin shouldn't overhear?

Todd crossed over to the table, glaring at Melissa.

I want to talk to Todd, but not in front of the demon. She turned back to her own table.

"Sit, sit. You only have a few minutes left for lunch," Martin said. A chair scraped against the floor. "Where have you been?"

Todd hesitated. "There was an inappropriate flyer on the bulletin board. Ms. Gibbons thought I put it there," he grumbled.

"Did you?"

"No!"

"My, oh, my." Martin spoke sympathetically. "Well someone must have put it there. Any idea who?"

"I have my suspicions."

Melissa spun around. "Don't you dare accuse me, Todd Simmons. I had nothing to do with it."

"I didn't say you did." He leaned across the table. "Feeling guilty?"

"Ignore him, Melissa," Mabel interjected. "He's a jerk." She grabbed up her trash and headed for the door. "I'm going back to work."

After Mabel was far enough away as not to hear, Todd mumbled, "Better than being a killer."

"Todd." Melissa searched her friend's face for any sign of the joy he used to have. None showed. "I would never do anything to hurt you. I want you to understand that. But you're hurting yourself. Eating yourself up inside. Whenever you want to talk to me, I'll be there." She turned to her food and fell silent as she munched on a stale cookie.

"Quite right, my boy," Martin said. "The girl is quite right."

Melissa raised her eyebrow. *Oh, really?*

"What?" Todd said.

"You're letting your passion consume you, your hatred control you. For instance, take the ketchup incident."

"What about it?"

"What would your grandmother say, that sweet old saint? Do two wrongs make a right?"

When the young man spoke, it was with resignation in his voice. "No. They don't."

"So you did something wrong. When you do wrong, it has a tendency to eat you up on the inside. Throwing that ketchup did no good. You simply ruined a man's shirt. Didn't change his opinion at all."

What's Martin up to? Melissa turned and stared at the demon. *He's almost talking sense.*

"What should I do, then?" Todd asked.

"Have you ever considered talking to the man, instead of throwing ketchup? More battles are won with words than with swords!" Martin's hands went out in a helpless shrug. "Perhaps he's never heard the other side. Plenty of good people think abortion is all right, simply because society says it is. They need to hear the truth. Mind you, I'm not necessarily saying you must talk to him ... but someone should. Everyone deserves to hear the truth. Frankly, I think the least you owe the man is a new shirt." He snickered. "We have some handsome ones over in Menswear."

After lunch was finished, Melissa headed back to the sales floor. Martin made sense. What he said was true. She'd have to ask Jonathan about this. Can demons speak the truth?

It was four-thirty. Melissa's shift didn't end until seven. She was taking a quick break, heading to the back for a soft drink, when she passed by Ms. Gibbons' office. Her stomach ached on remembering the look of disgust that the store manager had given to Todd when he was leaving at three this afternoon. *Todd isn't ready to listen to me, but maybe I can help him by talking to Ms. Gibbons.* She backed up and tapped on the door.

"Yes?"

Just as Melissa reached for the door, it popped open. Jonathan stood there. "Oh, I'm sorry," she said. "I can come back later, if I'm interrupting."

Ms. Gibbons sat at her cluttered desk. She smiled. "No, no. We were just chatting. Come in. What can I do for you?"

Jonathan opened the door wider, allowing Melissa to step into the room. "I'd better get back to work. I don't want my manager to get angry with me," he joked.

"Yes," Ms. Gibbons answered. "I hear she's a terrible ogre."

He smiled and nodded at Melissa as he exited.

"Well now. It seems today is the day for visiting the manager's office. What can I do for you?"

Melissa sat in the same seat she'd been in the day she was interviewed for the job. "It's about Todd."

The smile on the manager's face melted.

"Did you fire him?"

Ms. Gibbons paused. She rubbed the bridge of her nose. "The thought has crossed my mind. It would solve a lot of problems. But the answer to your question is ... No. I have not fired him ... At least, not yet."

"He's a good boy. Really he is," Melissa pleaded.

"A good boy?" Ms. Gibbons chuckled. "You sound like you're his mother."

Harriet had described Todd this way so many times, it was second nature to Melissa. "I'm a friend. That's all."

"I appreciate someone who sticks their neck out for a friend, but, as I said to Todd, he's treading on thin ice. I can't have someone bullying other employees, like he did to Mabel. Then there was the radio incident."

"You don't know he's guilty."

"Who else is there?"

The answer popped out before Melissa could stop it. "Martin."

Ms. Gibbons straightened up. "What in the world ... I hadn't even thought about ... well that's just plain silly. Why would Martin—"

"Why would Todd?"

Ms. Gibbons dismissed the notion. "Martin loves Todd like a son. He'd never do anything to hurt him. He'd confess to the crime before seeing the boy reprimanded."

Melissa squinted. "Are you sure?"

"What about the flyer?" Ms. Gibbons looked directly into Melissa's eyes. "Who did that?"

"I don't know." Melissa matched the stare. She sat more erect. "But if Todd says he didn't do it, I believe him."

Ms. Gibbons studied Melissa. Finally, the edges of her lips curled into a small smile. "He's very fortunate to have someone like you looking after him. But as I said, he's not fired."

Melissa inched forward in her seat. A big sunshine of a smile broke out on her face. "That's wonderful. Don't worry. I'm sure he'll behave himself from now on."

The phone on the desk rang. Ms. Gibbons answered it. "McCullen's Department Store. This is Lisa Gibbons. How can I help you?... Martin's gone home for the day. Can I direct your call to someone else?" She listened for a second, then Ms. Gibbons' face turned to stone. Her voice grew cold and stern. "Who is this?... This phone is not for personal use ... Hold on." She handed the phone across the desk. "It's for you."

Melissa brow creased. "What?"

"Take it. It's your friend."

Melissa placed the phone to her ear. "Hello?"

"Mel," Todd's timid voice called through the receiver. "I need your help. I'm in jail."

• *Twenty-Five* •

When Melissa left Ms. Gibbons' office, her manager was not in the best of moods. The thin ice was cracking beneath Todd's feet. The phone call had been brief. Melissa didn't have all the details, but Todd had been taken to the police station.

Something about graffiti ... stalking ...

He'd spoken in such haste, with so many half sentences and incoherent thoughts. The conversation was mostly gibberish.

Todd had told her that he first tried to call his grandmother, but couldn't get through. As a last resort, he called the store for Martin.

Lord, thank you that Martin was not at the store and that Todd asked for me. I was third in line, but at least he asked for me. That's something.

Receiving a grudging approval from Ms. Gibbons to leave work a couple of hours early, Melissa made her way to the same police station where she had been taken. She exited the bus directly across the street from the building and hurried in. As soon as she opened the door, her ears were assaulted by screaming.

"I don't care what he says! He's lying!" A man was accosting the officer behind the desk, the one who'd been there before, the fellow with the big neck. "He is dangerous and I expect him to be locked up!"

"Calm down, Doctor Winters."

Doctor Winters? Melissa scooted to the side of the room. *Doctor Winters must not see me!* Odds were he'd recognize her from the ketchup incident. *Can't let him put two and two together and come up with deeper trouble for Todd.*

"I don't want to calm down!"

"Well, well. Back for a visit?" A friendly voice called out. Officer Ramarez walked up behind Melissa.

Melissa smiled. "No. Well ... I guess. Yes I am. I'm here to see a friend of mine." She took the officer by the arm and directed her farther away from the main desk. "Todd Simmons? Do you know where he is?"

Officer Ramarez glanced over at the red-faced doctor, who was busy arguing his case. She nodded to Melissa. "Come on. I'll take you to him."

Todd was being held in a small room. He sat with his head in his hands at a table in its center. When Melissa entered, he jumped out of the seat.

"Mel!" He rushed forward and hugged her. "Am I glad to see you."

"I'll be outside if you need me." Officer Ramarez pulled the door shut as she left.

"What's going on?" Melissa asked. The two sat down.

"It's crazy. I didn't do anything wrong." Todd hit himself in the forehead. "Man! Gram's gonna kill me!"

"Not if you didn't do anything wrong." She placed a hand on the young man's shoulder. "Tell me what happened."

Todd took a deep breath and sighed. "Okay. You know I left work around three. I'd been thinking about the conversation at lunch."

Oh boy.

"Martin was right. Maybe I should talk to the people at the Center. They might be nice people ... just misguided. After all, Gramma use to work at a place like that, until ..." His words trailed off. He winced. "So I went to the Center."

Melissa shook her head. *Not a good idea.*

"But the closer I got, the more I realized, I wasn't sure what I was going to say. So when I arrived, I paced around a few minutes out front, trying to figure it all out."

"That's good."

"But that's when the trouble began. All of a sudden, a police car screeches around the corner. Before it even comes to a stop, the man storms out of the building, pointing at me and hollering, 'That's him! That's the kid!' I was so scared, I turned to run, but the police were standing right there. What could I do? 'That's him! He's the one! Arrest him!' The doctor was stabbing a finger in my chest."

"He must have recognized you from the other day."

Todd shook his head. "At first, that's what I figured. But, no. The officer says to me, 'Son. Where were you this morning, about 7:30?' He looked over to Doctor Winters, who nods back at him. Now I was confused. What did 7:30 have to do with the ketchup? I was starting to sweat. I tell them I was home.

"'No you weren't,' the doctor barked. He lurched toward me. The police officer placed a hand on his chest to hold him back. But that just made the doctor angrier. He starts waving a fist at me. 'I saw you. I recognize you!'"

"Recognized you from this morning?" Melissa furrowed her brow.

Todd nodded. "Then he points over to the building. There, spray-painted in big red letters, are the words 'Baby Killer.' It turns out that the doctor saw someone there this morning, painting the wall. But whoever it was, they raced off before he could catch him."

"And he thinks it was you?"

Todd cried out, "I didn't do it! Honest! Next thing I know, the officer is saying that we'll straighten this out down at the station. They loaded me into a police car and brought me here. You know the rest. I tried to call Gram. Then I called the store."

"Ms. Gibbons wasn't too happy about that."

"Why?" Todd's tone became defensive. "This has nothing to do with the store or my work."

"I know. But I think all the little things are beginning to add up, causing her a lot of problems."

Todd buried his face in his hands. "Man oh man. I'm dead!"

"I'm glad you asked for me, though." She sighed. "Look, I know things haven't been the best between us lately. I'm — I'm sorry if I've done something wrong. I didn't mean to. I promise that it won't happen again."

Todd remained quiet.

Not quite what I'd expected.

After a moment he declared, "I'm not the bad guy, you know."

Melissa tipped her head. "What?"

"I'm not the bad guy."

"Who said you were?"

"Everybody! People at church ... Mabel ... Gram ... you. It's not my fault that I have strong beliefs against abortion."

"I know you're not the bad guy. But you have to understand, some of those people you mentioned aren't the bad guys either."

Todd grunted. "You sound like my grandmother."

"She's very wise." Melissa smirked. At least the ice was broken between the two of them.

"Sometimes," Todd struggled for the words. "It's just ... man! Sometimes, I think people don't listen to me."

Melissa rolled her eyes. "I know the feeling." She paused. "Do you forgive me?"

Todd shrugged. "Of course I forgive you. I guess you were only doing what you thought was best."

"I was."

He smirked. "Besides, I've missed talking to you. You're like the sister I never had. Good old Mel."

The door to the room opened. Harriet Simmons entered, followed by Officer Ramarez and a tall, male police officer.

Todd jumped up. "Gram! How did you —"

Melissa interrupted. "I called Pastor Tom before I left work. He said he'd find her and let her know what had happened."

Harriet marched up to Todd. "What have you gotten yourself into now?"

"Nothing, Gram. Honest."

The officer pulled a pad of paper out of his shirt pocket and read. "At seven-thirty this morning, Doctor Henry Winters of the Southside Women's Health Center, witnessed a young African-American male painting disparaging comments on the side of the building. He claims it was your grandson."

Harriet's eyes lit, as if ready to explode. She pivoted back to Todd. "Of all the stupid ..."

He backed up like he'd rather face a room filled with police officers than his irate grandmother.

Harriet stabbed a finger in his chest. "How in the world ..." But then the expression on her face changed, going from angry to puzzled. "Wait a minute. Did you say, seven-thirty?"

The officer checked his notes. "Yes ma'am."

"This morning?"

"Correct."

Harriet shook her head. "Impossible. It wasn't Todd."

"Are you sure?"

"Sure as I'm standing here. I woke him up at seven-fifteen. At seven-thirty he was in the shower."

"Could he have slipped out a window?"

"At seven-forty-five we were having breakfast together and doing our devotions. You tell that doctor he must be mistaken."

The officer gave her a wary look. "He seemed pretty positive."

Harriet breathed in a lungful of air and puffed it out through her nose. "You ask that doctor if all African-American men look the same to him. Maybe that's the problem here. I will swear in a court of law on a stack of Bibles! My grandson was home this morning."

"Sorry ma'am," the officer stammered. "I didn't mean to doubt you."

"I understand. But I can assure you, the man is wrong."

The officer excused himself and backed out of the room. After several anxious minutes, he reappeared with Doctor Winters in tow. "Ma'am I told the doctor what you said. He wanted to have a word with you and another look at your grandson. I know it's not according to protocol, but didn't think you'd mind."

"Fine," Harriet answered. "We've nothing to hide." With her chin jutted out and eyes closed to narrow slits, she peered at the doctor with a measure of suspicion.

Doctor Winters stepped forward. "I don't appreciate being called a racist. There's not a racist bone in my body."

Everyone remained silent while the doctor scrutinized Todd. He slowly walked all the way around him. Todd held his breath.

"He looks ..." The doctor eyes searched Todd's face, every feature.

Melissa tucked herself farther behind the police officer.

Finally, Doctor Winters let out a big sigh and shook his head. "I can't be positive."

"See," Harriet exclaimed.

"But, what were you doing outside my clinic this afternoon?"

"Standing there," Todd answered.

"Don't be fresh," his grandmother warned.

Todd hung his head. "Sorry."

"Did you take the downtown bus the other day?"

Todd hesitated. His gaze swept from Doctor Winters to the police officers. With trepidation he said, "I don't know. What day? I might have. I work downtown."

"What does that have to do with this?" Harriet asked.

"My wife was on the bus the other day. She was being followed by a young African-Ameri-" He cut short his sentence.

Harriet glared at him.

The doctor stared intently at Todd. "But he looks so familiar." He tipped his head to the side. "Do I know you from somewhere?"

"I've never met you and I wasn't at your place this morning at 7:30." Todd answered, keeping his eyes focused on the wall in front of him.

Doctor Winters slowly shook his head. "Something's not right here. I know it. I don't trust you."

Officer Ramarez jumped in between Harriet and the doctor. "Since the young man has an alibi, I see no reason to continue holding him."

Doctor Winters stormed out of the room, with the male officer chasing after him. "My Center is under attack. My wife and I are being stalked! When will you—" His voice cut off as a door slammed shut.

Officer Ramarez gave the three who remained in the room a sympathetic look. "I'm sorry for any inconvenience. Why don't you follow me and we'll get you out of here."

• Twenty-Six •

Across the street from the police department stood an old elm tree, on the edge of the road. Its branches were filled with new green leaves, and one demon. Martin, invisible to the human eye, sat there in his full, inglorious form, giggling to himself.

"What are you up to, demon?" Jonathan, in angelic form, swooped down to perch opposite his nemesis.

"Just having some fun. That's all." He stared at the front of the building. "Look how easy it is to exploit these foolish human's fears. A letter sent. A picture taken. I could get that silly doctor to doubt his own mother."

"But look at the others." Jonathan pointed to the Police Station. "Like Harriet Simmons? There are humans who are not as easily manipulated by your games."

Martin shrugged. "Harriet Simmons is a lost cause. Too grounded in what she thinks the truth is." As Martin stared, his eyes began to glow. "But Melissa ... now that's a different story. I could have fun with her."

Jonathan growled. "Why are you even wasting your time on these trivial things? I thought you had a bigger mission."

"Oh, I do. But it's so much fun to play. I like sowing my seeds wherever and whenever I can. For instance ..." He continued gazing at the police headquarters. A lecherous look formed on his face. "Are you sure you're not interested in the girl? I hear she might be interested in you."

Jonathan shifted on the branch. "Mind your tongue, demon."

Martin threw up his hands in mock-surrender. "Fine, fine. I was just asking. You can't blame a demon for trying."

"Yes. I can."

Harriet, Todd, and Melissa exited the police station and walked down the street. Their conversation drifted across the road.

"Thanks for coming down, Gram."

"What about Melissa?" Harriet asked.

Todd smiled in his friend's direction. "Thank you, Mel."

"Mel?" Harriet groaned. "Are you still calling her Mel?"

Melissa laughed.

"Honestly!" Harriet shook her head. "If I find out that you were bothering that doctor's wife on the bus—"

"It wasn't me!"

"It better not have been."

Their voices trailed off as they turned the corner at the end of the block.

Martin's lips turned up in a mischievous grin. He pointed skyward. "I don't know why He's so interested in these humans. They're a lost cause."

Jonathan remained still and silent.

"What's the matter?" Sarcasm dripped from Martin's words. "God not allowing you to speak?"

"I know what you're trying to do, goad me into an argument." Jonathan shook his head. "It's not worth it. You'll never understand love or compassion. Mercy or grace."

"Blah, blah, blah." Martin laughed. "Any one of these humans would turn away from God in a heartbeat." His lips pulled tight and thin in a hard smile. His eyes gleamed with mischief as he scanned the street around them. "Now let's see. Who can I use to prove my point?"

Two people were seated on a park bench directly below—a well-dressed older man, busily studying some papers he'd taken from his briefcase, and a younger man, possibly in his twenties, dressed in jeans and a tee-shirt. He looked like your average blue collar worker on his way home after a day's labor. Both appeared to be waiting for the bus.

Martin wrung his hands in pleasure. "Let's see what fun we can have."

"Why?" Jonathan asked. "What do you possibly hope to prove?"

As they argued, a bus rolled up and the older man rose from the bench. When he did, something fell from his pocket.

"Wonderful!" Martin hopped off the branch and swooped down. "Opportunity arises," he proclaimed with a gleeful smile.

The young man, still seated, leaned over and picked up the dropped item. It was a wallet.

Oblivious to the fact he'd dropped something, the older man was up the stairs of the bus, fumbling through his pocket for the correct change.

Martin gazed at Jonathan. "Let me show you how weak these humans are."

Jonathan turned away and crossed his arms. "I'm not interested in anything you want to show me."

As the young man jumped up to return the lost wallet to its rightful owner, Martin whispered in his ear. "Look inside. See how much money it contains."

The young man obeyed. Ten dollars. That's all the wallet contained. The man hesitated, staring at the bill.

"Keep it," Martin urged. "Look at him." He pointed to the older man. "He'll never miss it."

The young man faltered. His gaze went from the wallet to the older man; impeccably dressed, well-polished shoes, neatly trimmed hair.

Jonathan grumbled. "I'm tired of your foolishness." He jumped down from the tree. "You shall not steal!" He called out. "It's the wrong thing to do."

The young man inched toward the door of the bus.

"You work hard," the demon countered in the young man's ear. "This guy probably makes ten dollars in ten minutes."

"But it's still wrong," Jonathan called into the other ear. "What about the other contents of the wallet? Pictures of his family. Loved ones. Treasures the man will never be able to replace. Are you willing to make this poor man suffer for ten dollars? Is that the way you'd want to be treated if you lost your wallet?"

The man looked down at the leather temptation in his hand. He sighed and placed a foot on the bus's bottom step.

Martin changed to a different tactic. In an instant, he was at the side of the older man, who was still searching for the correct change. The demon whispered in his ear. "Who's this bus driver think he is to rush you like this? No wonder you're struggling to get the money. He's making you nervous. Mocking you."

The older man's response was immediate. His face turned red with rage. "I don't care if you think I'm holding the bus up," he bellowed at the bus driver.

"You pay his salary," Martin quipped.

"I'll take all day if I want. I pay my taxes. Pay your salary."

"That's telling him. He's used to dealing with freeloaders. Not respectable people like you." Martin sneered, "Freeloaders. Welfare cases. Bah!"

The man's hand was trembling a bit. "I'm not like the welfare cases you deal with all day, you know. You just hold on until I'm ready!"

The bus driver had a bored, yet puzzled, expression on his face. "Uh-huh."

Meanwhile, Martin raced back to the younger man's side. "He's talking about you. Looks down his nose at you. Thinks he's better than you." The words spit out of his mouth like poison.

The older man, having finally deposited his change, was turning to walk to the back of the bus. As he did, he caught sight of the younger man. "What are you gawking at?" he growled.

The young man's lip turned up in a snarl. "Nothing!" He shoved the wallet in his pocket and walked off. "Nothing at all."

The bus pulled away.

Martin's face beamed with pride. "See how easy it is?"

Jonathan shook his head and rolled his eyes. "It's simple for you to influence those who don't belong to the Lord. What's that supposed to prove?"

Martin smiled. "Nothing. As you said, I have a bigger mission." He unfurled his wings, and with a great flourish, flew up to the tree branch and settled back on his perch. "Yes," he gave a smug smile. "Any one of them would turn in a heartbeat."

Jonathan grunted and gave his back to Martin.

The demon, head tipped up to the sky, sniffed at the air like a dog. "Can you smell it? It's the calm before the storm. No doubt about it." A warm breeze blew against his face. "Everything is quiet now. But the storm's coming." He grinned at Jonathan. "Coming soon. Are you ready?" Then he looked toward the young man walking away. "I am."

• Twenty-Seven •

Pain. Excruciating, gut wrenching pain. One moment, everything was peaceful. The next, every fiber of her body was on fire. Piercing agony. Bone crunching torment cut through her.

Spinning out of control, not able to stop it, not able to master the movement of her own body. *Run! Find help from somewhere. Anywhere.* But none came.

She was slipping away. Like water draining from a bathroom sink, her life was draining out of her.

Anything to stop this torture.

Just to have it over. To be done.

A distant voice cried out, "Oh God, help me! It hurts!"

Was that my voice?

Then another voice. Gruffer. Deeper. "Quiet down. It's going to be all right ... It's over."

The first voice answered, riddled with panic. "It's not over! It's not over!" The words echoed, time and time again. Sobbing, whimpering, she clung to those words — held them close to her soul. "It's not over."

Melissa awoke, screaming. She bolted out of bed and stumbled to the center of her room, clutching her pillow. Wide-eyed and shaking, she looked around. *My room. I'm ... in my room.* She raced for the bathroom and flipped on the light. The mirror revealed a sweat-covered face with terrified eyes. Melissa's chest heaved. Her heart pounded.

What was that all about?

She ran her fingers through her hair. "Foolish," she reprimanded the figure in the mirror. She then pulled herself up to her full five foot two inch stature, and announced, "There's nothing to be afraid of."

Right after she'd spoken, a strange noise sounded through the quiet apartment. Melissa froze. She held her breath and listened. All was quiet. Maybe it wasn't real. *My imagination.* It happened again, coming from her kitchen. Melissa leaned forward and tipped her head. The sound was familiar. What was it? She gasped. *Someone's pouring something into a glass.*

She pulled on her bathrobe, snatched the hairbrush off the dresser and crept to the bedroom door. A cold hand gripped her heart. With her weapon poised over her head, ready to attack, she peeked around the corner of the doorway. A shadowy figure was sitting in the dark, at her kitchen table.

What should I do? Should I call the police? The only problem with that idea was that the phone was on the other side of the kitchen.

She pounded a fist against her forehead. *Think Melissa.*

She tightened her grip on the hairbrush. *Flip the light on, and maybe scare away whoever was out there.* If they tried to attack her, she'd scream with all of her might and Mrs. Parsioni would come racing to her rescue.

She felt along the wall outside her bedroom door until she found the light switch. She paused. *What if Mrs. Parsioni is a heavy sleeper?* Too late to worry about that now. She flipped the switch and leapt out, ready for action, hairbrush poised above her head. Her mouth dropped open. "Jonathan!"

Her angel sat at the kitchen table, milk dripping down his chin, holding a half-eaten cookie, dunked into a glass. He had the guilty look of a small child caught with his hand in the cookie jar ... literally.

Melissa dropped the hairbrush and grabbed at her bathrobe, pulling it tightly around her neck. "What are you doing here?"

Jonathan grimaced. "These are ... great chocolate chip cookies. Did you make them?"

"Jonathan!"

He shrugged. "I happened to be going by and smelled cookies."

She glanced at the clock on the wall. "It's three in the morning. Who goes by at three in the morning?"

"Angels don't need to sleep." His faced brightened. "But I have to admit, I do have a weakness for chocolate chip cookies. They're best when they're warm." He wagged a finger in the air. "Here's a tip. If they get cold, stick them in the microwave for about fifteen seconds. But you have to have milk." He dunked the cookie into the glass in front of him, then bit off a big, dripping bite. "They're great with milk."

"So you come into my apartment in the middle of the night because you wanted cookies?" She sat in the seat next to him. "I kind of doubt that."

Jonathan took in a deep breath and let it out slowly. "You caught me. It's not just the cookies. I thought we could have a talk."

"Couldn't this have waited until morning?"

"I didn't wake you, did I?" The semi-accusing tone in his voice and his stare, told her he already knew the answer to that question.

"No."

"Good. Besides, I might not get to talk to you in the morning. You've been awfully busy lately." Jonathan raised the glass of milk to his lips and took a sip. He placed it back on the table, and ran a napkin over his face.

"What's that supposed to mean?" Melissa scooped up the bottle of milk and crossed to the refrigerator to put it away.

"It means you have very little time for me ... with you getting picked up by strange men —"

"That was before I knew any better."

"Getting arrested —"

"That wasn't my fault —"

"Being called to bail someone out of jail."

Turning from the refrigerator, Melissa crossed her arms and gave Jonathan a defiant look. "Friends help friends. Besides, it all worked out. They couldn't keep Todd. No evidence."

Without missing a beat, Jonathan said, "Setting off a fire alarm." The words lingered in the air like the foul smell in her jail cell.

"Oh," she whispered. Melissa turned away, her eyes avoiding his. "You know about that?"

Jonathan shook his head. "What were you thinking?"

"I was trying to help Todd."

"By breaking the law?"

"You don't understand."

"What? What don't I understand?"

"God sent me on a mission," she hollered. "To deliver His message. That's what I'm trying to do."

Jonathan stormed over to her. "By getting arrested?"

"I didn't get arrested!"

"You could have!"

Melissa groaned. "I'm trying to get Todd to listen. He has so much anger built up inside him."

"Melissa, you don't understand. You're—" Jonathan stopped mid-sentence. He raised his eyebrows and looked Heavenward. His lips twitched. It appeared as if he was involved in a silent conversation. After a few moments, he hung his head and mumbled something under his breath. "Never mind. Please, be careful. That's all I ask. Be careful."

"What was that?" she asked.

"What?"

She waved her hand in the air. "You were talking to someone, or someone was talking to you. Was that the Lord? Did He tell you what to say ... or did He stop you from saying something?"

Jonathan folded his arms and leaned against the counter. "That was the Lord, and the conversation between us was private. He was giving me instructions. That's all you need to know."

"That's not fair!"

Jonathan crossed to the table, picked up his glass and brought it to the sink. "I have to go. I'll see you tomorrow at work."

Melissa wrapped her arms around herself and stood there, gently rocking.

Jonathan raised an eyebrow. "What's the matter?"

"I had a nightmare," she whispered.

"Yes. I heard." He added with a shrug, "Humans have nightmares."

"I know, but this one was different." She shivered. "It felt so real. Mabel told me about one she had, where she was being chased through the store by Ms. Gibbons. Only it wasn't Ms. Gibbons. It might have looked like her, but she had fangs and wanted to bite Mabel in the neck. Todd says he has nightmares, too."

"Your point?"

"Their nightmares have one thing in common." She looked at Jonathan, waiting to see if he'd guess what it was. He remained silent. "Something or someone to fear. A monster, a person. But for me ..." She closed her eyes and shook her head.

He took a step toward her and spoke in a voice that sounded more like a mother consoling a small child. "What was it about?"

Melissa's lip quivered. "Pain."

"What happened in it?"

"... I don't know ..."

"Where were you?"

"I don't know ..." She turned away from him, heat spreading across her cheeks.

"Were you alone?"

Melissa gripped the edge of the counter with trembling hands. The frustration rose in her voice. "I don't know."

Jonathan touched her shoulder. "It's going to be all right. I'm here. Please, tell me everything."

Melissa took a deep breath and told him about the darkness. The pain. "I don't think I've ever experienced anything like that," she said. "I wouldn't even know what it was like."

There was a long pause.

"You've been through quite a bit," Jonathan finally said. "It's been my experience that human emotions can play tricks —"

"But what if I have experienced pain like that? What if it was from my life before Heaven?" She gave her head a vigorous shake, as if that would dislodge old memories. "Oh, I wish I could remember."

Jonathan sighed. "Sometimes it's best not to remember. Right now, all you have to do is focus on your mission."

"Yes. On Todd."

Jonathan groaned.

Melissa stabbed a finger in his chest. "Why don't you like Todd?"

"Who said I don't like him?"

"I can tell!"

"My feelings for Todd have nothing to do with this. I neither like nor dislike him. He's simply another human. All I can say is," he looked Heavenward, as if seeking approval. Then he nodded. "Be open to the Lord's leading."

Melissa shrugged. "I am."

She picked up a napkin and absentmindedly dabbed at some cookie crumbs on the corner of Jonathan's mouth.

Jonathan brushed her hand away. "Melissa, are you listening to me? Be open to the Lord's leading."

Her forehead creased. "I am," she answered. "I am."

• *Twenty-Eight* •

Dr. Henry Winters slapped the twenty-dollar bill on the counter at the hardware store. A clerk, who looked like he'd been a fixture there since the place opened eighty years ago, retrieved it from under his angry glare. The doctor wasn't upset with the clerk, nor with the store.

It's the whole situation.

The fact that his clinic had been getting such negative publicity. First, there was the ketchup incident. He grumbled. His wife never got the stain out of his shirt. His favorite shirt! Then there was the break-in, with the pulled fire alarm, those terrible flyers scattered all over the floor, plus the vandalism. Then there were the phone calls and the threatening letter.

And now the graffiti.

It all added up to one big headache.

On top of that, he himself had to come down to the store and buy the cleaning supplies to remove the offending words.

I am a doctor! Not a handyman!

The clerk handed Dr. Winters his change. "There you go. Have a nice day."

Henry stormed out the door. As if the day wasn't bad enough, in his hurry, he stepped off the sidewalk and splashed into a deep puddle.

"Wonderful. Just great." The cold water seeped into his shoes and socks. He hobbled over to a bench and sat down.

With grumbling effort, he removed a shoe and poured its contents onto the ground. Then he removed his sock and wrung it out. When the left foot was done, he repeated the procedure with the right one.

'Baby killer! Murderer!' Those words spray-painted on the side of his building made his blood boil. *Lies! Utter nonsense!* "How can people be so ill informed in our enlightened society?" He slammed his left shoe down on the bench. "Murderer indeed!"

All I do is remove the POC or a small amount of fetal tissue. This shouldn't offend anyone. He puffed his chest out with pride. *If anything, what I do should be considered a great resource to society. I supply a needed service to a disenfranchised element of the community — the poor women who suffer from unwanted pregnancies.* He smiled. *And if I make a good living while doing so, all the better.*

What had gone wrong? Everything was done according to plan. The Southside Women's Health Center had slipped into town almost unannounced. Not that they'd done anything underhanded or dishonest. The Board of Directors simply wanted to open with as little fanfare as possible. 'No publicity is good publicity' was their mantra. But now they were getting more of it than they bargained for, and were worried. Too much attention, too quickly.

At the emergency meeting last evening, Dr. Winters had explained, "In these incidents, the clinic would be viewed as the victim, not the bad guy."

He had argued this point for three hours. Unfortunately, the Board didn't agree with him.

"Bunch of cowards," he grumbled.

His shirt pocket vibrated. He pulled out his cell phone and checked the number of the incoming call. His head dropped to his chest and he moaned before answering. *Jack Evans. Speaking of the Board of Directors. At least he's one of the members I can tolerate.*

"Hello, Jack." There was no joy in his voice. "Yes ... yes. I know you feel a news conference is the best way to go ..."

Doctor Winters rubbed his temples, seeking to ward off a headache. "I disagree ... but ... but ... Jack!" He spoke sternly into the phone. "I understand the Board's position. I simply disagree that we could best explain the truth with such an event. These are isolated incidents. Nothing to be alarmed about ... Why am I opposed to a news conference? Stories can be slanted you know. The wrong twist put on something and we come out looking like the bad guys."

Even a moron should be able to understand that.

He shifted the phone to his left ear. "Nonsense! Who cares what a few right-wing lunatics think? Better to let the stories die off. There's always another big news item on the horizon. When it hits, it'll push us out of the spotlight ... I'll think about it and get back to you tomorrow."

He ended the call, leaned back and stared at the sky. *I'll think about it.* He sighed and shook his head. *Sure I will. Bunch of cowards!*

After wringing out his socks again, he put them, and his shoes, back on. He stood up and grimaced. It felt like an ocean of water was squeezing out of the cushioning in his shoes. He groaned and shook his head. *I give up.* He fell back down on the bench. *Maybe I should chuck these stupid shoes in the gutter.* He paused. *Is that ...* He sniffed the air. The delicious aroma of coffee wafted on the breeze. It probably came from the café next to the hardware store.

Tempting. He closed his eyes and took a deep whiff. This particular chain was overpriced. *But I can afford it, and I deserve it.* He got up and headed that way, making a squishing squeak with every step.

"Well, hello there," a friendly voice called out from behind him.

The doctor turned, as if to greet an old friend. Instead, it was a stranger. A white-haired man had taken up residence on the bench he'd just vacated. His friendly greeting had been directed into a cell phone.

What an annoyance, Dr. Winters sneered. *Broadcasting his whole conversation for everyone to hear.*

"Listen dearie, I picked up the lettuce, but they're out of tomatoes."

It's just plain rude.

The old man gave his forehead a quick slap. "I heard. Can you believe it?"

Why don't people talk in private? The doctor turned back toward the café.

"Why they're allowed to stay open I'll never know."
Why you're allowed to have a cell phone, I'll never know.
"There should be laws."

Dr. Winters reached for the café's door.

"I hear they tell every girl who walks in there that they're pregnant, just to do the abortion so they can make money."

The doctor's breath caught in his throat. He released the door and let it swing closed, remaining on the outside.

The old man continued his phone conversation. "What?"

Henry took a couple of steps toward the bench.

"Dead babies in the freezer?" The old man's high-pitched voice verged on hysteria.

A cold chill shot up the doctor's back.

"Well, all I can tell you is, we need to do something about this. Yes, indeedy. Someone has got to take a stand. We need to get a petition going. Drive them out of the community. They deserved to be broken into. They deserved the graffiti." The man rose from the bench and tottered past Doctor Winters. "The people who are attacking the Southside Women's Health Center are heroes. Heroes I tell you." He opened the café's door and stepped in. The door closed behind him.

Doctor Winters' stomach churned with acid. He crossed over and fell back onto the bench. *Are they serious? Fetuses stacked in a freezer? What's next? Townspeople storming the building, armed with torches and pitchforks like some dumb monster movie?* He sighed. *What can we do?* These accusations were ludicrous, but how could they combat them? He pulled out his cell phone and punched in a number.

"Hi, Jack. This is Henry ... I know we just hung up, but," he scratched his head. "I've reconsidered that news conference idea. Maybe you fellows are right. Maybe the public needs some educating."

So much preparation had gone into this. Saturday, Martin had walked into the stock room, where an irate Ms. Gibbons was mumbling to herself, flipping through a pile of papers. "Something wrong?" he asked.

She tossed the pile down on top of a box. "It's all wrong. Someone messed up big time. The inventory of these twelve boxes has been misfiled, some of them aren't even what we ordered. On top of that, overstock items have been labeled and packaged incorrectly."

"Oh, my. How in the world did that happen?"

She shook her head. "This has to be taken care of before we open on Monday."

"I tell you what. I would gladly come in tomorrow for a couple of hours in the afternoon, and get this done for you. But, I'll need a strong back to assist." He smiled. "May I suggest young Todd?"

Lisa Gibbons looked doubtful. She shook her head. "He's more trouble than he's worth. I'm beginning to wonder if I should have hired him at all."

Martin raised a hand in protest. "No, no, no. He's a good worker. Just has his head on backwards over this abortion thing. But he'll be a valuable asset to me ... on Sunday."

Ms. Gibbons hesitated. "Are you sure?"

"Trust me." Martin smiled.

The store manager paused for a second before nodding her approval. "Thank you. You're a godsend."

• *Twenty-Nine* •

It was Sunday afternoon. Martin peeked into the break room where Todd was sitting, munching absentmindedly on a bag of chips. The store was closed and he had the young man all to himself.

His demon lips curled up with delight. *The stage is set. Time for my act.* He put on a worried expression, and slightly mussed his hair to add to the harried picture. Then taking a deep breath, he pushed the door open and made his grand entrance. "Oh my. Oh my!"

"Are you okay?"

Martin paced back and forth in front of the young man, clutching a rolled up towel. "Yes. I suppose I am. It's just, I have so much on my mind, and now to hear about this." He pinched the bridge of his nose and shook his head. "It's terrible. I don't know what to do."

"What?" Todd hopped out of his seat and followed the man around the room.

Like a sheep being led to slaughter. Martin opened his mouth to speak, but paused and nervously began to chew on the tip of his thumb. "No." He took a step away from the boy. "I can't. It ... it would only upset you."

"What? What would upset me?"

"But ... No. I shouldn't burden you."

Todd pulled the old man over to the table. "You're my friend. Sit and tell me."

With obedience and a dramatic sigh, the sly demon sat. "Are ... are you sure? I wouldn't want to burden you. I mean, I know how sensitive you are about—"

"Martin!"

"Okay, okay. As I said, I have other matters on my mind. But when I heard about this ... it simply upset me even more."

"Martin," Todd warned. "Get to the point."

"I was trying to figure out what to do about ... this," he looked down at the towel, then quickly covered the bundle with his hands, as if not wanting Todd to see it. "I was walking through the television section. Thought I'd check out one of those big screen TVs. The store's closed. No one's around. What harm would it do? I was watching, when a news blurb came on. One of those silly teasers, designed to make you want to watch the six o'clock news."

Todd thumped the table with his palm. "Martin!"

"It was that doctor!"

"What doctor?"

"The one from the abortion clinic." The words dripped with disdain.

Todd's back stiffened. "What about him?"

"He's holding a news conference today. Something about the terrible acts of violence against a poor public servant like him."

"Public servant?"

Martin nodded. "He intimated that he'll be making an important announcement. Something about a brand new location."

"New?"

With his head hanging low, Martin peeked at the boy through his eyelashes. "Yes ... bigger. More efficient."

Todd grit his teeth.

A long, sad sigh issued from the demon. "He said they'd be able to process more clients. Just what we need. Another clinic to kill babies. I tell you, it infuriates me! If I were a younger man—" He brought his fist down hard on the tabletop, then shook his head and slumped his shoulders in defeat. "But, alas. I'm old. Not strong."

"Yes ... you're ... old." Todd's brow creased.

"Someone," Martin whispered, "Someone should do something about that man. He needs to be stopped." A few seconds went by as the demon watched Todd's facial expressions.

"When did you say this news conference was being held?"

"Today." Martin looked at the clock on the wall. "In an hour as a matter of fact. I might go, at least to protest ... register a complaint, but," he glanced down at the towel, "I have another problem."

"What is it? Is there anything I can do to help?"

Inwardly, Martin giggled. *Yes. You young fool. Fall into my trap.* "Oh ... I don't know." His rapidly blinking eyes darted about the room. He ran a nervous hand through his hair and muttered quietly to himself. Then, looking as if he made up his mind to share some important information, he pulled his seat closer to Todd. "I was over in Housewares, looking for some new towels for my apartment, when I found this." He placed the towel on the table and carefully unwrapped its layers, revealing its contents.

"A pistol!" Todd's eyes widened.

"Yes. It was lying under a couple of bath towels. How in the world it got there, I couldn't tell you." He shivered. "It frightens me just to possess such a thing." Martin pushed the towel and gun away from him, and closer to Todd.

These stupid humans are so gullible. So full of pride.

Todd gazed at the weapon.

"I don't know what to do with it ..." Seconds ticked by. *Could the boy be that dense?*

Todd finally spoke. "I'll take care of it for you." His face darkened.

"You?" Martin exclaimed, as if the idea had never occurred to him.

"Give it here."

The pistol scraped along the top of the table as Martin slid it closer. "Do you know what to do with it?"

"Yes."

Martin took Todd's hand and placed it on the gun. "Be careful," he said. "It's loaded."

Todd's fingers wrapped around the stock. He caressed the weapon like it was a great treasure. "What time did you say the news conference was?"

"Soon." Martin stretched the word out. "Very soon."

· *Thirty* ·

It was almost four on Sunday afternoon.

Melissa sat about half way down the left side of the bus, which was a couple of blocks from the store, gazing out the window. *Was that Todd?* A young man raced along the sidewalk. *He walks like Todd. It can't be him. We're supposed to be meeting at four. Unless I misunderstood what he said.* She craned her neck to follow the figure as it disappeared from her view. *Whoever it is, they're in a big hurry to get somewhere.*

That morning she'd approached him after worship service. "How about lunch?"

Todd shook his head. "No good. I've got to put a couple of hours in at the store."

"But it's not open."

"There's been a mix up in some stock or something, and Ms. Gibbons wants it straightened out before we open tomorrow."

"Your grandmother is okay with this?" Melissa gave him a dubious look.

"I know what you're thinking. She doesn't approve of working on Sundays. But she said it would be okay, just this one time, since it's kind of an emergency, and I went to morning worship. Besides, it's only for a couple of hours." Todd puffed out his chest with pride. "And I was asked for, personally. Someone must think I'm doing a pretty good job."

Melissa half smiled. With all the trouble he'd been in lately, why did Ms. Gibbons ask for him? She tipped her head. Something didn't seem quite right to her.

"How about we get together afterwards?" Todd suggested.

"That sounds great."

"Around four? Meet me at the store."

Melissa agreed. Now that they were back on friendly terms, this was her opportunity to help focus him on what was important—God's love and forgiveness.

Melissa arrived at the closed store. She knocked on the front door. Nobody answered. Then she pressed her face on the glass, checking out the darkened interior. There was no movement within.

Without warning, Martin's smiling face popped up in front of her. "Boo!"

She jumped.

"I'm sorry, my dear," he said as he unlocked and opened the door. "I didn't mean to frighten you. Just a little joke that's all." He stepped back and let her in.

"You didn't frighten me," Melissa answered with a slight cracking in her voice.

"Of course not."

She walked past him and into the store. When Melissa turned to asked Martin where Todd was, she cringed at the look he was giving her. Like a cat watching a trapped mouse.

"I mean, how could an old man like me scare you? You know what everyone says, 'Old Martin is harmless.'" With a snicker, he walked into the bowels of the store.

Melissa followed. *Just take me to see Todd.*

"Sorry it's so dark in here," he said. The farther they walked down the long aisles away from the front entrance, the gloomier it grew. She looked behind her. The light from the store's windows shrank in the distance.

Not like when it's opened. Melissa shivered.

Martin took a sharp left and headed through the Woman's department. As Melissa rushed to follow, racks of dresses and skirts, all filled with shadows of imagined hands and arms, reached out and brushed against her.

"I guess I should be offended that everyone considers me so harmless," he said. "Then again, maybe it's a good thing."

He came to an abrupt stop. Melissa almost fell over to avoid hitting into him. He spun around. Looking over the top of his glasses, his lips pulled into a tight grin. "If they think you're harmless, they don't know how much trouble you can cause." He gave a low laugh.

Melissa backed up a step. Something jabbed into her shoulder. Screaming, she spun around and struck her assailant. A swimsuit mannequin's head fell off and rolled across the floor until it came to rest at Martin's feet.

He bent over and picked it up. With a look of deep concern, he said, "Oh my. I'm sorry my dear. I guess I'm not as harmless as they say." He giggled. "Old Martin is just having some fun with you."

"I'm all right," she said.

Martin tipped his head to the side and smiled, slyly. "I'm sure you are."

She took a nonchalant step to the right, drawing her body behind a rack of blouses. "I was looking for Todd. I was supposed to meet him here."

Martin's grin disappeared. "Oh my. I thought you had come to help put away the shipment. Todd's not here."

Melissa tensed. "Not here?"

The demon ran a nervous hand through his white hair. "I'm worried about that boy. Yes, I am." He walked away from Melissa, toward the back of the store.

She chased after him. "Where is he?"

"Gone. Stormed out of here."

"What?"

"Yes. Just a few minutes ago."

Then that was him I saw from the bus.

They had reached the electrical supplies department. Bulbs and extension cords lined the wall behind Martin. Several lamps cluttered the counter. "He was all upset about that doctor's news conference. Said he was going to go down there and take care of business."

"That's not good."

"No indeed. But the worst part is," Martin paused. "He has a gun."

Melissa gasped.

"Who knows what he'll do?" Martin shook his head. "Poor Todd."

"Where did he get a gun?" Melissa gritted her teeth and tried to calm her trembling hand.

The shadow of a smirk crossed Martin's face, but it was quickly replaced with that phony look of deep concern he was so good at. His sad eyes cast a glance down to the floor. He gave a melancholy shake of his head. "I wish I knew. Where do any of these troubled youth get their weapons? Tragic, I tell you. Tragic."

"Where did he get the gun?" she asked again, this time more slowly, her tone no longer hiding her anger.

Martin looked like the cat caught with yellow feathers sticking out of his mouth, who dares to say to the owner, 'Canary? What Canary?' "I told you. I don't know."

Melissa blurted out, "I'm sure you don't, you demon!" *Oh, no!* But it was too late. The words were out there.

Martin's mock look of sadness and concern dissolved, replaced with one of genuine shock and confusion. "What did you call me?"

"Nothing." Melissa took a nervous step away from her foe. "It-it's an expression. That's all."

"No. You called me ..." he paused, tipped his head to the side and scrutinized Melissa more closely. His eyebrows rose and fell as his mouth formed words, but no sound came out. Finally, he wagged an accusing finger at her. "You know."

"I don't know what you're talking about." Her eyes darted from side to side, searching for the easiest way of escape. *Why did I follow him all the way back here?* Her heart sank. Martin stood between her and the way out. It was like Parker's car all over again. Very vulnerable. Very alone. She swallowed and tried to skirt around him. "I think I'll go look for Todd."

Martin moved to block her path. His questions came in rapid succession. "You know who I am? Why do you know? How do you know? Who told you?"

A drip of sweat rolled down the small of Melissa's back.

"Did Jonathan tell you?"

"He didn't tell me anything!" She yelled with a sudden surge of defiance.

"I don't believe you." Martin stepped closer. "He must have told you."

"I'll-I'll see you tomorrow at work." Again, she tried to slip by, but his hand shot out and grabbed her arm. As it did, a jolt of electricity sparked between them and a transformation took place, similar to Jonathan's outside of Parker's car, yet this one wasn't complete.

Martin shimmered back and forth between his earthly and supernatural bodies. At times, human and demon features merged and overlapped. His hand clutched the side of his head. After a few seconds, he pushed Melissa away and fell back into the counter behind him. He returned to the old man form. Through rapid breaths, he gasped, "What? How?"

Then there was a flash in his eyes. His face glowed. He straightened up to the full height the old man's guise could muster and scrutinized Melissa. He hissed, "Ahh ... that spirit. I recognize that spirit."

Melissa took a step away from him. "I don't know what you're talking about."

"Of course you do." He sneered. "Don't treat me like a fool." The demon slowly nodded as he stared at Melissa. Then he spoke as if addressing an old friend. "It's been a long time."

"You know me?"

"I'm surprised you're back here ... now. Why?" He scratched his head and paced back and forth in front of the girl. "Why?" Facing her, his eyes narrowed. "Why on earth would Jonathan do such a thing?"

She jutted her chin out and smirked, "Jonathan didn't send me. God sent me."

"Really?" Martin chortled. "Interesting."

"I'm His messenger."

Martin laughed long and hard. "Well, messenger." He wiped a tear from his eye. "Looks like you're going to fail your God."

He did not transform into his demonic appearance. No. But the old man changed none the less. Gone was the good humor and joviality. Gone was the weak-looking façade. A stronger, more threatening one took its place. He strode toward Melissa. With each menacing step, she found it harder to breathe. "You are a pretty thing, aren't you?" He smiled a toothy grin.

Though still in human form, his demonic eyes shone through. "Why don't you and I have a little … fun?"

Melissa's legs almost went out from under her. Her left hand gripped the edge of the counter for support.

He was only a couple of steps away now.

Her right hand fumbled along the counter top.

"Poor child. Are you all alone? Don't worry. I can take care of you." He stepped closer. His foul breath caressed her cheek. "I like to take care of little girls like you."

"No!" She grabbed a lamp off the counter and swung it with all her might. It connected with the side of Martin's head, sending him hurtling to the floor. Melissa raced down the deserted aisle away from the demon.

His scream shot through the store like a bolt of lightning, shaking Melissa deep to her bones. A series of profanities echoed from wall to wall. "Young whelp! You'll pay for that. You'll pay!"

Melissa darted through the jewelry department. She was all alone. No one to help her. Her heart thumped out of her chest. *Run, run!*

"Don't bother with the front door," Martin called out. "I locked it, remember? I have the key."

Is he lying? On the outside chance that he was, she didn't stop running. Jonathan said he was good at lying. She reached the door. Pulled on the handle.

She whimpered.

He wasn't lying.

"Melissa," came the voice, in a sickeningly sweet musical lilt. "Where are you?"

Melissa spun to face the darkened store. Coming to the front entrance was a mistake. Her eyes had to readjust to the lack of light. The aisles looked darker than ever.

"I want you."

She raced for the nearby men's department and dove under a rack of dress shirts.

"Poor Melissa. All alone. No one to help her." The voice seemed to be coming from all around her.

She struggled to take deep, long breaths. *Quiet. Stay calm. Stay calm.*

"Melissa. I know why you're here."

Somewhere to my left? Is that where he is? What's over there? Toys ... video games ...

The store had changed into a house of horrors, every shadow containing hidden dangers. The mannequins' unblinking glass eyes watched her, each one with the deadly potential of being Martin.

"Poor Todd," Martin's voice called out. "He never had a chance you know. It wasn't his fault. No indeedy. Do you know who's fault it was? It was God's fault." His words dripped with hatred. "God deserted him. Oh sure. I may have given him the weapon ... may have manipulated that silly doctor into thinking someone was out to get him ... but it was God who deserted Todd. Just like He's deserted you."

Melissa crawled through art supplies. *The loading dock. I can escape through the loading dock.* The loading dock door had a push bar. It always opened from the inside.

Her new destination was on the other side of the break room. If she could just get there. She peeked around the endcap of an aisle, through a display of glittery unicorn stickers. All clear. She moved forward.

Martin went on, with feigned dismay. "Todd will probably spend some time in jail. Testimony will be given about how the doctor had received death threats. The wife and police will talk about a young African-American male who had it in for the poor doctor. If Todd kills the man, he'll get life in prison. Maybe the death penalty ..."

Shut up!

"Everything is falling apart. Isn't it? I don't blame you, though. After all, are you really equipped for such a task? He never should have sent you. My master never sends a child to do a demon's job. Makes you wonder if God really even cares for you."

Melissa was almost there. The door was just a few yards away. She slid on her belly down the cold tile floor.

How ironic. All the games of hide and seek I played with Jonathan in Heaven ... they weren't quite like this.

Ten more feet. She pushed forward. Just eight more feet.

Wait!

The back of Melissa's neck tingled. Something was wrong. Dead wrong.

Martin! Where's Martin? He's stopped talking?

She froze along the back wall of the store and pressed her side into a display counter.

Stopped crawling.

Stopped breathing.

If she could have, she'd have stopped her heart from pumping. Anything to be as quiet as possible.

Her head rose along the gray wall of the counter to get a better view of the store. She braced herself for the distinct possibility that the demon might be on the other side, smiling back at her. She bit her bottom lip as her field of vision broke over the top.

Nothing.

She breathed a sigh of relief.

Maybe he's on the other side of the store.

The door to the back room was right across the aisle from her. *Does it squeak? God forbid!*

She pushed off her knees to her feet and, crouched over, headed for the double doors.

Just inches now ...

Her hand reached up and touched the door on the left. She winced, bracing for the squeak. No noise.

She opened it a small crack and squeezed through. Once on the other side, she slowly shut the door.

I'm going to make it. She began to breathe again, as she smiled and turned to walk down the hall.

"Gotcha!" Martin stood in the inky blackness of the hallway, his grinning face mere inches from hers.

Wide-eyed, Melissa fell back through the doors, slammed into the counter across the aisle, and collapsed to the floor.

Martin gave a hollow laugh. His face twisted with maniacal pleasure. "Aren't we having fun now?"

Grabbing the counter, Melissa pulled herself up and faced her attacker. She touched the corner of her mouth. Blood came away on her fingertip.

Then, something inside her changed. She clenched her teeth. She curled her hands into fists. She narrowed her eyes to glare at Martin. "I don't care what you said to Jonathan."

The demon paused. His head tipped to the side. "Said to Jonathan?"

"You'll never have me!" She stabbed a finger at the demon. "I heard you in the break room. You said he could never win. That I belonged to you." She waved a fist in his face and, in what might be her last act of bravery, shouted, "Never!"

"*You* belong to me?" Martin laughed and laughed. "What a fool you are."

"I may be a fool, but I'm strong enough to stand against the likes of you."

"Poor Melissa. God never should have sent you here so ill prepared. I am so sorry he doesn't treat you with more respect than that." The demon took two steps toward her.

Lightning streaked from the store's ceiling. It crashed into Martin, tossing him high into the air. As he hurdled out of control, he transformed fully into his demonic form, pulled to a stop, and hovered. "I was wondering when you'd make your appearance," he sneered.

The bright light swooped down, circled around Melissa and took up a defensive position in front of her. Jonathan stood there, fists clenched.

Melissa released the white-knuckle hold she'd had on the counter.

Jonathan glanced back at her, at the blood. His face contorted in rage. "Demon!" Jonathan streaked through the air. His strong hand clasped around Martin's neck. "What did you do to her?"

Martin slammed his arm against Jonathan's, breaking the grip. He then pushed his fists into the angel's chest, sending him reeling backwards. "Have a care, angel. I will not play the fool for you any longer," the demon rasped. "And for your information, I didn't do anything to her. She did it to herself. Hit into the counter."

Jonathan raised a doubtful eyebrow.

"Ask her, if you don't believe me."

Melissa shook her head. "No. He never touched me."

"See." A look of smug satisfaction crossed the demon's face. "I told you. I know the rules. I follow them." He pointed an accusing finger at Jonathan. "You see that you do, too."

Jonathan took up his position next to Melissa. "Don't you dare question me, you son of the pit. Now be gone!"

"Gladly!" The demon spun around and headed upwards and into the shadows. "I have other fish to fry. This is so delightful. So many lives to play with." Martin flew straight at the ceiling and disappeared in a puff of foul smoke.

"Good riddance," Jonathan growled. He turned to Melissa. Though the rage was gone from his eyes, a sternness remained. "I told you to watch out for that demon. You have no idea how dangerous he is. What were you doing here, anyway?"

"I was supposed to meet Todd, and ... Todd!" She raced for the loading dock's door.

"Wait!" Jonathan called after her.

"No! You don't understand. He needs me."

"Stop!" Jonathan rushed after her.

Melissa was already down the hall and out on the loading dock.

Jonathan transformed back into human form to give chase. Before he'd gone too far, a voice called out to him.

"Hold."

"But, my Lord. Melissa —"

"Let her go."

"But she needs me."

"Not yet. Besides, you have another task. It's time."

Jonathan sighed.

"Trust me, Jonathan. Trust me. All will be well."

"Yes, my Lord." He bowed his head. "You have never failed me."

• *Thirty-One* •

Melissa pushed her legs to run faster. Her shoes beat against the pavement. What terrible thing would Todd do when he found Doctor Winters?

One block from the Women's Health Center, the regular street noise was drowned out by a mob of voices which sounded like a semi-truck rumbling down the road. With each step, the voices became more distinct, more angry. Melissa turned the corner onto the street where the Center was located and slammed into the wall of people. Red-faced, shouting, screaming people, blocking her way.

This clinic has brought out strong emotions in more individuals than just Todd.

Men and women, young and old, packed the area. Police officers formed a fragile line to keep the bulging crowds from overflowing into the traffic lanes.

Melissa pushed her way forward and found herself in the center of a shouting match.

"Stop killing babies!"

"Stay out of a woman's right to choose!"

"Murderer!"

"Religious fanatic!"

Signs stabbed at the air above the crowd.

'My Life. My Choice.'

'It's the Holocaust all over again.'

Melissa scanned the sea of people. Standing on the front stairs of the Center, looking over the crowd with a bewildered expression on his face, was Dr. Winters. A group of well-dressed individuals stood in front of him, staring out at the mob. A couple of police officers were there, keeping the crowd back a few feet from the steps. The doctor waved his arms in the air, as if pleading for quiet, for order.

At least he's still alive. Maybe Todd won't show up.

"Do you believe in life or death?" A short elderly woman, white haired and smiling sweetly, stood beside Melissa. She wore a flowery, blue dress.

What a silly question. It would be foolish for someone to say they didn't believe in one of those two things. But it was obvious, the woman wanted Melissa to choose one. She nodded. "I like life."

"Good." The woman deftly stuck a pin on Melissa's shirt.

Melissa looked down. 'Life,' it read. She gave the woman a kind smile and moved away.

Todd. Where's Todd? She looked left and right as she pushed through the crowd. Letting out a deep sigh, she shook her head. Why? There were so many questions. So many whys that needed to be answered. For instance, why had Jonathan let it happen? Why had he allowed Martin to give Todd a weapon? Why?

But there were bigger questions, too. Why hadn't God stopped this? And why had He even allowed Todd's mother to go into that abortion clinic to begin with?

At the far edge of the crowd, she spotted the top of a head that looked like Todd's. The person was making their way toward the steps of the building.

"Todd," she screamed. Her voice was a drop in a vast ocean, swallowed by the flood of noise around her.

The more she pushed her way through the mob, the more it closed in on her — waves of people hitting against her, blocking her way, suffocating her. Finally, she got close enough. Sure enough. It was Todd. As he trudged forward, toward the doctor, Todd was cradling something under his shirt.

The gun?

Melissa waved her arms and screamed. It was no use. She couldn't be heard, but only watch him, helpless. *What do I do?*

Sadly, there was no fire alarm to pull. She pushed forward and accidentally hit into a large woman holding a sign that read, 'Back Alleys and Hangers are for the Dark Ages!'

"Watch where you're going!" The woman's mouth curled up in a sneer. A group gathered around her, all eyeing Melissa.

"Sorry." Melissa tried to move away.

The woman stabbed at the button Melissa was wearing and pushed her back. "Lousy right-wingers think you own the streets."

Her friends all cheered. Shouts of 'You tell her!' and 'Gestapo witch!' egged the woman on.

Melissa lifted her hands in surrender. "Please. I just want—"

"I know what you want." The woman threw down her sign. "You want to throw us back into the dark ages! Take away our rights. Take away all we've fought for!"

Her supporters cheered even louder.

Melissa retreated a step backwards. Over the woman's shoulder, off in the distance, Todd was still on the move. Melissa's chest tightened. *How can I get past this woman and get to Todd?*

"What's the trouble here?" A police officer walked up; an older man, with gray hair poking out from under his cap. Several officers were patrolling through the crowd, breaking up small skirmishes and escorting people away.

"This rube tried to knock me down," the woman growled.

"No. I accidentally hit into her. That's all."

"I'll take care of it." The officer took Melissa's upper arm and guided her away from the fray, but in the opposite direction of Todd.

"Please let me go," she pleaded, as the officer skirted through the crowd.

When he was closer to the outer edge of the commotion, he stopped. "What are you doing here, Melissa?"

Melissa stiffened. "Do I know you?"

"I met you at the police station. You seemed like a nice girl." He smiled at her. "Reminded me of my daughter. Too nice to get caught up with some of the crazies here. Mind you, I'm not saying they're all crazy. But some of them definitely fit the bill." He glanced back in the general direction of the woman she'd just had the confrontation with.

"Please. I have to get to the front of the Center." She wrung her hands.

The officer eyed her suspiciously. "Why?"

Melissa hesitated. *How in the world do I tell a police officer that my friend has a gun and is planning on shooting the doctor? I don't want to get Todd in trouble.* She stifled a sarcastic laugh. What a ridiculous thought—get Todd in trouble. As if shooting a doctor wouldn't get him in enough hot water. "No reason ... I just have to."

She peeked over her shoulder, toward the steps. No sign of Todd. She scanned the crowd. *Where is he?*

Finally, she spotted him. Her forehead wrinkled. Something wasn't right. He was headed away from the stairs, and not under his own power. Someone was walking along beside him, an arm wrapped around his neck guiding him. *They've caught him. He won't shoot anyone.* Melissa smiled, but it lasted only an instant. Todd was caught. *What happens to someone who's found with a loaded pistol, in a crowded public place?*

"Looking for someone?" The officer stared off in the general direction she'd been looking.

"Yes ... no ..." She groaned. *How do I get away from this man?* "It's—"

"There you are!" Jonathan raced up, out of breath. "I can't believe we got separated like that."

Melissa wrinkled her nose. "Separated?"

"Yes," Jonathan continued with a strained smile, while his eyes danced back and forth between Melissa and the officer. "Separated. You shouldn't wander off." He turned to the officer and chuckled. "A bit of a scatter brain. Here we are, on our way to a restaurant. I turn my head for one second and poof! She's gone."

"Poof! She's gone." The officer mimicked Jonathan, then turned to Melissa. "You know this guy?"

"Yes. Yes." Melissa took a quick step to Jonathan's side and laced her arm through his. *This is my best shot to get away, and back to Todd.* She gazed up at Jonathan and pasted a happy smile on her face. "I'm sorry. I heard all the commotion and wanted to see what was happening." She glanced at the mob. "I guess I got turned around."

The officer nodded slowly. "No harm done. You two have a nice day." He looked at Jonathan. "Keep an eye on her."

"I will." Jonathan gave a reassuring smile. He grabbed Melissa's hand and turned to leave.

Melissa rolled her eyes. *Still going in the wrong direction.*

Loud cracks exploded in the air. They reverberated off the surrounding buildings.

Oh, no. Melissa's heart sank.

• *Thirty-Two* •

The crowd froze. But just for a moment. Before the echo of the shots had died off, pandemonium broke out. Screaming people raced in every direction. Protest signs fell to the ground and the lines between enemy camps were ignored. Everyone ran.

Three shots. Was that three shots? With the echo off the buildings it was so hard to tell.

The officer who'd been escorting Melissa, now ignored her and fought his way back through the confusion, his hand on his holstered revolver.

Oh, Todd. What did you do? She searched the crowd, leaping up to see over people's heads. Her stomach tightened into a knot. God had sent her here to save Todd. She'd failed Him. She failed them both.

By the steps to the Center's door, several police officers huddled around a small group of civilians.

What happened? Is someone lying on the ground?

Jonathan grabbed Melissa and began to pull her away.

"What are you doing?" She dug her feet in.

"We've got to get out of here."

"No. I've got to go back to the front door!" She broke loose and took a step toward the crowd.

"There's no time for that." Jonathan blocked her way.

"You don't understand. Todd is there."

"No, you don't understand. There's something we need to take care of." He wrapped his arm around her shoulders and marched her away.

Melissa fought him. She dragged her feet. She twisted her body, trying to break free. But it did no good. With his eyes set on some distant point, Jonathan moved her farther and farther away from the chaos.

Sirens blared all around them. Police and rescue vehicles sped down the road. When Jonathan had dragged her for a few blocks, he released his grip.

Melissa shoved him away. Face burning, breathing hard through clenched teeth and rubbing the spot on her arm where Jonathan's iron grip had been, she yelled, "You hurt me!"

"Sorry. I was concerned for your safety back there."

"But you pulled me away. I wasn't done yet."

"Done with what?"

"My mission."

He heaved a sigh. "Your mission? That's why you're here."

"I know. That's why God sent me —"

"No," Jonathan snapped. "That's why you're here." He pointed at the sidewalk.

"Why I'm here?" She pointed to the same spot. He nodded.

Melissa looked around. He'd dragged her to an intersection in a rundown part of town. Closed up shops, dusty old stores, an occasional small restaurant. Nothing special. She shrugged. "I don't get it."

Jonathan pointed across the street to a bar. She and Todd had passed this way several times on the walk to or from work. She'd had asked Todd why people would stumble out of places like this, struggling to control their movement. Oh, yes, there were high-class eateries that sold alcohol. Many national restaurant chains, who cater to families, also have bars in them. Clean, bright places, with different themes from western to hard rock. But this was not one of them. This was a corner bar, a relic of the past. Old and run down, with a paint-chipped exterior and a tattered awning over the front window. Shadows from the larger, surrounding buildings gave it a dark and dank feeling.

She furrowed her brow and gazed at the big neon sign in the front window, which flashed the name of a local beer. "I don't understand."

Jonathan spoke slowly. "Being a messenger from God means we sometimes have to go places where we'd rather not be." He looked back at the bar. His steady gaze fixed on the front window.

She followed the general direction of his line of sight, checking out the interior of the establishment. A large wooden bar ran along the back wall of the room, where several patrons sat on tall stools. A television placed on top of a filing cabinet was tuned to a local ball game. The area between the bar and the front window was cluttered with six or seven tables, some occupied with couples, others empty.

Up against the windows was a row of booths. Again, some of them were empty and others were occupied, mostly with groups or couples. One booth, though, at the end of the row — the farthest away from any other activity or human contact — contained a lone occupant.

Melissa gasped.

"Recognize anyone?" Jonathan asked.

"Yes ... I do."

"Why don't you go in and say hello."

She took a step toward the bar. "But what about Todd?"

Jonathan rolled his eyes. "Don't worry about Todd."

"But he's my mission."

"Says who? Who told you that Todd was your mission?"

Melissa hesitated.

"You did," Jonathan said, his voice filled with accusation. "Somehow you convinced yourself he was your mission."

"But, but ... he needs me."

He patted her on the shoulder. "This world is filled with needy people. It's wonderful to help as many as we can. But there's someone else who needs you right now." He nod- ded toward the window. "Go. I'll see you in a while."

As Jonathan turned to walk away, Melissa grabbed his arm. With a slight crack in her voice, she said, "Aren't you coming with me?"

"I'll be ... around." He gazed deep into Melissa's eyes. "Remember your mission. Remember what the Lord told you to say."

"I remember."

"Melissa!" The force behind his voice almost knocked her down. "Be prepared not simply to say the words ... but to mean them." He hurried off.

Melissa pushed open the bar's door and stepped in.

· *Thirty-Three* ·

The air was filled with various odors and the murmurings of conversations. Melissa flinched when the people at the bar cheered for something that had happened on the sports event blasting on the television. She made her way to the booth where a woman sat, elbows resting on the table, staring into the half-filled glass in her hands.

Melissa cleared her throat. "Hello, Ms. Gibbons."

Lisa Gibbons peered over the top of her beverage. Her back stiffened. "Melissa? I never would have expected to see you here."

"I could say the same thing. May I sit down ... or are you waiting for someone?"

Ms. Gibbons waved the glass at the empty bench across from her. "Sit. Sit. I'm not waiting for anyone. Though it is the night for unexpected company. A friend of yours left a few minutes ago. Jonathan."

Melissa's eyes widened. "Jonathan was here?"

The woman gave an amused smile. "Yes. Nice boy. We've had some interesting conversations at work."

"About what?" Melissa raised her right eyebrow.

Ms. Gibbons studied the air in front of Melissa's face. After a moment she said, "Life. He talks to me about life." She paused. Her shoulders drooped, as if a heavy weight were pressing against them. She signaled a passing waitress. "Another drink."

As the waitress walked away, Ms. Gibbons raised her glass to her lips and emptied the contents in one long swallow. Then she tipped her head to the side and smirked. "Looks like you've discovered my little secret."

"What secret is that?"

The waitress returned and placed a glass of a light brownish liquid on the table. Lisa Gibbons picked it up and swirled it around. "I like to drink." She grunted a giggle. "Some might say I need to drink." She took a sip. "Life's funny. But, speaking of life, do you want anything?" She motioned to the beverage. "I mean, you are old enough. I know that because," she raised her glass to Melissa and proclaimed, "today is your birthday. Twenty-one. Correct?"

"It is?" Melissa's eyes widened.

"Of course! Silly girl. I noticed your date of birth that first day, on your application. June 12. Don't you even remember when your birthday is?" Ms. Gibbons took another drink. When she was done, she replaced the glass on the table with a heavy thud. Her face darkened. "I do."

Melissa gave a nervous laugh. "I guess you're good with numbers and dates. I've never been, myself."

Ms. Gibbons chuckled. "You're a ..." she waved a hand through the air, "... special one. Aren't you? Don't remember your birthday. Don't recognize a fire alarm when you see one ... No last name." She peered deep into Melissa's eyes. "Who are you?"

"I'm ... Melissa. That's all." Her forehead wrinkled up as she studied her manager. Ms. Gibbons' blood-shot eyes twitched from side to side. Her hand had a slight tremble to it as she lifted the glass to her lips. Melissa whispered, "Is there anything I can do for you?"

"Do for me?" Ms. Gibbons gazed out the window for a moment, then turned back and sighed. "You seem like such a lovely young lady." Pools of tears formed in her eyes. "But some things are better left unsaid."

"Are you sure?"

The woman sat back and looked at the ceiling. As she did, a tear rolled down her cheek. "It's something I've never told anyone ... But this whole business with Todd." She closed her eyes and slowly shook her head. A few seconds passed before she opened them again, stared at Melissa and smiled. "You know. If I'd ever had a child ... I'd have named her Melissa. I always loved that name." She said her name in an almost reverent tone. "Melissa."

Melissa forced a smile.

Ms. Gibbons shook her head. "I thought I'd been handling this so well on my own. The years of grief ... building inside me. The suffering ... the guilt."

Melissa fidgeted. "I don't understand. What—"

Words poured out of the woman like water through a broken dam. "Then you come in to my office—Today's your birthday—Mabel and Todd arguing—the radio—that awful poster on the bulletin board ... I tried to drive home today and got caught in a traffic jam down by that clinic." She bowed her head. "Your name is Melissa ... I can't escape. Can I? Lately everything keeps driving me back to it!" She looked across the table. A tear traced down her trembling cheek. "I try to forget ... try to move on." She pressed a fist against her forehead. "Why does it hurt so much?"

Melissa found herself struggling to hold back tears. "Have I done something to upset you?"

"No ... Not on purpose." Ms. Gibbons covered her face with her hands. Then she wiped her cheeks dry and coughed to clear her throat. "It seems that everything happening lately has served to bring back bad memories."

"What memories?"

The woman sighed. "I've never shared this with anyone. Maybe it's the alcohol loosening my tongue ... I don't know ..."

"Please, tell me."

Lisa Gibbons closed her eyes. "Today ... is an anniversary. A twenty-one year anniversary. Every year, on this night, I try to drown my sorrows ... try to forget." She gave a scornful laugh. "Every year, my foot!" She picked up the new drink a waitress had set on the table and took a sip. "The years are getting shorter. Drowning my sorrows is happening more often. It doesn't help."

"Maybe talking about it will." Melissa reached across the table to squeeze Lisa's hand.

The woman bit into her lip and gave a single nod of her head. "You see, I ... I was pregnant. Today is the day I aborted my baby. My Melissa." Ms. Gibbons' hand fumbled across the table and stroked Melissa's hair. Her alcohol breath blew on Melissa's face. "I always imagined she'd have looked just like you."

Melissa's mouth went dry. Why had Jonathan wanted her to come into this bar and talk to this woman? She searched deeply into Ms. Gibbons' eyes for answers. Then, her head jerked back. *It's not possible.* Lisa's features were a reflection of her own. Older, more seasoned. A few wrinkles and lines from the experiences of life ... But her face. The eyes she searched were ... her eyes.

"I-I told you I liked the name Melissa," Ms. Gibbons said. She waved a hand in the air. "It's kind of silly how it all came about. When I was a child, not more than five or six, I told my parents, 'When I grow up, I'm going to have a little girl named Lisa.' They laughed. Told me it could be kind of confusing, having two Lisas in one house. When I got a new doll, I named it Lisa." Lisa Gibbons stared off into space. The edges of her mouth curled into a melancholy smile. "'My Lisa'. That's what I'd call her. 'My Lisa, MyLisa. Eventually, 'My Lisa' turned into Melissa. My Lisa. Do you get it? They almost sound the same."

Melissa nodded.

Lisa Gibbons lowered her gaze to the table and whispered, "Melissa ... My Lisa." After a moment, she looked up at Melissa and tipped her head to the side. Her eyes locked onto Melissa's. "Melissa —"

A sudden commotion by the bar broke the connection. The patrons were protesting the interruption of their televised game by a news alert. Melissa glanced up at the screen. There, on the television, was a picture of the front of the Southside Women's Health Center. The caption read, "Shooting at Local Health Center."

Melissa gasped and her hand covered her mouth. *Todd!*

"They tell you that an abortion won't hurt," Ms. Gibbons mumbled. Her eyes were tightly closed. "But mine did."

The captioning on the bottom of the screen read, *'Dr. Henry Winters of the Southside Women's Center, has been shot ...'*

"I can remember it like it was yesterday," Lisa said. "I lay there on that table, my legs in the stirrups."

Melissa winced. That cold, metal table she and Todd had seen during their night excursion.

'The doctor has been taken to All Saints Medical facility for emergency surgery.'

"I was screaming 'Oh God! Help me! It hurts!'"

Wait. What? That sounds familiar.

Tears flowed freely from Lisa's eyes. "The ... the doctor ... the doctor. He didn't have what you'd call a great bed-side manner. He barked, 'Quiet down. It's going to be all right ... It's over.'"

Melissa's voice choked as she whispered, "It's not over. It's not over."

Lisa Gibbons' eyes snapped open. She sat back. Her jaw dropped. "How did you—"

'We've no further information on the doctor's condition, but will keep you informed as facts come our way.'

Melissa stared at Lisa Gibbons. Same hair color. Same eyes. Same chin. She slowly shook her head. *It can't be. It can't be.*

'The police are looking for any and all leads on the shooter– a young African-American male ...'

"Melissa. You're always saying, God loves."

Melissa blocked her ears with her hands.

"Can he love someone who—"

"No!" Melissa slammed a fist into the table.

People seated at the bar turned to look.

"But—"

"How? How can He forgive you?" Melissa's lip trembled. "You're a murderer! A killer. How could God ever ..." Sputtering, she shot up from the seat, shoving the table against Lisa.

The woman slammed into the wall behind her, mouth hanging open.

"You killed your baby!" Melissa screamed.

Lisa slumped forward. Her head sank into her hands and she began to sob.

Melissa raced from the table, knocking into patrons as she fled. As she stormed through the exit, she hollered back, "You killed me!"

· *Thirty-Four* ·

Melissa ran as fast and as hard as she could, trying to get away from that bar, away from Lisa Gibbons. *Don't want to think about it. It's not possible. No.*

She ended up in the park, the same one where her mission began. The sun was hanging low in the sky and the shadows were stretching far across the walkway. The park was empty except for the occasional walker or jogger. Jonathan would probably tell her it wasn't safe for her to be there at this time of day.

"I don't care," she snorted.

The tip of a pine tree's shadow touched a park bench. The exact spot, the exact seat where her adventure had begun. Melissa approached. She ran a finger along the bench's back before sitting down. Next to her sat the ghost of Harriet, smiling at her.

"What are you looking for? Smurfs?" Harriet said.

Melissa hung her head. A tear fell to the ground. *Why me? How could she possibly have killed me? What did I ever do to her?* She gave a bitter laugh. *How ironic. I sound like Todd. I can almost understand why he'd want to shoot someone.* Her shoulders slumped. She buried her head in her hands and wept. "Shoot someone ... Poor Todd."

But then, she stiffened. It was as if a cold electric current ran up her spine. Using her arm, she wiped away the tears. *No, not poor Todd. Stupid people!*

"It's stupid people," she spoke through gritted teeth, her face flushing hot. "The world is filled with stupid people. The Parkers, the Mabels, the Lisa Gibbons'. They bring on the pain. The suffering."

And there are billions more just like them! She bit her bottom lip and slammed a fist into the bench. "They don't deserve it. They don't deserve God's love. They don't deserve—"

About thirty feet away, a man was happily mumbling a song to himself as he skipped along the path.

Stupid, silly song.

As he crossed in front of her, she blinked out the tears that clouded her sight. Martin.

He was almost all the way past the bench, smiling and whistling, when he seemed to catch sight of her. His face shone with astonishment. "Melissa?"

"Martin," she said flatly.

He stood, staring at her. "You look ... you look terrible." He stepped toward her. "What's the matter?"

"Stay back, demon."

Martin halted. His shoulders slumped. In a sign of surrender, he turned his hands, palms up. "I mean you no harm."

"I'm sure you don't," she said sarcastically.

He looked around. "I'll sit over here." He pointed to a bench directly across from her. "I promise I won't move." The little man sat down. "Believe it or not, I'm just concerned. That's all."

Melissa shifted on the bench. He did appear genuinely concerned. There could be no doubt about that.

"You don't look like you should be left alone right now. That's all." He glanced around. "Where's Jonathan? Isn't he here to take care of you?"

Take care of me? He's the one who sent me in to talk to her. The only answer she gave was a vigorous shaking of her head.

Martin gave a furtive glance up and down the sidewalk. "I know you think of us as being on opposite teams and all of that, but ... everything isn't always what it seems, and sometimes the things we've been told aren't quite the truth."

Melissa tried not to listen, but had to wonder, could this demon be right? God was supposed to be good and would never do anything to harm her. Yet here she was. She had believed Lisa Gibbons was a nice woman, yet ...

"What are you doing, demon?" Jonathan stormed up the sidewalk.

Martin raised his hands, protecting himself from Jonathan's attack. "Nothing. Absolutely nothing. I found her here. She looked so distraught. I was concerned. That's all."

"I'm sure you were." Jonathan planted his feet, like stone pillars, on the sidewalk between Melissa and the demon.

Martin leaned to the side, to catch a glimpse of Melissa. "I have to wonder though ... what would make this poor girl, who is generally so happy ... so miserable? Unless ..." he paused and turned his head, slowly looking from the girl to Jonathan and back again. A smile spread across his face.

"Demon. I'm warning you," Jonathan growled.

Martin continued, great compassion oozing in his words. "She knows."

"Knows?" Melissa cocked her head.

"Yes. You know the truth."

"Demon!" Jonathan took three steps in Martin's direction.

"And what truth is that?" Melissa slid over on the bench.

"The truth that you are Lisa Gibbons' dead child." Martin said the words as if this were information the whole universe knew ... everyone but Melissa, herself.

A cold vice closed around her heart.

Even this demon knows the truth about me.

Martin shook his head and made a sympathetic clicking noise with his tongue. "What a terrible tragedy. To be given the great gift of life and to throw it all away. Foolish people. But what a greater tragedy, to find out like this. Betrayal!"

"I'm warning you ..." Jonathan marched up to Martin.

"Not by someone who supposedly loves you," the demon continued. "Oh no. You'd have thought a merciful God would have informed you of all the details. Would have told you how your loving mother didn't want you, had you ripped from her body and discarded like last week's leftovers."

Melissa wilted into the bench. She touched the side of her head where a sudden pain throbbed.

"Ah, yes. The pain. You remember the pain."

Jonathan grabbed Martin by the throat. "I've had enough of you!"

Martin wriggled under the hold, but he didn't stop talking. He spit his words out in Jonathan's face. "Why? Because I'm lying? But I'm not, am I? Every word I speak is the truth. Isn't it? Tell her! God sent her here to suffer the pain of discovery. He could have told her. Could have spared her the anguish." The demon's eyes flashed at Jonathan. A sadistic smile crossed his face. "But there's more, isn't there?"

"Silence!" Jonathan tossed the old man, like a rag doll, down against the bench.

Melissa jumped to her feet. "No. Let him speak."

Jonathan turned to her. "Demons are liars! They twist the truth!"

"Let him speak." She marched up to Jonathan. "Is there something you don't want me to know?" Melissa searched his face for a sign of the truth he wanted kept secret.

Jonathan turned away.

Gasping for breath and rubbing his throat, Martin struggled to stand. "I'm sorry Melissa. I'm sorry I'm the one who has to tell you the truth. But I suspect you already know, don't you? Oh, the betrayal! Your own angel here. The one who's supposedly protecting you. He knew. He knew all about you. Yet, he sent you into that bar ... that trap, to find out all by yourself. What kind of a friend ... what kind of a loving God does something like that?"

The words stung like a swarm of bees. Melissa spun to Jonathan. The look on his face said it all. He stood, head bent, eyes closed, teeth clenched.

It was true.

God and her angel ...

Melissa turned and ran away.

Martin watched as Melissa escaped down the path, regarding her as hunted prey, weakening, almost ready for the kill. "It's over," Martin spoke gleefully.

"No, it's not." Jonathan said as he stared at his departing friend.

"Give up. I won twenty-one years ago. I'll win tonight." He laughed, a dry hoarse laugh. "Your God has really messed up this time." In an instant, he transformed into the hideous creature. Wretched wings carried him skyward and he flew off. His laugh lingered in the tree branches.

• *Thirty-Five* •

Melissa wandered from street to street. Eventually she found herself in front of McCullen's. The downtown shops were all closed, the streets were all empty. *Like my heart feels.* She frowned at her reflection in the front window. Eyes red from crying, face empty of hope, drained of color.

That's my life now. Hopeless.

Another figure reflected in the window, walking up behind her.

"Are you all right?" Jonathan stopped a couple of feet away.

"I'm wonderful. I just found out that my mother killed me ... didn't want me. My best friend knew all along and never told me. I had to hear it from a demon."

"I'm sorry," he whispered.

"On top of that, I've been telling the whole world about God's love." She spit the words out. Her head sank to her chest. A tear fell against the pavement. "And no one listened." Her hands formed into fists. "Maybe they shouldn't."

Jonathan stepped forward and touched Melissa's shoulder. "Child."

She pulled away, walked off the sidewalk, into the edge of the street. "Don't touch me. And don't call me that. I am not your child!"

"But—"

"Why didn't you tell me?"

"It's not as easy as all that."

Melissa laughed, scornfully. "Really? You couldn't work it into the conversation? 'Here we are Melissa, on Earth, and oh by the way, your mother killed you?' Would that have been hard to do?"

"You don't understand!" Jonathan growled and turned away. "Why couldn't you be happy and content in Heaven? Why did you have to know where you came from?"

"Is that the solution? Ignorance?"

"That's not what I'm saying."

"Then what are you saying?"

Jonathan opened his mouth to answer, but stopped. He looked to the sky. His head tipped to the side.

"What? What's He saying to you?" Melissa marched up to him, grabbed his shoulders and shook with all her might. "Tell me! What's He saying? I have the right to know!"

Jonathan looked down. "I have to go."

"Now?"

"Yes. There's something—"

Melissa punched his chest. "Go! Get out! I don't need you!" She turned her back on him and walked a few steps away.

"But you don't understand."

"All I know is you lied to me. You didn't tell me the truth! How can I trust you? How can I ever trust you again?" The more she spoke, the hotter her face grew. She began to shake. With a growl, she picked up a rock from the gutter, screamed and hurled it at the store's window. Shards of glass exploded in all directions. An ear-piercing alarm sounded.

"Melissa—"

Before Jonathan could say anything else, she sprinted away. *Why should I listen to him? It would probably be another lie.*

• *Thirty-Six* •

The door to her apartment slammed against the wall. Melissa stormed in and stomped to her bedroom. She flung herself on the bed. Over and over she punched her mattress. Then, burying her head into her pillow, she screamed. "Nooooo! Why? Lord, tell me why!" She rolled onto her back and stared at the blank, white ceiling. "Tell me why," she whispered.

Like a dead woman set out for her viewing, she lay on her bed. *For all practical purposes, I am a dead woman.* "Lisa Gibbons' dead daughter," *Martin said.*

Ripped from her mother's womb. *A mother who never wanted me. A mother who figured death was better than life for me.* Yes, she was a dead woman, existing in some state of purgatory.

Melissa pushed off the bed and crossed the floor. At the window, she fell to her knees and gazed out. The noise from the streets was remote, as if she was outside her own body watching everything happen. Watching life go by.

Empty. What an awful feeling. So alone.

Cars and buses chugged along. People walked by. Laughter and honking. Nothing mattered now. A mother with her small toddler skipped down the sidewalk.

So happy ...

Strains of music blew in through the window with the evening breeze. A hymn. Evening service had begun.

Should I go? Why? What good did church ever do for me? Then again, I do like the music.

Finally, music won over weeping. In a trance-like state, she headed out the door of her apartment, down the stairs.

"Sweetie, are you okay?" Mrs. Parsioni walked through the outside door, juggling bags of groceries.

Melissa passed by, not saying a word.

The couple dozen people who attended the Sunday evening service were scattered around the large sanctuary. Arriving late, she'd be able to avoid contact with anyone there. *Why bother?*

As soon she sat in the back pew, the music ended. With a grumble, she rose to leave.

The pastor spoke. "Tonight, I'd like to ask you a question. Which brother are you?"

With a deep sigh, Melissa sank into the pew. *Might as well stay. Better to sit here than in my apartment.*

He continued. "If you remember, last Sunday we talked about the parable of the prodigal son. You know what? I don't think we've given that story the right name. We always focus on the son who took his inheritance and ran away. He squandered every cent on bad choices, and bad living, until he found himself literally in a pig sty."

Melissa crossed her arms and rolled her eyes. So many humans were just like that—squandering, wasting, killing all the good things they have. *They all deserve to live in pigsties.*

He shook his head. "He had so much. Suddenly he found himself penniless, friendless, and starving. Life didn't seem worth living. He felt empty. Dead inside."

Melissa snorted. *I know what that feels like.*

"But, what about the other son? The one who never left his father, or so he says. The one who had so much. So much wealth. So much love. He was always with his father, always enjoyed the benefits of being a child of his dad."

A single tear rolled down Melissa's cheek. Until God sent her here, she was constantly in His love. Her head bent low, until her chin almost touched her chest. *Why God? Why?*

"You wonder if this son ever knew how good he had it. But he was angry. When his brother came home, he felt envious. He was the perfect child ... or so he thought. He felt that his brother, who'd walked away from his father was less deserving."

Melissa stirred.

"But he'd been lying to himself. He had left his dad as much as the younger brother had. Maybe not physically, but spiritually. Somehow, he'd blinded himself to his own sinfulness. His sin of pride was as bad as his brother's sin. What about his sin of unforgiveness toward his brother? What right did he have to not forgive? His brother had done nothing against him, personally. Only against his father. How many of us are like that? We forget two things. Number one — All sin is ultimately against God. Not us. Number two — If we look at ourselves, we'll see that we 're sinners too. If God is willing to forgive us, why in the world would we think we have the right to not forgive someone else?"

Melissa rubbed her hands against her lap and stared at the pew in front of her. *Is it possible?* She shifted around in her seat. *Am I a sinner?*

"Let me ask in closing, what I asked a couple of minutes ago. Which son are you? Are you the one who's holding a grudge? You've walked so close to the source of all blessings, but when someone else wants to walk where you're walking, you say, 'No way! You're not worthy of my Father's love?' Or, are you the brother who ran away? You've fallen into sin, and feel like there's no way out? Well, I have good news for you. For both of these brothers there is a way out."

Melissa looked up, anxious to hear what the Pastor had to say, what the solution was. What acts of goodness or penance could she perform that would lift her from the emptiness she was feeling?

"But, it's not by their own power. No! Look at the story." The pastor glanced down at the open Bible in front of him. "In both cases, it wasn't the person who earned forgiveness. It was the father who gave it. Yes. The prodigal came running back. He had been practicing a speech all the way. 'Father. I have sinned against you. I am no longer worthy to be called your son. Make me a hired servant.' He knew that even the servants in his father's house had it better than he did."

Melissa nodded.

"But," the Pastor continued, "when he began his speech, the father interrupted him. Before he came to the part, 'make me as one of you servants'. No! The father would not even hear these words. The son had come seeking forgiveness. He was a child of his father. The father forgave."

The pastor pointed out at the congregation. His finger swept back and forth, from pew to pew. Did he stop and hover over her a second longer than the other people?

"The father forgave and our Father forgives!"

With great dramatic flare, the pastor swept his arms through the air, issuing orders to imaginary servants. "Put the best robes on him. Prepare the banquet. We party! My son has come home!"

He returned his attention to the open Bible. "But what about the older son? He heard the party and refused to go in. Listen to this. The father went out to him." The pastor repeated the words with great emphasis. "He went out to him! 'Son. Don't you understand? Your brother was dead, but now is alive. He was lost, but now he is found!' No matter which child you are, no matter what sin you've been caught up in, if you've wandered for years or just for a day, it's still wandering. God has good news. He died for you. They nailed Him to a cross for you. He willingly — yes, willingly — died. No one took His life, He gave it ... for you! Redemption!"

The stained glass window of Jesus was right beside Melissa. His nailed-pierced hands were turned out for all to see.

"Redemption," she whispered.

"For God so loved the world ... That's you," Pastor Tom continued. "If you were the only one here, you'd be the world."

Melissa reached toward the window, toward the nail prints. Tears flowed from her eyes.

"He gave His only begotten son, that whosoever believes in Him will not perish, but have everlasting life."

She lowered her head. "What a fool I've been. What a fool ..." She wept for the rest of the service.

"Child? Are you all right?" Harriet stood next to her, the deep concern on her face reflected how terrible Melissa must have looked.

"Oh, Harriet ..." Melissa struggled to speak through uncontrollable sobs.

Harriet slid into the seat beside her and pulled Melissa's head down onto her shoulder. "It's all right child. It's all right. Whatever it is, God can take care of it."

When Melissa finally regained control of herself, she said, "I've done a terrible thing. An awful thing."

"You?" Harriet stroked her hair like a mother would a small child. "Come now. You're on a mission from God. Remember?"

My mission. Todd! She wept louder. "I've failed! I've failed!"

Harriet patted her head. She pulled a tissue from her pocketbook and handed it to Melissa.

Melissa sat up and wiped the tears from her face. "The pastor asked which son we were. I'm both. I'm both. To be in the very presence of God, and to know his joy. That was me." She nodded at Harriet, vigorously. "I came here, thinking I was so much better. Talking about forgiveness ... yet can I forgive?" Tears blurred her vision again. She had screamed at Ms. Gibbons. Screamed how much she hated her. "But I'm the other brother, too. I've walked away. I've walked away. When was the last time I told you God loves you?"

"But you've told me, child. You've told me," the older woman said in a soothing voice.

Melissa pressed her hands against her chest. "This hollowness. This terrible feeling. This is separation from God. I don't like it. I've turned my back on Him."

"Even though you've turned your back, He's still there." It was Pastor Tom talking. The church was empty now, save for the three of them. "Melissa, God never leaves us nor forsakes us. He's there for you."

Melissa chewed her lip and lowered her head. "How can He be there for me? I failed my mission. And Todd ..." Her words faltered.

Harriet perked up. "What about Todd?"

"I failed him. The gun."

"Oh ... You know about the gun?"

"Yes." She glanced toward the door and gave a determined nod. *I may have failed Todd, but it isn't too late for Ms. Gibbons. At least I hope it isn't.* She hopped out of the pew.

"Where are you going?" Harriet asked.

"I'd like to talk to you some more," the pastor added.

"And I'd like to talk, too," Melissa spoke as she rushed away. "But I have some unfinished business to attend to. Some very important business."

· *Thirty-Seven* ·

Melissa stood on the street corner, peering down the various avenues. What was the fastest way back to the bar? Things looked different at night. Giving an affirmative nod at one of the roads, she headed off in that direction.

Hurry. She looked at her watch. Twenty minutes had passed since she left the church. *Feels like two hours.*

She found the spot to where Jonathan had dragged her and peered through the window of the bar. Her face fell. The booth was empty.

"She's gone." Jonathan walked up.

Melissa kept staring at the window. *No. She's got to be there.*

He stood silent, scraping his shoe on the sidewalk. "Listen," he finally spoke. "I didn't mean to disappoint you. I'm sorry if you feel—"

"No," Melissa interrupted. "I was wrong. I didn't trust God. He knows best. He has His reasons for revealing things in the manner that He does."

"Praise God," the angel whispered in reverence.

A deep crease formed between Melissa's eyebrows. "He had to teach me something ... something about love ... forgiveness ... redemption."

"Have you learned?"

She nodded. "But what about Ms. Gibbons? I've failed her."

"Not yet."

"How can you say that?" Melissa cried. "I failed her. Instead of showing her God's love ... I told her I hated her!" She looked down at the ground.

"Child, there are various elements in delivering a message from God. Number one is timing. We deliver the message in God's time." He looked skyward. "Yes," he said to the unseen. "It's almost time. It's almost time."

Then he focused back on Melissa. "Secondly, you deliver the message. Not your interpretation of it."

"I did."

"Did you?" Jonathan's eyes pierced into her. "Did you? Think back. What did God tell you to say?"

With mechanical precision, Melissa recited the words. "The Lord loves you, and —"

"No. Don't speak. Think! Remember. Look back to that day, when you were standing with the Lord."

Melissa's forehead wrinkled.

Jonathan grabbed her arm. "It's time. Head down Fifth Street ... Go north." He moved behind her and, like a bulldozer, pushed her. "Toward the river. Toward the bridge."

"Why?"

"You'll know when you get there."

"Where will you be?"

"I'll be there." His face was grim. "I have a task to do. You have a task to do."

The angel transformed. Majestic wings unfurled. He bent his legs slightly, and leapt skyward. The wings took over and he flew. "Fifth Street! Now!"

Melissa ran with urgency, as if Jonathan was still pushing her on. The life and death tone in his attitude prodded her forward. *What am I going to find? What does God expect of me?*

Fifth Street circled the edge of the downtown area before it exited the city and swept over a wide expanse of the river. *What did he mean, 'Not your interpretation of it'?*

There it was, off in the distance. The bridge loomed large and dark. Its metal supports disappearing up into the night sky. The river wasn't too wide at this spot, and the bridge extended well beyond its banks, crossing over not only the water, but the jagged rock-lined shore as well.

Melissa puffed for air, her breaths synchronized with the beating of her shoes on the pavement. She scanned the roadside for Ms. Gibbons. There was no sign of her. *Maybe Jonathan is wrong. Maybe I should turn around and go back to town.*

Just then, a noise, a sobbing, caught her attention. Up ahead, about half way across the bridge, a figure leaned precariously over the edge. It was Lisa Gibbons.

Melissa raced on.

The large steel supports arched over the great expanse. Lisa's hands white-knuckled one of these beams. Two other figures were there. Jonathan and Martin, fully transformed to their supernatural states, floated above the woman, half hidden in the bridge's framework. They appeared to be speaking, one poised on each of her sides.

"You are valuable. This is no way to end it. The Lord loves you. There is always forgiveness," Jonathan said.

"It's over. You are a failure," Martin hissed. "No one loves you. You killed your child. There's nothing you can do to make up for it. You don't deserve to live." Tendrils of black smoke wrapped around Lisa's head, pulling her closer to the abyss, urging her to jump.

Melissa halted about ten feet from the woman. Cars sped by as if nothing out of the ordinary was happening. *Probably invisible to ordinary people.*

Lisa balanced on the edge of the bridge, running a trembling hand through her hair.

Melissa cast a wary glance over the side. It had to be a forty-foot drop. The water was shallow, too shallow to cushion Lisa's fall. That was, if she even hit the water and not the rocky shoreline.

"God loves you," Jonathan was imploring.

"How could God love you?" Martin retorted.

"How could God love me?" Lisa echoed.

"You're a murderer," Martin rasped. The tendrils of smoke pushed into her ears.

"No!" Jonathan yelled.

"I'm a murderer," Lisa moaned with robot-like precision.

"You robbed a small child of life."

"Yes. A murderer."

Melissa's eyes darted between the angel and demon. A bitter cold seemed to rise from the bridge itself and flow through her until it froze in her throat. *Jonathan's losing this fight.*

Martin glanced over at Melissa. His eyes blazed with satisfaction. His face was covered with a devilish grin. "Even Melissa says you don't deserve forgiveness."

Lisa groaned. A tear dropped from her face and disappeared into the darkness below. "Even Melissa ..."

"No!" Melissa exclaimed. It was like a knife cutting into her heart, to hear her own words being used in such a way.

Startled, Ms. Gibbons turned and looked.

"Stay back!" Martin hissed.

"Stay back!" Lisa screamed.

"Melissa," Jonathan cried out. "I'm losing her!"

The words were like a trapdoor opening beneath Melissa's feet. Wide-eyed, she looked up at Jonathan. Here was an angel of the Lord. Her angel. If he couldn't do anything for Lisa Gibbons, what in the world did he expect her to do?

I'm a nothing. A nobody.

"What can I do? Tell me," she pleaded. "What can I say?"

Lisa gave an incredulous look up at the sky. "I know I've had a few too many, but what's your excuse?"

"Excuse for what?" Melissa asked.

Lisa pointed in the air all around her. "For talking to the pink elephants."

"She can't see us. Only feel our influence," Jonathan explained. "She needs to hear from you."

Melissa took a cautious step forward. "The Lord loves you —"

"That's not what you said in the bar." Martin smiled.

"That's not what you said —"

"I know what I said!" Melissa clutched at her aching heart. How do you take back something you said? How do you undo damage already done?

"You said I was a murderer!" Lisa pointed at Melissa.

"A murderer," Martin laughed, his face turned skyward. "An unforgiven murderer!"

"But —" Melissa wrung her hands.

Lisa Gibbons slammed a fist into the metal beam. "That's what you said. A murderer!" Her eyes blazed at Melissa, drilling into her with anger, before she turned her attention back to the dark river. "A murderer."

Melissa withered back a couple of steps, like a flower in the hot desert sun. *I am such a fool. How in the world could God have ever trusted me?* "What's the use?" She moaned and closed her eyes in defeat. "I've failed. God never should have sent me."

"That's not true," Jonathan said.

A tear rolled down her cheek and she slumped against the side of the bridge. "I'm such a failure."

"No," Jonathan's lips moved like he had hollered, but it sounded more like a whisper.

Melissa looked over the edge of the bridge at the water ... The inviting water ...

She tipped her head. *Where did that thought come from?* And yet, she'd failed Todd. Now she failed Lisa Gibbons. Maybe the best thing was to end the struggle.

What an odd thing to think.

"God is not the author of those lies." Jonathan spoke from somewhere far, far away. "Nor is He the author of the foul thoughts you are having. Look!" There was an urgency in his voice. "Look," Jonathan demanded while pointing to Melissa's side.

She hesitated. Why bother? She was such a failure. What could she possibly see that would change any of that? But it was her angel asking ... She struggled to turn her head. What she saw caused her mouth to drop open. She gasped. Martin had taken up his station next to her ear, a gleeful expression on his face. Tendrils of black smoke oozed from his mouth and were encircling her head.

Overwhelmed by nausea, she leaned over the bridge railing, her stomach spasming with dry heaves. She looked back to Jonathan. He was saying something to her. His lips were moving, but the sound wasn't getting through. Something was blocking them.

• *Thirty-Eight* •

"Such a failure," Martin said.

I shouldn't listen to him. But there's such a sweet seductive quality to his voice.

"First Todd ... now Lisa ..." he said.

It was true.

"How many others will you fail?"

I failed Todd.

Lisa Gibbons climbed onto the rail.

I'm failing Lisa Gibbons.

Melissa watched Lisa Gibbons balancing on the narrow beam. It was as if she were watching a play on a stage — not able to do anything to change what was going to happen. Worse yet, not caring to change what was going to happen.

"Lisa Gibbons will be leaving you soon." Martin smiled. "Maybe you should go with her."

No! And yet ... In agony, she clenched the sides of her head and fell to her knees.

Jonathan's face was blood red. The muscles in his neck tense. His mouth moving as if he were desperately screaming something.

"Give up. Give in," Martin said, his face lit with utter joy.

How is this happening? Melissa leaned forward. The cold, steel side of the bridge was the only thing holding her up now. Martin whispered one poison lie after another into her ear.

I have to find the strength to fight this attack! She pressed her fists against her forehead. *I can't. I can't.*

"You've failed God."

Wait. Melissa's eyes opened wide. *I'm not strong enough. But I know someone who is.* She lifted her face to the dark sky and cried out, "God! Help me!"

In an instant, a flash of brilliant light slammed the foul demon against one of the support beams, swinging his head back with a loud crack. The shock wave knocked Lisa backward onto the pavement.

The tendrils of lies surrounding Melissa's head dissipated. With her strength returning, she slowly lifted herself off the ground.

Jonathan gave a satisfied grin. "All you had to do was ask."

"But how did he get such a hold over me?"

"Don't doubt God. Don't doubt the mission you're on. Demons will use any crack to gain a foothold." He cast a concerned glance at the other woman. "Now, you help Lisa Gibbons."

"How?"

Lisa stood up and moved back to the railing. Martin recovered and flew to her side, leaning closer and closer, whispering his noxious fumes into her ear. "Jump. Die. Life is over."

"Ms. Gibbons." Melissa ventured a step closer.

"No," Lisa warned. "I'll jump! I swear, I'll jump!" There was a wild look of desperation in the woman's eyes.

She's far beyond reason.

Clutching the side of the bridge, Lisa gazed over the railing to the rocks below. "I'm so tired. So tired. I want to rest."

"This isn't the way," Melissa pleaded.

Ms. Gibbons' head snapped in Melissa's direction. "Why not? You said it yourself. I'm a murderer. I don't deserve forgiveness."

"I was wrong. I was so wrong."

"But I killed my baby. My Melissa." She sobbed uncontrollably. "I didn't mean to ... didn't want to. I was so alone. I didn't know what to do. It seemed like the only way."

"You were alone?" Melissa's voice softened.

Lisa gave a vigorous nod. "The father abandoned me. Said it was more responsibility than he could handle." Lisa sniffed.

"My parents said it would ruin my life, having a baby at my age ..." Pleading eyes looked deep into Melissa's. "What could I do? I was so afraid."

"She's talking to you," Jonathan said. "That's a good sign."

Martin growled at Melissa. "None of that matters," he whispered in Lisa Gibbons' ear. "You killed your child. You don't deserve forgiveness."

"I don't deserve forgiveness ..." Lisa put her leg up onto the steel beam.

"No!" Melissa reached out.

"Tell her," Jonathan hollered. "Tell her God's message."

"There's peace in death," Martin's words enticed the woman.

Melissa shook her head. "But, I've said it a hundred times already!"

"No, you haven't," Jonathan answered. "Think of what God told you to say."

Melissa chewed her lower lip. Jesus had said, "Say, The Lord loves you, and Jesus forgives you ..."

Wait. Melissa closed her eyes. *Was that what He'd said?*

"Jump," Martin cried.

"Hurry," Jonathan urged.

"It's too late," Martin laughed. "She's mine. I told you she was mine."

Melissa clenched her teeth. *I can't fail this woman.* She looked to the sky. *Lord, we can't fail her.* She blocked her ears with her hands, cutting out all the sounds and distractions. She thought back to that day.

Jesus was giving her the message. "The Lord loves you, and I forgive you."

But surely by 'I forgive you,' He'd meant Himself—Jesus—hadn't He? Melissa took one last look at this pitiful human before her ... her mother. The one who had prematurely ended her life on this planet. Was it God's forgiveness she was seeking right at this moment? Or was it ...

"Wait," Melissa screamed in a voice so loud that it jolted Lisa Gibbons.

"What now?" Martin griped. "I have a suicide going on here. Why do you keep interrupting me?"

"You're not going to stop me," Lisa whimpered. She began to climb onto the railing. "I deserve to die."

"Please! Before you do anything, let me tell you a story."

Lisa Gibbons hesitated. She looked at Melissa with bewildered, bloodshot eyes. "A story?"

Melissa stepped closer. "This day ... twenty-one years ago, the doctor told you to be quiet. Said it was all over."

"I told you that at the bar."

"It's not over ... it's not over." Melissa said. "That's what you said."

Lisa spoke in a halting voice. "Where did you hear that?"

"It's what you were saying over and over. You were sobbing. You realized what you had done. You were sorry. Your heart was breaking. It's been eating at you for twenty-one years! It's not over. It's not over."

"How? How did you know?" Lisa backed away from Melissa.

Melissa gulped hard. *This is going to sound unbelievable.* "I was there."

"Oh, come on," Lisa Gibbons scoffed.

"How else would I know?" Melissa stepped closer. "Have you ever spoken to anyone about this?"

The wrinkles between Lisa's eyebrows deepened. "No ..."

"This is going to be hard for you to believe." Melissa took another step. "I am your daughter. I am your Melissa."

Distrust and disbelief covered Lisa's face. Her voice trembled. "No."

"Yes. How else would I know what happened in that room?" Melissa sighed. "I don't pretend to understand it all, but somehow God allowed me to remember that day, so that I could be here right now to help you. You kept weeping, It's not over ... it's not over."

Lisa Gibbons peered deep into Melissa's eyes. "But you died."

"I died." She slowly nodded her head. "But God let me come back for this moment, to help you, and also to teach me about forgiveness ... redemption."

"Foolishness!" Martin whispered.

Lisa Gibbons' face closed.

Martin's words still have some control over this poor woman.

"I know it's hard to believe," Melissa said. "Hard to understand. But think about it. Think about how naïve, how innocent I was when you first met me."

"You're not much better now," Lisa snickered.

"I think you're getting through," Jonathan encouraged.

"I'd never been to Earth before. I live in Heaven. God sent me with a message for you."

"Why in the world would God send me a message?" Lisa said in a mocking tone. Melissa had been slowly inching forward. They were now standing face to face. "Besides," Lisa said. "I've heard your message a hundred times. Nice words, but—"

Melissa shook her head. "You don't understand. I messed up the message."

"No, you didn't," Martin exclaimed.

"Yes, you did," Jonathan countered.

"It's not God's forgiveness you're looking for, though you need it. You need it very much." Melissa looked into her eyes. "Lisa Gibbons. The Lord loves you ... and ..." she hesitated, a catch in her voice. "I forgive you."

The two stood in silence. Streams of tears flowed from Lisa's eyes, streaking mascara down her face. "Melissa? My Melissa?" She reached up and caressed Melissa's hair.

Melissa nodded. "Your Melissa."

For a moment Lisa Gibbons trembled. Then she threw her arms around her daughter and sobbed uncontrollably. "I am so sorry. So sorry."

Melissa held the woman, tight. "I forgive you. I forgive you."

The moment was cut short by an explosion of profanity from Martin. He spiraled wildly up into the night sky above them. "I was so close! It's not fair. It's not fair!"

Through clenched teeth, Melissa looked up at the demon. "She's not yours. You were wrong."

Lisa pulled back from the embrace and sniffed, "What are you talking about?"

Martin's eyes burned bright red. "Stupid little girl!" He snarled and shook violently. Letting out a blood-curdling scream, he launched himself at the two.

Jonathan was there in an instant. He took up his position in front of Melissa and acted like a shield between the demon and the two women.

Martin slammed against Jonathan and, with a mighty explosion, ricocheted off and out over the river. He pulled himself to a stop and hovered about thirty feet away, eyes flashing and teeth bared.

Melissa cringed. She grabbed ahold of Lisa Gibbons. With arms wrapped around her, half for comfort and half for protection, she looked over to her angel.

What in the world?

Jonathan stood there, arms crossed against his chest in an almost casual manner, a calm smile on his face.

"Mocking me, angel?" Martin spit the words out. "I am not the weakling I've pretended to be. That was for the puny human's benefit. No! Now you will feel my full fury."

With a calm smile, Jonathan pointed directly below Martin and shook his head. "I don't think so."

The demon looked at the air beneath his feet. His countenance changed. Raging red eyes melted away to fear.

It began as a noise, like rushing water, growing louder with each passing second. Then the bridge started to vibrate. Melissa clung to Ms. Gibbons. She peered over the safety rail. About twenty feet below Martin, a small swirl appeared in mid-air, like a whirlpool in the sea.

The noise was deafening.

The swirl increased in size, doubling, tripling, spinning faster and faster, until finally the vortex engulfed the sky. Its center was pitch black. The darkness expanded, swallowing even the shadows around it.

"No!" Martin cried. He scrambled to get away, clawing at the air itself. The black hole pulled him closer and closer. Finally, he was swallowed up. In an instant, the night sky returned to normal.

Melissa trembled.

"Are you all right?" Lisa Gibbons placed a hand on her shoulder.

"Did you see—" Melissa stopped short. The two battle-scarred and weary women fell against each other and sobbed.

Jonathan towered over them. He smiled down at Melissa. "Good job." Then he wrapped them both in his wings.

• *Thirty-Nine* •

A single spotlight illumined the pulpit area, casting peaceful shadows through the remainder of the sanctuary. Melissa stood in front of her favorite stained glass window. She traced the figure of Jesus with her finger. The window seemed to have a supernatural glow, the effect of an outside streetlight.

All was quiet, especially when compared with her time on the bridge.

"You did the right thing, suggesting Pastor Tom could help Lisa." Jonathan sat in the back pew, looking toward the front of the church. Lisa and the pastor were there. In view, but out of earshot. "He's a Godly man."

Melissa's gaze drifted around the church.

"Are you all right? You seem lost in thought."

"Just feeling ... sad. My mission is over." She cast a questioning glance to her angel.

He nodded. "Don't look so forlorn. You get to go back home."

She sighed.

"What's the matter?"

What do I say? "I'll miss this place, these people."

"The good news is you'll be seeing many of them again." Jonathan gave an encouraging smile.

Melissa sat down beside him. "While we're alone, I have some questions."

"Okay."

"First of all, why didn't you tell me?"

"Tell you what?"

"That Lisa was my mother."

Jonathan nodded Heavenward. "It was His call. He knows best. Things had to unfold in their own time. If you had known sooner, what would you have done? Told her?"

Melissa shrugged.

"Besides, you always said you wanted to know what it was like to be human. That means pain, suffering, temptation. Those are a part of the equation. You couldn't have truly forgiven her unless you had a taste of what she'd been through."

The door to the sanctuary squeaked open. Harriet Simmons stepped inside.

Oh, no. Todd!

All Melissa could think was that her friend was probably being held in a dark, dank cell, where he'd remain for the rest of his life. *Poor Harriet.* She jumped out of her seat. "I am so sorry. I failed you. Failed Todd."

Harriet tipped her head. "Failed? What are you talking about?" She waved an arm, as if swishing away Melissa's words. "Never mind that now. Could you come outside for a minute?"

Melissa followed Harriet through the door, and a warm smile spread across her face.

Todd stood at the bottom of the church steps. His hands were shoved into his pockets. He stared at the ground, rocking back and forth on his heels.

"Todd!" Melissa raced down the steps. She hit into the young man, knocking him backwards, and clung to his neck. "The police let you go?"

He pushed her away, holding her at arm's length. "Police?" He looked up and down the road, nervously, as if he expected a cruiser to be bearing down on him.

Harriet grabbed his sleeve and shook it. "Did you do something I don't know about?"

Todd raised his hands to protect himself from his grandmother's attack. "No, honest." He turned to Melissa. "What are you talking about?"

Melissa's stare shifted from Harriet to Todd. *Am I the crazy one here?* She turned to Jonathan, who'd followed them out of the church. He offered no help as he stood at the top of the stairs, leaning against the railing. His right hand was covering a grin.

Melissa turned back to Todd. "But the protest ... I saw you —"

"You were at the protest?" Todd scratched the back of his head. "It was nuts there, wasn't it?"

"Todd! You had a—" She stopped herself and glanced at Harriet, cautiously.

Harriet frowned. "Gun? Is that what you were going to say?" She shook her head. "Fool boy, carrying a loaded weapon into a crowd like that. You were lucky you didn't kill someone ... or yourself!"

Todd's chin dipped down to his chest. "Sorry."

"I don't understand," Melissa said. "I heard shots."

"That wasn't me."

"Must have been some other crazy person," Harriet said, half under her breath.

"I was so angry," Todd continued, seeming oblivious to his grandmother's comment. "When Martin found the pistol ..."

Melissa shuddered.

"Foolish old man. Giving you a gun." Harriet shook her fist. "When I get my hands on him, I'm going to give him a piece of my mind."

"I don't think you'll have to worry about Martin anymore," Melissa said.

Jonathan cleared his throat.

"Why?" Todd asked. "Is he okay? Did something happen to him?"

"Yes ... No ... I mean—"

"What are you saying?"

"I—"

"I'll tell you what she's trying to say." Jonathan walked down the steps and came to her rescue. "Martin won't be with us any longer. I saw him a couple of hours ago. He's gone on a trip."

Phew. Thank you, Jonathan.

"A long trip," Melissa added.

Jonathan shot her a chastising look.

"That's too bad. I liked the guy," Todd said.

Harriet shook her head. "Giving my grandson a gun." She grumbled. "What kind of a fool is he?"

Melissa said, "The gun! You were at the rally. I saw you. What happened?"

Todd let out a long sigh. "I was so angry. I wanted to kill him."

"Dr. Winters?"

He nodded. "I was making my way toward the front, to where he was standing. I hid the gun under my shirt. It was so heavy ... like a bowling ball. All I kept thinking was, I'm gonna get caught. I'm gonna get caught. It felt like everybody was gawking at me, like they all knew what I planned on doing. Finally, I was right there, standing in front of him. It would've been so easy."

"What stopped you?" Melissa asked.

"People were pushing and shoving all around me." Todd closed his eyes and shook his head. "Screaming and yelling. It was crazy. They were all filled with such hate." He hung his head. "It was kinda like looking in a mirror. Was I like them?" Todd shuddered. "You and Gram have been telling me I was being eaten up on the inside."

"Nice to know you listen," Harriet said.

Looking down at the ground, Todd closed his eyes and shook his head. "In the end, I couldn't do it. I couldn't bring myself to kill the killer."

"I didn't raise a murderer," Harriet said. "Thou Shalt Not Kill!"

Todd looked at his grandmother and said quietly, "While I was standing there, those words echoed through my head. If I killed him, would I have been any better than he was?"

"But I saw them taking you away," Melissa said.

"Huh?"

"I saw someone escorting you out of there."

Todd chuckled. "And I'm glad he did. I stood there scared to death. All of a sudden, I felt like I couldn't hide that gun anymore—like everyone was looking at me, looking at it. I started shaking. Then a cop—"

"Policeman," his grandmother corrected.

"Policeman saw me. He was over by the steps, giving me the eye. All I could think was 'I'm busted for sure.' He started a slow walk toward me. What could I do? Run? That would be a sure sign of guilt. Besides, in that crowd I wouldn't get too far. He was only a couple of feet away, when this hand comes down on my shoulder. I jumped out of my skin, almost pulled the trigger."

"And almost shot yourself in the belly! Lug-head!"

"Gram." Todd rolled his eyes.

"Who was it?" Melissa asked. "Who grabbed you? Was it the police?"

Todd shook his head. A grateful smile spread across his face. "It was the pastor. Don't ask me how or why, but he was looking for me. In that crowd, he was looking for me."

"It was the Holy Spirit." Harriet raised a hand to the Lord.

"And guess what? The pastor knew the policeman." Todd polished his knuckles against his chest. "He introduced me as a fine young man from his church. We shook hands. Then the pastor and me walked away. We didn't stop until we got back here."

"That's wonderful," Melissa sighed.

Todd tipped his head and gave Melissa a puzzled look. "What were you doing down there?"

"Looking for you. I'd heard about the gun and was worried you'd do something ... something ..."

"Stupid," Harriet said. "That's the word you're looking for. S-T-U-P-I-D." She turned to Todd. "See. God had more than one angel looking after you."

"I guess he did." He kicked at a small stone on the sidewalk. "But I still get so angry when I think about that place ... and what they do."

"And you should," Jonathan chimed in. He placed a hand on Todd's shoulder. "But what matters is how you deal with that anger and what your response is to places like that."

Todd nodded. "That's what the pastor says. We're gonna meet. He's gonna help me with some things."

Harriet looked at Melissa. "He wanted to come down and let you know he's all right."

"I'm glad."

Todd turned to leave. "I'll see you tomorrow at work."

"Oh." Melissa frowned. "I don't ... I don't know if I'll be working there anymore."

The young man tipped his head to the side. "Get fired?"

"No, nothing like that. I might be moving on."

Todd's shoulders slumped. "I'll miss you. My little sister."

Pools of tears formed in Melissa's eyes. "There's one thing you've got to remember."

Todd chuckled. "I know. I know. God loves me. He forgives me too."

Melissa peered up at her tall friend. "Never forget that! But there's one other thing." She jumped forward and wrapped her arms around him, crushing her head into his chest. She held on tight. "I love you, too. You're my big brother!"

Todd stood paralyzed for a moment, arms dangling out to the sides.

"Hug her back, dummy," his grandmother said.

He did. "I'll miss you, Mel." After a moment, the embrace ended. Todd backed up a step and wiped away a tear. "I don't know why this is so emotional. Even if you quit the store, you'll come back and visit. I'll see you again."

"You never know."

"Come on, sweetheart," Harriet said. "I've got to get home." She said her farewells to Melissa, then she and Todd turned to leave. "You know with nice friends like that, how do you end up listening to an old dummy like that Martin?"

"Gram!"

"Seriously. Sometimes I don't think your head's on straight."

"I know."

She reached over and took his hand. "But I love you ... Lughead. You've brought such joy to my life."

"I love you, too, Gram."

The two disappeared down the sidewalk.

Melissa and Jonathan headed back into the church.

"I wonder how Todd knew I was here?" Melissa said.

"That's easy," Jonathan said. "I called him. Figured you'd like to say your goodbyes."

Melissa smiled. "I thought you didn't like Todd."

Jonathan slipped into the back pew. He grimaced. "It's not that I don't like him, I was just afraid you were getting too caught up in his situation and would miss your mission."

"Thank you." Melissa gave his hand a gentle pat. "What a stroke of luck that Pastor Tom was at the protest."

Jonathan looked at the ceiling and grinned.

"What are you smirking about?"

He chuckled. "That wasn't luck."

It took her a moment. "That was you?"

Jonathan nodded. "When you raced out of the store to find Todd, I flew off to find the Pastor. Just as you saw me and the demon seeking to influence Lisa on the bridge, so I influenced him. Fortunately, being a man of God, he was much more open to God's will."

"I only wish I had a chance to intercept Todd and speak to him. Maybe I could have stopped him from even going."

"Don't worry. Todd has an angel of his own."

"Really?"

"His grandmother, Harriet."

Melissa gasped. "She's an angel?"

Jonathan laughed. "In a way. Nothing beats the influence of a strong Christian in your life. All those years of a Godly up-bringing weren't wasted. Even as Todd was heading for the news conference, his grandmother's voice was speaking to him, shouting in his mind, reminding him of Bible verses he'd learned as a child, pushing him to do the right thing. By the time he got to the rally, he was under such heavy conviction, I doubt he could have pulled the trigger." Jonathan shook his head and chuckled. "Throwing a baggy of 'blood' on someone is different from killing them."

Melissa glanced to the front of the church, where Lisa and the pastor were deep in conversation. "We've certainly given Pastor Tom enough to keep him busy. Speaking of influencing ... At the bridge, I didn't even realize Martin was whispering in my ear until you pointed it out."

"The devil's ways are crafty, subtle. Most people never know he's there. Thankfully, you did the right thing. You called out to the Lord! He'll always help. You simply have to ask."

Melissa fell silent.

"Anything else?"

"Yes." She turned her whole body to face him. "At the store, when you rescued me from Martin, he said he knew the rules. What rules?"

"Demons have limits," Jonathan explained. "They can't go around attacking and harming anyone they want, not physically at least. They need permission from God or from the individual themselves. Martin knew he couldn't touch you."

Melissa's head tipped to the side. "The bridge?"

Jonathan nodded. "He broke the rules. He paid the price."

A deep crease formed between her eyebrows. "Then why bother hunting me down in the store like he did? If he couldn't touch me, he couldn't accomplish anything."

Jonathan snorted. "He accomplished just what he wanted to accomplish. He made you doubt. That's what demons do. He used the time to talk, to sow his seeds. He filled your head with doubts about your abilities and God's love."

The two turned to face the front of the church. Melissa leaned back. "How stupid of me."

"If you think about it, in almost all of his conversations, that's what Martin did. He misdirected, suggested sinful behavior, made people doubt themselves and God."

She shook her head. "I never had a chance."

"Don't be too hard on yourself. He was toying with you. With a demon's supernatural abilities, you never could have truly hidden from him in the store. Impossible. But, as for never having a chance, you had the same one that all humans have. It's right there." Jonathan pointed at the figure in the stained-glass window. "Jesus is the hope of the world. People walk away, are led away ... However you want to describe it. Jesus offers redemption."

"Redemption." Melissa gazed at the nail-pierced hands. Then she nodded toward the two seated in the front of the church. "I take it, when I overheard you and Martin talking, the 'she' he said he owned was not me at all. It was Lisa."

"Correct."

She chewed on her bottom lip. "He made it sound like he knew her ... He knew me."

Jonathan sighed. He closed his eyes and tipped his head back. A pained expression crossed his face. "He did. Twenty-one years ago ... he was the demon whispering to Lisa, telling her there was no hope if she had that little baby. He convinced her to have the abortion." He leaned forward and rested his elbows against the pew in front of him. "I was her angel. I battled for your life." He shook his head as if he could shake the memory from his brain. Then he turned a smiling face to Melissa. "The Lord allowed me to watch over you. Be a part of your life in Heaven. You have to understand, though. All those times you wanted to know of your past ... I couldn't say a word. To tell you about your former life meant I'd have to admit my failure ... I'd have to open your heart to all that pain." He grunted. "Martin didn't realize the rage he unleashed in me when he dared to suggest some type of unnatural relationship between us." He sat up straight and puffed out his chest. "I am and ever will be your angel!"

Melissa leaned over and hugged him. "I couldn't ask for a better one." She stiffened and gazed at her friend. "Wait a minute. You said I never had a chance when I was hiding from the demon in the store."

"That's correct."

She stood and slowly crossed to the wall, chewing on her thumbnail. She spun around and placed her hands on her hips. "What about an angel? Any chance?"

Jonathan sputtered. "Are you serious? Of course not."

"Really." Melissa stretched the word out. She glared at him. "All those games of hide and seek we played?"

"Oh ..."

"All those times hiding under the trees or in the bushes? You could have found me right away?"

"I ... umm ... Well, it's ..."

Lisa and the pastor's voices grew louder as they strolled toward the back of the church.

"Oh look. They're done." Jonathan hopped up and rushed over to them.

Melissa smiled and followed along.

Pastor Tom shook Lisa's hand. "I appreciate you coming to see me, and look forward to meeting with you Thursday at seven-thirty. Don't forget, the Lord loves you." He placed a hand on her shoulder. "He truly does."

"Thank you," Lisa said. "I'll see you on Thursday." She turned and walked toward Melissa.

Jonathan stepped over to the pastor and the two began to talk.

Melissa wrapped an arm around Lisa and guided her in the opposite direction, out of the pastor's hearing. "Are you okay?"

"I think 'okay' is a couple of steps away from where I am." Lisa shook her head. "But I'm better." She glanced over at the men before continuing. "I ... I don't know who you are. I know what you said ... at the bridge." She leaned closer and whispered. "Who you say you are, but that seems impossible." She turned away and shook her head. "Maybe it was the alcohol. I don't know."

Melissa squeezed Lisa's shoulder. "It's all right."

Lisa touched her hand. "Part of me wants so desper- ately to believe you are who you say you are, but ..." Her words broke off. She turned, and with her eyes narrowed to slits, as if trying to peer into Melissa's heart, to see the truth, she asked, "How?"

"Did you tell the pastor who I was?"

Lisa chuckled. "Are you serious? He'd have me institution-alized. Did you tell Jonathan?"

"He already knows."

"Really?"

Melissa shrugged. "He's an angel."

Lisa Gibbons' head jerked from side to side, from Melissa to Jonathan. Her forehead creased with deep furrows. Finally, she said, "I can see it. Yes."

"Seriously?"

"Sure. Why not?"

The two fell silent, simply standing there, gazing at each other. When Melissa spoke again, a sadness had crept into her voice. "I think I'm going to be leaving soon. My mission is done. The Lord will be bringing me ... home." The word caught in her throat. *Home? Is it...?*

"I wish—" Lisa broke down. "I wish that your home had been with me."

"Me too. But it wasn't."

Lisa's features contorted. She looked away.

"Don't be upset. Remember what I told you," Melissa said. "The Lord loves you. No matter what. We can't change our past, but He loves us in spite of it."

"Yes." Lisa gave a long, hard look around the sanctuary. "It's been a long time since I've stepped in a church." She chuckled. "Kinda surprised the roof didn't cave in."

Melissa cast a wary glance upwards.

"I told the pastor I used to go all the time, when I was a kid. Before ..." Her words drifted off and she hung her head. "I even went forward at an altar call, once. It was at a youth retreat. I was twelve." She sighed. "Back then it was so easy to believe in God's love. But now ..." Despair entered her eyes.

"Ms. Gibbons. God loves you."

The woman's features tightened.

She's either holding her guilt in or holding God's love out.

"It's true," Melissa said. "He told me. He loves you. And if you ask Him, He'll forgive you. There's nowhere you can run that's too far from God's forgiveness. But there's more!" Melissa paused. She took a deep breath. Then gazing into Lisa Gibbons' eyes, she said, "And I love you. I forgive you ... Mother." Her lip quivered. It was the first time she'd spoken the word, but it felt right. "Mother."

Lisa trembled. An ocean of tears opened up. "Thank you. Thank you. I don't deserve ..."

Almost simultaneously, the two reached a loving hand toward the other's face, and wiped the tears out of the other's eyes.

"That's the wonderful thing about God's love," Melissa said. "We don't deserve it, but He offers it. Are you going to be all right?"

Lisa nodded.

Jonathan walked up from behind them. "Melissa. It's time to go."

"I hope to see you again, Mom."

Lisa's eyes lit up. "When?"

"You listen to Pastor Tom. Believe in the love of God that he'll tell you about and I'm sure we'll see each other again."

The two embraced. Melissa held on as tight as she could.

"Ready to go?" Pastor Tom approached.

Lisa wiped a tear from her eye. "Pastor Tom is going to give me a ride home."

"That's nice." Melissa smiled.

The four walked out of the church. Lisa and Pastor Tom climbed into his car. Melissa's eyes stayed locked on her mother as the car drove off, not looking away until it was well out of sight.

"It's all right." Jonathan placed a hand on Melissa's shoulder. "You'll see her again."

Melissa remained quiet.

"Are you ready to go?"

She hung her head.

"Is something wrong?"

"No." She paused. "But before we leave, could I go back to the apartment and say goodbye to Mrs. Parsioni? It won't take much time. I promise."

Jonathan considered the request and nodded. "All right."

· *Forty* ·

Melissa shuffled down the sidewalk, not speaking to Jonathan the entire walk. Leaving Earth was going to be hard enough. She'd made some good friends here, and connected with Lisa Gibbons, her mother.

Heaven. Home. Something was wrong. Should she go back? Would she be welcome? Did she even belong there?

I want to feel joy, to feel happiness at returning. But I'm no longer the innocent child I was. I've suffered temptation. I failed.

She hung her head.

All those things I told Lisa Gibbons about God's love and forgiveness. Are they true for me, too? Could He possibly forgive someone who's walked with Him in Heaven, strolled with him through the fields of flowers, and then ...

Her apartment building loomed large in front of her.

"I'll wait here." Jonathan sat down on the steps.

Melissa dragged herself up to her apartment, and collapsed on a seat at the kitchen table. She'd lied to Jonathan. Though it would be nice to say goodbye to her landlord, she would rather stay in her room. Hide here. Her mission was accomplished, and yet there was a heavy weight pressing on her heart. She buried her head in her hands. *I don't deserve ...*

"Child?"

Melissa jumped up. Jesus was standing there. He looked at her, his eyes filled with love and compassion. *That look. How could I have ever forgotten it?*

"What is it, Child? Why do you weep?"

She took two quick steps toward Him, but came to an abrupt stop. Shame-faced, she turned away. *He's got to be disappointed in me.*

"Melissa?" His footsteps creaked on the floor as he walked up behind her.

She couldn't bring herself to look at Him. *Maybe I could return to Heaven and be a servant.*

"Child?" Jesus placed a gentle hand on her head.

Instinctively, she reached up and took hold of it. Her fingers ran across the scar.

"Lord. I have sinned," she stammered out. The dam of tears burst from her eyes. She spun around and fell down before Him, grasping His feet, focusing on the nail prints. "I'm sorry. Please forgive me. I'm no longer worthy to—"

Jesus' touch on her shoulders silenced her. He lifted her up and placed His hand under her chin, raising her face, forcing her to look at Him. Would she see anger there ... disappointment? But there was none of that. Only love.

Her lips quivered into a smile.

"Oh, my child. I love you. You are mine." Jesus wrapped His arms around her, engulfing her in his embrace. "You are mine."

Melissa closed her eyes and clung to Him. Joyful tears flowed. All her cares, all her failings, flowed out with them.

For a wonderful minute, His unconditional love washed over her like the warm rays of the sun.

She opened her eyes again. A smile burst across her face. Miraculously, they were back in Heaven, standing by the Temple, surrounded by a crowd of people. Eager eyes watched her, friends with happy faces. Jonathan stood amongst them. He gave her a look of encouragement.

I'm home!

Jesus gazed down at her. He stretched out His palms, revealing the nail scars. "You are forgiven, because you have asked. You are worthy because I am worthy."

The angels above Him began to shout, "Worthy is the lamb that was slain!"

"I love you. You are my child!" He ran His hand along Melissa's face, wiping the tears away.

"You were lost, but now are found." Jesus raised His head and looked to the cheering crowd. "And now, let the celebration begin. My child has come home!"

THANK YOU!

I hope you enjoyed *A Message to Deliver*! I need to ask you a favor. Would you help others enjoy this book too?

Recommend it. Please help other readers find this book by recommending it to friends in person and on social media.

Review it. Reviews can be tough to come by these days. You, the reader, have the power to make or break a book. Loved it, hated it – I'd just enjoy your feedback. Please tell other readers what you thought about this book by reviewing it at one of the following websites: Amazon, Barnes and Noble, or Goodreads.

My goal is to have 100 honest reviews on Amazon. Will you help me reach that goal?

And I'd love for you to connect with me on my website: www.JeremiahPeters.com

Thank you so much for reading *A Message to Deliver* and for spending time with me.

In gratitude,
Jeremiah Peters

Resources

Dear friends, If you're looking for a pro-life organization, here's a short list of some national groups. You could be searching for a variety of reasons. For example, many such groups use volunteer workers, and you'd like to donate your time. Or you may find yourself dealing with a pregnancy or the effects of an abortion. I give you the following list. It is far from complete. As a matter of fact, you may find other similar groups in your local area.

Elliot Institute www.afterabortion.org
Abortion Recovery Int'l www.abortionrecovery.org
CareNet www.care-net.org
Heartbeat Int'l www.heartbeatinternational.org
Birthright Int'l www.birthright.org
Christian Family Care www.cfcare.org
National Right to Life www.nrlc.org

Beyond these organizations, there is someone else ready to help you. Of course I am talking about God.

Parts of this book take place in Heaven. There are even angels and demons involved, and I'm sure some will take me to task for my portrayal of Heavenly things. But you must remember, this is not a book of theology. It's a book about forgiveness: Forgiveness from God, forgiveness of others, and forgiveness of self. Whether you have aborted a child (or are thinking about it), or perhaps there is a sin in your life you struggle with. You wonder, "Can God forgive me?"

Here's some wonderful news. God says, "I love you, and forgive you."

Remember, there's nothing you can do that He can not forgive. Psalms 103:12 states, "As far as the east is from the west, So far has He removed our transgressions from us."

Forgiveness isn't about us being perfect, or even attempting perfection. Forgiveness is a gift from God, offered through the sacrifice of His Son, Jesus.

"For God so loved the world that He gave His only begotten Son, that whosoever believes in Him will not perish, but have everlasting life." John 3:16

I urge you, if you have not sought forgiveness and a restored relationship with God, do so today.

Discussion questions

1. Which character in the story do you identify with the most? Why?

2. Do you think a human can come back from Heaven? What about Lazarus (John 11:43)? The centurions daughter (Matthew 9:23-26)?

3. Jesus spoke directly to Melissa. Does God still speak to us today? If so, in what ways?

4. Melissa comes to Earth with the innocence of a child and then finds herself changed through the circumstances of the world. What are some ways you can see this in your own life? Is it possible to regain some aspects of our own innocence and strengthen our faith in the process?

5. Read Psalm 139:13-17. What can we learn from this passage about the creation of a new life? Who is involved and to what degree? What does God think about each new life? About your life?

6. Both Melissa & Mabel have trouble dealing with Mabel's abortion. If you learned that a close friend had an abortion, how would that change your relationship? If the friend was struggling with the consequences of that decision, what would you say to her?

7. Melissa discovered there was a birth defect involved in Mabel's decision to abort her child. What do you think? Is there any time an abortion is justified? Do birth defects matter?

8. Is violence against those we disagree with right or wrong? What about the Old Testament? Didn't God call for violence in the OT? Read Exodus 34:12-14 and Numbers 33:50-56.

9. Melissa had an angel. What place do angels play in the lives of Christians? Read Numbers 22; Luke 1; Acts 5:19; and Acts 10:1-7. What is the purpose of angels in these passages?

10. Can demons harm you? Can they possess a Christian? If Satan is the author of lies, can he ever speak the truth? Read Matthew 4:1-10 and Mark 8:33.

11. Read Ephesians 4:31-32. Todd allowed his anger about the past to control his present. Are there issues in your past that you can't let go of? Do you let decisions made by others control you?

12 Read Psalm 32:1; Mark 11:25; Acts 3:19; 1 John1:9; and Psalm 103:12. Is there a sin that can't be forgiven? What sin committed against you have you had trouble forgiving? Have you ever committed a sin, and had trouble forgiving yourself? Which sin does God have trouble forgiving?

13. Have you ever had to forgive someone that hasn't asked for your forgiveness?

14. What effect does unforgiveness have in a person's life?

Acknowledgements

There are some people who need to be mentioned
for their help with this book.

To my friends who critiqued the book: Debra Bock,
Christa Handley, Clarice James, Cheryl Cates,
Reggie Thomas, and Kate Vachon. Thanks for the
kind and encouraging words.

To my personal editors, my daughters: Jessica
Nilsen and Jamie Wixson. I am so pleased that they
have grown up to be avid readers, devouring book
after book. It gave them that unique ability to help
their dad.

To Jennifer Peters, my wonderful daughter-in-law,
who worked patiently with me in getting this book
into print.

Most of all, to my wife, Jodie, for supporting me
through the process, and prodding me to keep
going the many times I was ready to give up. When
my quirky personality got in the way, she was there.
I am eternally thankful.

A portion from the sale of this book is donated
to pro-life organizations.

Here's a sneak peek at Jeremiah Peters' next book. This cozy mystery, which is book one in the **Jack and Jill Mystery Series**, will be available in early Summer, 2019.

The List

After serving as a U.S. Marine, Jackson Hill thought college life would be a cake walk. That all changed when he met two different women. One was the girl of his dreams. The other was dead.

JEREMIAH PETERS

JEREMIAH PETERS

Chapter One

I never knew death could be so lifelike. Over in Iraq, it was anything but.

Here, though . . .

She looked so peaceful seated against the rear of the library building. Serene. Her skin had an almost translucent glow from the single light bulb that hung over the service entrance. Her long, dark hair curled around the sides of her face and draped over her shoulders. If it were a couple of inches longer, I wouldn't have even noticed the knife in her chest.

I shook my head hoping this was just a dream, a nightmare from which I'd awaken. No luck.

But maybe she wasn't dead. Maybe she was just hurt. Stupid thought. The knife pointed to death.

But what if I was wrong?

I jumped off the corner of the cement slab that acted as the library's loading dock, where I'd stopped to retie my running shoes. "Hey! Are you okay?"

No response.

I inched forward and cupped my hand above my eyes, shielding them from the stark light. Her sweater had a large red stain on it, circling the knife's entrance. A puddle of blood stretched across the cold ground. I lifted her wrist to check for a pulse. Nothing.

In the stillness of the dawn, I offered a silent prayer.

Clouds of steam escaped my mouth and ascended into the dull predawn sky. Most of my fellow students at Springsbury College were still sound asleep.

A dead body behind a Dumpster . . . The media is going to have a field day with that.

In the past few months, two other girls had been found in a similar state. One was about seventy miles away. The other, thirty. The media announced we had a serial killer running rampant through New Hampshire. With the bodies being left the way they were, they dubbed him The Dumpster Killer.

Just then, a small cry, like a dove cooing, sounded from behind me. I spun around and raised my hands, expecting to see a wild-eyed murderer, wielding a blood-stained blade. Instead, across the narrow road that ran behind the library stood a young girl, her back to the woods. The morning mist played around her feet.

Freaky. It was like something out of one of those horror movies where the children rise from a cornfield or dark woods, seeking vengeance on the adults. I had the queasy feeling that at any moment the girl's elf-like voice would call out to me, "Jackson Hill, I've come for you."

Instead, "Oh," was all she said.

After a moment of dazed confusion, I lowered my hands.

What in the world is a kid doing on campus this early in the morning?

She stared at the body. "Do you have a cell phone?" Her voice was cold, almost detached. Certainly not elf-like.

I patted the pockets of my running pants. "No. Why?"

She rolled her eyes as if to say, 'How dumb can you be?' "Someone's got to call the police." She started to leave but turned back. "You stay here. Don't touch anything."

What did she think I was? Stupid? Of course I knew not to touch anything.

She disappeared around the corner of the building.

That was weird. If I were her, I'd have been frightened out of my wits. Yet here she'd been, in the early morning, behind a building with a strange man and a dead body. Why hadn't she run off, screaming at the top of her lungs?

Then I had a terrible thought. I tensed as a cold wind bit into my face. It was a silly notion, really. Probably fed by the shadowy morning fog and eerie quiet.

Who's to say the serial killer had to be a man? Or even an adult?

■■■

The police arrived and cordoned off the area with yellow tape. A few cruisers and an ambulance were parked on the narrow road. About a half dozen latex-gloved officers were busy at work, I assumed looking for clues, occasionally bagging some object. A steady stream of traffic flowed through the back door of the library. The Dumpster sat silently to its right. The stark flashes from the photographer's camera lit the building.

I leaned on the front edge of the dock, as far away from the Dumpster as I could get.

Where's the chalk?

On television, they always do a chalk outline of the body? And how would they accomplish this with the deceased leaning against the building? Would the chalk line flow from the ground to the wall?

I mentally chastised myself. Here I was in the middle of a crime scene, worrying about chalk outlines. The scrape of plastic against metal jolted me to reality as the ambulance attendants pulled a body bag from the back of their vehicle.

I jumped to my feet. Something wasn't right. Where was that young girl? Had she escaped? I relaxed and sat back down. There she was, behind one of the cruisers.

"You Jackson Hill, the one who found the girl?" A baby-faced officer approached me.

"Yes, sir."

"You're going to have to answer some questions. Don't leave." He spoke in a voice too stern for his youthful look. "You want to sit in one of the cruisers?"

"No, sir. I'm fine."

"Would you like—"

A voice bellowed from the sidelines. "What's the meaning of this?" A tall, silver-haired man fumbled with the tape, trying to gain access to the area. He looked like he'd just crawled from his bed and thrown on wrinkled clothing from the hamper.

A woman followed him. Her long, blonde hair was slightly gray. She had high cheekbones and a slim figure. In her youth, she must have been quite a beauty. She placed a hand on the man's shoulder as he struggled with the tape. From the tender touch, I assumed she was his wife. "Let me—"

He yanked his hand away. "Ms. Fielding, I can do this."

Okay, so it's not his wife.

"I know." Crestfallen, she backed away. "I'm just trying to help."

Finally, in a great fluster, he tossed the tape over his head and marched toward the center of the action, with the woman close on his heels.

My baby-faced officer raced over.

"Who's in charge here?" The newcomer glared at the scene.

A large, muscular gentleman with close-cropped red hair, approached. He wore a dark sports coat and light brown trousers. "I'm Detective Phillips." He nodded toward the young officer as if to say, 'I'll take care of this.'

Looking grateful, the babyfaced officer hurried away.

"And you are?" Detective Phillips asked.

The man straightened up. "Dr. Roland Spiner. The president of this college."

The woman hovered behind him, remaining watchful, but silent.

"Well, Dr. Spiner, until Detective Thomas arrives, I'm in charge of the investigation."

"Investigation? What investigation?"

The z-i-i-i-p-p-p of the body bag cut through the air.

Dr. Spiner seemed to catch sight of the activity behind the Dumpster for the first time. His mouth dropped. "What? But—but this can't be happening."

Detective Phillips consulted a small notebook. "Her name was Emily Hamilton. Mean anything to you?"

Ms. Fielding gasped.

Dr. Spiner stared at the body. "Should it?"

"She was a student here," the detective said.

The color drained from the man's face. His legs gave out, and he fell against one of the cruisers. "No . . . no . . ."

The detective lurched forward to catch him as he slid down the side of the car, but the woman beat him to it.

"Easy," Detective Phillips said. "Do you want a seat in the car?"

Semi-dazed, Dr. Spiner stared at the scene behind the Dumpster. "How could this happen?"

He allowed the detective to take him by one arm as Ms. Fielding held tight to the other. They guided him to the cruiser's door, and the two crawled into the back seat. Before his head disappeared through the opening, he gave one last look at the body. "What's this going to do to our enrollment?"

That was cold.

Speaking of cold, my backside was chilled from sitting on the cement. On top of that, I had to go to the bathroom. I shifted my position and glanced around. All the officers seemed engrossed in their work.

No one will miss me if I sneak away for a second.

As I ducked under the yellow tape, a voice called out. "Hey, you!"

Before I had a chance to answer, someone else joined in. "Hey, kid? You deaf or something?"

Two officers marched toward me. The shorter one, who looked like he had trouble buttoning his shirt around his bulging stomach, spoke. "Where do you think you're going?"

"To the bathroom."

His partner sniffed and wiped his nose. He looked like he'd give the college president a run for his money to win the Who-was-Dressed-Most-Shabbily Award. "You can't just walk away. You got to tell someone!"

"Sorry, sir."

"You the one who found the body?" the short one

huffed.

I nodded. "Yes, sir."

He placed his hand on my shoulder and guided me to the loading dock. "This is a crime scene. You're a part of an investigation. You walk away, it don't look too good."

The tall one pulled a slightly used tissue from his pocket and blew his nose. "We don't know where you're planning on going unless you tell us."

"Sorry, sir, but –"

"Boy! Kids today." He shook his head. "Where do we get them?" His words were directed to his partner, but it was obvious I was meant to hear this condemnation of college students in general and of me in particular.

"Yeah. Not too bright."

"You know . . ." The tall officer balled up the tissue and stuck it back in his pocket. "Once they graduate high school and go off to college, they think they're all grown up. Then again . . ." He eyed me suspiciously. "You're too old for a typical college brat."

"Yes, sir."

"A little young for a teacher?"

"Well, I—"

"Late starter, eh?" The short one with the belly poking through his buttons gave a sympathetic look. His insinuation was obvious. Somehow, I must have been too stupid when I graduated high school to go right to college.

Maybe it was because of the early hour. Or the fact that I'd found a dead body. Or a lack of food. Whatever the reason, my temper rose. "Well, sir," my volume increased. "You're right when you noticed I'm older." I stuck out my chest, "I served time in the marines before starting college."

It's funny, at one moment I'm trying to forget my time in the service, and at another, I'm wearing it like a badge of honor. The words poured from my mouth like water through the crack in a dike. Unfortunately, I didn't have a little boy to stick his finger in the hole. I'd like to come up with another reason for my anger. But, there was only one I can attribute it to—stupidity. I don't know . . . Maybe these two simply rubbed me the wrong way. Whatever the reason, I kept going.

"That, sir, is why I am older. And may I also add, as a marine I've been trained to respect those in authority. I'd appreciate it if the authorities respected me."

Suddenly, the area grew very quiet. The surrounding officers' conversations came to an abrupt halt. All eyes focused on me. Even the girl by the cruiser was gawking.

A thick cloud of embarrassment hung over my head.

The silence dragged on until the taller officer snickered. "Wow! A marine."

"We're sorry," the other said.

The two smirked.

"We promise to treat you with all the respect you're due. Don't we, Officer Daniels?"

They laughed.

"Everything okay here?" Detective Phillips walked up.

Others who'd stopped to watch this spectacle took this as a cue to get on with their jobs.

"Yes, sir. Everything is fine," the short one answered. "General Patton here needs to pee."

The detective gave a stern look. "I've got a job for you. Dr. Spiner and his secretary are in your cruiser. Their homes are on the other side of the campus. I don't think he's in any shape to walk back. Take care of them."

"Will do, sir." He walked away.

Officer Daniels smirked. "But we weren't done with—"

The detective glared at him. "You're done. I'll take care of Mr. Hill. Get going."

"The two climbed in the cruiser and drove off, smiling and laughing as they did.

"Don't be too hard on them," Detective Phillips said. "They're just coming off a twenty-four-hour shift. A little sleep deprived."

"No problem." What else could I say?

Another car pulled up. A man got out and slowly scanned the scene. He nodded at Detective Phillips. "Wait here." The detective trotted over to the newcomer. I slapped myself on the forehead.

Idiot!

In a low whisper, I mimicked my voice. "I'm a marine

so treat me right! Next week, I'll be the king of England."

Idiot!

I sighed. There wasn't much I could do about it now.

Settling back on my perch, I watched as Detective Phillips greeted the man. Then grim-faced, the two talked. Several officers approached the pair, asking questions, receiving instructions, or showing something they'd recovered.

By his attitude and the way everyone treated him, it was obvious this must be the fellow Detective Phillips told the president about, the one who would be in charge. Occasionally, his eyes wandered in my direction. He wasn't looking at me though, but at the Dumpster. At least that's what I wanted to think.

The sun was beginning to peek through the trees. Students lined the yellow tape, curious, all wanting a good view of the proceedings.

How long was this going to take?

Finally, the man broke off from Detective Phillips and approached. "I'm Detective Thomas. You are?"

"Jackson Hill."

"You found the deceased?"

"Yes, sir," I answered, meeting his steely stare.

Detective Thomas stood about six foot two or three. He looked to be of average-to-thin build. "I have a few questions for you."

Did his mouth move? I couldn't tell. It was like speaking to a statue.

"I'll answer as best I can."

"What time did you find the body?"

"I found Emily about six am." I was kicking myself that I couldn't be more precise.

"Emily?" The man showed no signs of emotion, not even the flickering of an eyebrow. "Did you know her?"

I shook my head.

He paused, his gaze fixed on me. It was quite uncomfortable. What was going through his head? "You say you found the body around six?"

"Yes, sir."

"What were you doing out at that hour?"

"Jogging. I was in the military and—"

"So I heard."

Was that a dig? Had someone already told him of my stupid and embarrassing declaration?

I continued, deciding to ignore his comment. "I got in the habit of early morning runs." As I continued with the whole story of how I found Emily, he just stared at me. No movement. He looked like a statue. The Great Stone Face.

I finished.

"Thank you. That's all for now. You'll have to come down to the station for a more complete statement. We'll be in touch about that. Give Detective Phillips your contact information. Meanwhile, please don't leave town without letting the police department know." He stepped away.

I leaped forward. "One other thing."

"Yes?" He turned back.

As inconspicuously as possible, I glanced in the direction of the cruiser, where the young girl stood. She appeared nervous, fidgeting, half hiding behind the car's side.

"I . . . er . . ." I made my way around the detective so that the cruiser was behind me. "If you look over there," I mumbled, "You'll see a girl by the cruiser. She looks like she's trying to hide. Do you see her?"

His eyes barely moved. "Yes."

"She was there, too," I announced in a somewhat dramatic whisper. "When I found the body."

For a nanosecond, I thought I saw a glimmer of something on his face. Maybe an emotion. But it quickly disappeared. "And?" he said.

"She appeared out of nowhere, acting like she was guilty of something. It seems odd to me . . . a high school kid wandering around that early in the morning."

I couldn't tell if the detective was taking me seriously or not. It almost looked like he smirked. Then he paused, and the petrified look returned to his face. With a coldness in his voice, he said, "Thank you, Mr. Hill." and walked away.

"Get those cameras behind the line," Detective Phillips barked.

The Manchester television station had arrived. They scurried around like hungry field mice, trying to snatch up tidbits of information. Who could blame them? How often did a serial killer come their way?

I was on the receiving end of dubious stares, both from reporters and fellow college students. Let's face it, if I were them, I'd be staring, too. Being the only civilian on the wrong side of the yellow tape made me fair game. I felt like a freak in a sideshow. 'That's the guy! He's guilty,' was probably what they were thinking.

"It's wasn't me!" I wanted to yell. "What about the girl?"

To suspect her was crazy, I knew that, no matter what my earlier fantasies had been.

The onlookers parted, making room for the ambulance to leave. Their faces showed shock and disbelief. A couple of girls were crying. One found comfort in the shoulder of the young man next to her.

Could this possibly be happening? Here was someone who was so alive just a few hours ago. And now . . .

I caught sight of Detective Thomas over by the cruiser. He was interrogating the girl, leaning over her and speaking in a low tone. She shook her head. Her eyes welled with tears.

Then something happened that took me by surprise. Detective Thomas signaled to an officer. They loaded the girl in the cruiser. The officer got in and drove away.